Colorless

Miranda Smith

authorHOUSE®

AuthorHouse™
1663 Liberty Drive
Bloomington, IN 47403
www.authorhouse.com
Phone: 1 (800) 839-8640

Published by AuthorHouse 06/05/2017

ISBN: 978-1-5246-8781-6 (sc)
ISBN: 978-1-5246-8780-9 (e)

Library of Congress Control Number: 2017906876

Print information available on the last page.

Any people depicted in stock imagery provided by Thinkstock are models, and such images are being used for illustrative purposes only. Certain stock imagery © Thinkstock.

This book is printed on acid-free paper.

Introduction

Every day I walk down the same hallways, breathe a breath of fresh air, and straighten myself for the day that is about to come. My simple appearance and my normal life don't make me stick out at all. My cheeks quickly turn red for a second, and I pat down my hair. When I think about my life so far, all I can remember is being with my best friend. Maybe that's because I don't really have anyone else. I'm lucky to have her, actually. Her name is Katelyn Matthews, and she has brown hair and green eyes. Unlike me, she doesn't wear glasses. Katelyn has long eyelashes and is tanned. When I think about myself, however... I have brown hair and brown eyes with pale skin. I blend in, I guess. I'm not fashionable and I'm not very unique. Every time we have a school assembly, or I see my classmates out with their friends, it makes me think about how much I don't have; how much I really seem to be missing. Everyone else is always noticed for their talents, but I'm just... talentless. "What's so special about me?" I always ask myself, or "If I did have something special about me, what difference would it make? There will always be people better than me." Maybe I'm way too hard on myself, but truthfully, and yes, I will admit it, maybe it's just a way of hiding my jealousy and embarrassment. Why can't I be noticed?

Chapter Uno

Spanish Class

I'm not exactly sure why we have Spanish in the morning. You can't actually expect people to learn when half of their brain is still asleep, can you? Take me, for example: trudging down the hallway in my plaid khakis and red shirt with my school emblem on it, yawning and bumping into people on a Friday morning. There's no use trying to hide my poor appearance. That will only make me more noticeable. There are black bags under my eyes, and I can't seem to think correctly. My hair is unfortunately frizzy today, and I did not think to put it up this morning. There are other students who look similar, but that thought doesn't seem to give me any more confidence. Just standing a few feet away from my classroom door, I run my fingers through my hair, trying to pat it down. Although this probably does nothing to help me, I know that I need to look at least somewhat presentable in front of my teachers. As I stand in the doorway of my classroom, I see the familiar white board and markers. Vocabulary words are taped onto the walls across the room. The desks are set up on different platforms; the ones in the back leveled the highest. The aisle that is most near to the teacher (which I like to call Aisle A) is usually quiet, and helps if you want to take notes; however, Aisle F, in the back of the classroom, is usually noisy, and it's hard to take notes when there's a lot of noise, at least in my opinion. I feel a nudge on my arm, and realize someone just shoved past me to get into class. It seems I'm just a ghost at this school. I walk over to the desk in the middle of the classroom and slowly take my seat. My book bag lies on the floor next to me, and the desk I use is made out of wood. Black and brown streaks fill the top of my desk, but the wood is nonetheless beautiful. The legs of my desk are made of metal, and as I try to put my book bag on the desk, my leg hits something. Pulling my leg onto the seat, I glance at the place where a bruise will form. Quickly getting my books out of my book bag, I quietly sigh, as my leg is throbbing just a bit. As I get my Spanish vocabulary book out, my teacher enters the room from the closet.

"Hola mi amigas and amigos. Welcome to clase de espanol. First I want you to take down the notes that I wrote on the board, and afterwards you will complete a worksheet that I left in your desks. There will be no homework, since I don't like giving homework on Fridays," says our teacher.

This year we have 6 new students in our grade, so he will probably give them an easier worksheet to do, since they aren't as familiar with the language as the rest of us. Spanish isn't that hard for me. I was brought up in a Spanish family, but never actually learned the language. It's very helpful to learn it now, though, considering I have a lot of cousins in other countries. I scroll through endless amounts of vocabulary words in my notebook, thinking about how much we've done within the first month of school. It's actually quite impressive. The many vocabulary words listed on the board are written in green marker. It might take me half of our class time just to write them down.

Looking around the room, I notice that Katelyn, my best friend, is absent today. Usually she sends me a message asking me to gather her homework, but she didn't… That's abnormal for her. Though, we haven't talked much in the past few weeks, actually. It seems like whenever I try to talk to her, she manages to get out of the conversation. Now is really the only time I've been pondering over it. Am I a bad best friend for not noticing? Shame quickly spreads throughout me, leaving my cheeks tinted red. Last week she only came in for two days! I tried texting her last week, but I don't know whether she got my message or not. This week, she hasn't come to school at all. Maybe instead of texting her, I should actually call her. Katelyn always has her phone with her, so I don't understand why she didn't respond. Could I possibly have said something to offend her? Maybe she *did* tell me why she wouldn't be in class and I just wasn't paying attention. I let my head fall onto the desk and begin to feel drowsy.

"Paula! Please pay attention!" shouts Senor Augment.

I look up immediately, seeing the frown on my teacher's face. Did I fall asleep? If I did fall asleep, why didn't anyone wake me?

"Alright, now that you seem to be awake, how do you say a name in Spanish?" he asks, still frowning.

I quickly blush because I fell asleep. Although I caused this situation myself, I wish this didn't have to happen. It's a bit embarrassing, as I can see everyone looking at me with smirks on their faces, nearly laughing.

"A name in Spanish is el nombre," I reply with a slurred voice.

Not expecting my voice to come out like that, I shut my eyes closed and breathe in and out, trying to calm myself. I need to wake up before my next class.

"Yes class, a name in Spanish is le nombre. It is not spelled or pronounced the same as a name in the English language. Please, on our next quiz, do not fail to forget this. You are dismissed."

It's funny how time manages to lose track of us. If we stop paying attention for just one second, we might miss something that's really important. I smile at my frivolous thought and put my books back into my book bag. I quickly get up, but find myself feeling a bit faint. My vision begins to fade, and I nearly trip over myself. When I regain my vision a few seconds later, I shake my head. Perhaps I should go to the nurse? This isn't something that usually happens to me… I shake off this thought and continue on my journey to math class, which, in my opinion, should've been first in our schedule. I guess this year isn't making too much sense, after all. I start to sprint to my next class, and remember that we aren't supposed to run. I trip over something and my glasses slide across the floor. I manage to grab them before more students come rushing out of the classrooms. There are hundreds of students in this school, and I'm just one of them. It relaxes me to know that I most likely will not be paid any attention to, but it's also disappointing. I have a sinking feeling in my chest, and realize I'm getting depressed over nothing. So what if I'm not popular, or don't have many friends? There's still Katelyn… Then again, she might not want to be my best friend, either. I stare at the tiles for a few seconds, and when I look up, I notice that there aren't as many people in the hallway as there was before. As I spin around in circles trying to remember where I have to go, I recall that I have Pre-Algebra in second period this year. Yes, that means questions with variables, such as $2y+4y = 12$. I know what we're doing is nothing compared to Algebra, but it's a big change. I'm in the Seventh Grade, Advanced Math. In the Eighth Grade we begin Algebra. I change my direction, and quickly walk to my math class. We're taking a test today, and that seems to lift my spirits. If I finish early, I might be able to finish my book! My mom told me to go to sleep last night, so I couldn't read the rest of the story. Let's just say I was too busy pondering for another few hours on how the book would end that I managed to only get 5 hours of sleep; and now I'm here, about to take a test, too tired to really think straight. Entering the room with some of the other students, I take my seat at my desk in the middle of the classroom. It's a black desk with a smooth top, and is perfect for writing with a pencil. The chairs are wooden and somewhat uncomfortable, but I've gotten used to them. Unlike my Spanish classroom, the floor is leveled and not made like a very wide staircase. The first five questions are pretty easy, each taking maybe a minute or two each. The 10 after that are a bit harder and take longer than expected. By the time class is nearly over, I have five really long algebraic questions and only 15 minutes left. Where's the time for me to read my book there? My brain wanders for a minute, thinking about the plot of my book, and then I remember that I need to focus on my test. The rest of the questions aren't necessarily hard, but confusing. Within 10 minutes I finish 4 questions. I sigh as I reach the last question; the last question is a word problem. I'm usually good with word problems, but this one was quite difficult. I don't remember learning what happens when you have more variables alone than numbers to work with. What do I do?

My hand is sweating with 4 minutes on the clock. The pencil has lost its sharp point, and the paper is wrinkled. Eraser marks spread across the paper. I still have 50 pages in the book to read! And now I only have 3 minutes left! My heart beats faster.

"Focus, Paula, focus," I say to myself.

I scribble down variables mixed with numbers, but the answer doesn't make sense. Something is better than nothing, right? I just hope I get a good grade. Quickly placing the paper on the teacher's desk, I rush out of the room with my book in my hands. Finally, what I wanted to get to. It's a murder mystery. I quickly read a few pages and almost knock someone down from not paying attention. I quickly apologize, and rush to the end of the hall, desperate to find an empty place to read. Alas, the hallway is starting to become crowded. I decide to keep reading, which is probably not the best idea on my part. Every ten seconds I find myself looking around to make sure no one trips over me. How am I supposed to remember what happens in the story if I can't read the book in peace? I guess it's for the best, anyway. I have to get to my next class. Still, it's too bad I have to wait to read the rest. There will be thoughts and ideas in my mind left untouched.

* * *

In reading class we spend the time looking up information for our next essay on a book we recently read. The genre of the book was fiction and it was extremely detailed. If you didn't pay close attention, you most likely wouldn't understand what you read. This is why we have discussions in class: it allows us to examine the topic of the book more thoroughly and achieve a greater understanding of it. My brain feels tired from a lack of sleep and completing algebraic equations, so it takes me a bit longer to do the class work. Although it seems like an interminable journey, reading ends and our science teacher enters the room with a book in her hands. Normally we would move for the first few classes and then stay in homeroom being taught different subjects, but that doesn't seem to be happening this year. I look at my science teacher once more and notice that there are papers within the textbook.

"Everyone will be completing this worksheet and you must hand it in before class ends. If you don't, you will receive an automatic zero. I do not encourage you to work with other people, but if you think that it will work better for you, you may," informs our science teacher.

After giving us all a worksheet, she explains the directions and leaves us to do our work. We can use our textbooks to find information, so I know I'll get a good grade on this worksheet. Science gives me a bit more difficulty because there's a lot to remember, and a lot to remember means a lot of studying. After I complete the worksheet, I give it in and read a few more pages of my book. I remember that we have lunch next, and become a bit more relaxed. Perhaps I can take a quick nap at my table. Though, I'll have to find someone to wake me...

Luckily, for lunch we have assigned seats, which make everything so much easier. Well, almost. Sometimes people come and ask for your seat, and if you don't give it to them, they become angry. The doorway of the cafeteria is large because of the large number of students we have. The cafeteria is most definitely the biggest room in our school, but it also seems to be the one with the least space to move around in. Since there are so many students, the cafeteria doesn't seem nearly as large as it really is. At first, everything is quiet, but I can hear the tension spreading throughout the atmosphere. As I take my seat, I notice everyone is getting up and moving to different spots in the room. It isn't uncommon, but usually most people stay in their seat. Apparently, today is not one of those days. I have about 4 people left on my table when there are usually 8, including myself. I don't mind sitting with 8 people, but it often gets too noisy. Sometimes the girls try to speak over one another, and the lunch room sounds like a battlefield. Today, however, the noise seems to be coming from one area in the room. When I hear a lot of shouting from behind me, I turn around. No one is shouting at me, but they are fighting about something. It seems that there is a debate team meeting during lunch. I guess that means sleeping is off of my to-do list. I can't even read my book with this much noise. When this thought hits me, I decide that maybe speaking to someone really wouldn't be so bad.

I begin talking to the girl next to me. Though, I have to admit, I don't know her name. Even though we've only been in school for a few months, it seems that there are a lot transfer students. Her hair is dark brown, and she has amethyst eyes. I've never seen amethyst eyes before.

"Hey, my name is Paula," I inform the girl.

She squints at me, almost as if she can't see. Her face quickly changes, however, and I smile at her.

"Hi, my name is Cornelia," She replies while smiling back at me.

"Are you new?" I ask.

"Yeah, just came in this year as a transfer student," Cornelia responds quietly.

I thought so.

"I don't exactly know what's going on, and my schedule seems to be a bit messed up, so… Do you have any advice about what I should do?" she asks.

I pause before I speak, thinking of what to say. School can be complex at times, but I guess, if you follow a few rules, you should be fine. Though, I've never been to another school before, so I don't know whether these apply to other schools.

"Well, lunch is normally quieter than this, but today we have a debate team meeting. Usually you can read a book or try to take a nap, but during these meetings it's best to look busy. Sometimes people ask you for your opinion and that can be a problem. Also, for P.E., we often play games like dodge ball. You need to participate, but just try not to get hit by the ball. Trust me, it hurts," I say, groaning.

"Thanks. You're pretty smart about the lunch thing. You saved both of us."

There's a weird look on her face, but I can't decipher it. Oh well, nothing to worry about, right?

"Sorry about that…" I reply meekly.

"It's cool. Anyway, lunch is over in about 5 minutes.

Guess we don't have much time to talk. I suppose I'll see you around school, Paula. Bye!" she says, smiling.

She waves to me as she leaves her seat and quickly puts the rest of her lunch back in her bag.

"Bye!" I respond.

Maybe my tips are a bit selfish, but truthfully, you never know who you will meet. I mean, heading to history was a bit easier after that. Without my best friend in school, I have no one to talk to about the schoolwork, and that makes everything a bit more stressful. Though, with Cornelia around, it looks like seventh grade might be a bit more bearable. In my history classroom, the desks are small and no one sits together. The room is quite big, and the walls would've been a pretty white if they didn't hang so many posters up. Don't get me wrong, I love looking at artwork and facts from so long ago, but it'd be nice to have a change of scenery, too. History is interesting because it seems like our teacher knows more information about the Civil War than the text book itself. I'm truly amazed at how one person can keep that much information in their head. Compared to the teacher, I'm simply an amateur. Our teacher says History is the time when we can seriously study a topic and learn to be informed voters. It's also the time that I count how much homework I have. Let's see:

Math - Page 267 in the workbook
Science - 25 questions on page 439
Vocabulary test in Spanish on Wednesday

I have until Monday to do the work, but I usually complete it on Sunday. It's more or less my work day. We have 45 minutes left of history. Right now we are learning about the Civil War and what led to it. There are five different sections for this one chapter, so it is a lot of reading, I suppose. The notes aren't that hard to take if you know what you need; though, the tests are difficult because they focus on details that you wouldn't think would matter. I guess it's because they think that without these key parts, the Civil War might have been different. I like to think of these key parts as a series of paths. At first you start with two paths, but soon the paths grow and grow. By the time you get to my age, there could be millions to hundreds of millions of paths waiting for you to choose just one. For example, today I could've stayed quiet during lunch, which would've led to consequences such as maybe I wouldn't have made a new friend, or maybe I would've gotten stuck in the debate. Not only do our choices depend on who we are, but they also depend on other people. Within choices there are intertwining paths that you can't avoid. Sometimes you will meet someone who will change your life forever. Maybe you'll learn something which will inspire you to try a bit harder. There are so many paths made out for us; millions, trillions maybe, and we have to choose just one. It may sound hard, but sometimes choices can be easy. When I get older, I want to be a veterinarian. That choice might change too, but if I do decide to stay with that, I'll make sure my full heart is poured into it. These thoughts engrave themselves into my mind. One day in the future I'll remember this, and maybe then I'll think about how far I've come. I suddenly feel dizzy and goose bumps appear on my arms. Maybe having thoughts like these without 8 full hours of sleep isn't such a good idea. Then again, I can't control my thoughts. I read somewhere that we have millions of thoughts per second, and we might not even know it. It is funny how we can be so inobservant towards ourselves, but observant towards our atmospheres.

"Hello students. My name is Mrs. Washington and I am someone who helped the American Revolution. In your notebooks I want you to right with your quill how this First Lady helped the American cause. You must also name her first name. After you do this, write how families with different views may have affected the Civil War," said Mrs. Marley.

Mrs. Marley often does things like this. She will make a character out of previous knowledge, and act as if she were this character herself. I write down my answer and raise my hand to let her know that I'm done. Sometimes at the end of class, the first person to raise their hand gets a prize. Mrs. Marley comes over to check my work and places a sticker on it. Class passes by like this: sometimes we talk about the chapter and sometimes we go a little… Off of it. With a few minutes left of class, she tells us to type up what we said so that we can get a grade for it. Some of the kids groan, but it doesn't bother me too much. I already know I'm going to get a good grade because I got a sticker. We leave the classroom a bit early, desperate to get to our last class, English. If you know what rules you must use to speak proper English then I assume you will be fine. English isn't difficult for me most of the time…

My English classroom has rules and ideas for writing spread across the walls. One of the posters gives you more unique words to use rather than sad, happy, or mad. We take our seats and do some pages in our textbook that Mr. Hemming has given us.

"Write down the rules on textbook page 34 in your notebook please, and do all of the work on the next page. Afterwards you will do workbook pages 53-54. When you are finished, quietly read a book," says our teacher.

Although our teacher usually goes over it with us, he probably is annoyed with our books. This chapter has taken us 3 weeks when it only should've taken us 1 week to complete. Glancing at the clock, I realize we only have 5 minutes to 2:00 p.m. I begin counting in my head. The work he just gave us was actually assigned a few days ago, but it isn't due until Monday. I already completed the work, so I have nothing to do right now. After we hand everything in, we are going to have a test on Tuesday. I nearly forgot to write that down. Once I finish writing my homework down, I continue reading the book, but quickly become disappointed.

"After a failed attempt at finding out the criminal, we decide to take a different route. It's a dangerous and crazy adventure ahead of us, but I know we can do it."

I turn the page and realize that the rest of the pages are advertisements for all of the other books in the series. I stayed up a few hours last night just considering what might happen!

"My mother probably won't take me to get more books for awhile too," I mumble with a frown.

In my spare time, if I don't have anything to do, I'll often start writing down numbers in my notebook. Often, however, I notice it just makes the days seem longer than usual. I wonder if time passes more slowly when we want it to pass quickly. In that case, I wonder if when we want time to slow down, it moves more quickly than ever. It's a bit of a depressing thought, but I am nonetheless curious. Before I know it, class has ended and I'm on my way to my mother's car, which is parked in the front of the school. Before I go outside, I realize it's raining. I can see the grey clouds in the sky, gloomy and depressing. My mom's car is silver; similar to the clouds, but at least the car is shiny. The clouds look like cotton balls of depression. I make a mad dash to my mom's car, swinging the door open with my book bag covering my head. I nearly hit the car with my book bag, but manage to get inside without looking as if I took a shower with my clothes on.

"How was your day, honey?"

"It was fine, mom," I respond with a sigh.

We drive by a few houses when I notice one that's familiar.

"256 Oceanic Drive is for sale. People don't normally move in this neighborhood… But that name seems familiar," I think aloud, "Wait, Katelyn! This is their house! Why is it for sale?"

"Didn't Katelyn tell you? I thought for sure you guys have been talking about it. She's moving to North Carolina," My mom answered.

My heart sinks down into my chest, and I immediately think that this is some sort of prank… I mean, it can't be true, right? I look through my mom's windshield and see the rain, making the sky look blurry, as if the sky wasn't blurry enough with the clouds out. I open my book bag with an apparent migraine and take out my phone. I call Katelyn, and, for once, she responds. I quickly begin to speak, but as I hear the faint pace of her breathing into the microphone, I know that I already have my answer.

"Hey, is it true you are moving to North Carolina? Why didn't you tell me?" I ask.

"My family has been busy with the preparation plans and I just got caught up in it," Katelyn answers.

"Is that why you've been avoiding me?"

"I just didn't know how to tell you," She responds quietly.

"How soon are you leaving?"

"Saturday…" Katelyn replies.

"You mean *tomorrow* Saturday?"

"Maybe…"

"I can't believe you didn't tell me! It's been weeks Katelyn! Weeks! Maybe, Katelyn, if you would've told me before, everything would've been ok, but now I can't even see you!" I reply with a grumble.

"Just come over to my house tomorrow. Please."

I purse my lips and say "Mhm…"

After that, Katelyn hangs up. I groan and put my phone away. She could've told me weeks ago, but instead she doesn't say one word about anything. Then again, maybe it's my fault for not asking. Either way, as a good friend, I should go tomorrow. It's only right. It's one of my best friend duties. The drive home, short, but oh so stressful, taught me something. You need to trust your friendship. If something happens where you two are pulled apart, it's for a reason. Maybe it's a test of some kind. Whoever is meant to be in your life will stay in it, and whoever isn't, won't. Let's just hope we can both be strong tomorrow… But as I walk into my home, my face reflecting the rain, I know I won't be. There's a difference between the rain and my tears; the rain comes from an unknown location. The water evaporates from a river, or maybe the ocean, but with my tears, you can taste the feelings. You know that it comes from despair and depression; but it can also come from happiness. I've heard people say to other people in movies, "You know what you're feeling; you just don't want to admit it to yourself." How would they know that? What if you're completely lost? Obviously I should feel sad. I should feel depressed. But as I look up into the sky, I know that these clouds will soon fade. Maybe the sun will come shining through, but what if you miss the clouds? What if you don't want them to go? Those fleeting moments when the sky cries are precious, even if they aren't perfect. I'm spewing nonsense; I must be. But one thing I know, throughout all of this nonsense, is that pain isn't all that it seems. You don't just feel "sad". There are other feelings mixed in with that. There must be; because there is no word that can explain how I feel right now.

Chapter Two

Dreams and Alarm Clocks

I drape my purple nightgown over me, my hair sending droplets of water down my back. My back shivers with each drop, and I quickly grab a towel to dry my hair. I tip-toe to the sink and brush my teeth. While walking back to my bed, a chill gets sent down my back. I see my lilac sheets on my bed, my brown, polished drawers, my wooden shelves, and the purple walls, which all give me a sense of nostalgia. The windows have a white, wooden frame. I lie down and pull the sheets over, feeling a sense of warmth envelop me.

"At least there's some sort of warmth in my life," I think to myself.

A tear rolls down my cheek, and I know that I need to let everything out; but if I do, what will happen? These feelings are something that will affect me… and if I let something this small affect me, what will be left when I come in contact with a real problem? Though, I suppose, this is quite big. When I feel another tear rolling down my cheek, I notice that it is cold. Aren't tears supposed to be warm? Perhaps I haven't been crying enough... Maybe my tears have simply been waiting to be let out... When I think back to my childhood, I don't recall having anything personal to cry about. I lost my father when I was young, but I never got to know him. How can I care for someone deeply when I haven't really met him? I quickly shake the thought off and return to my thoughts about Katelyn. Why should I cry? I'm losing my best friend, but we can still contact each other... That doesn't mean that it will be the same, though. A sharp pain comes from my heart, and I realize that nothing will be the same. How am I supposed to see her? I punch my bed, but it doesn't make much of a difference. I'm not very strong, and I don't think I ever will be. I mean, look at what's happening right now. A small laugh escapes my throat, but a tear escapes my eye. My head is trying to understand what a life without Katelyn as my best friend would be like. She's always been there for me. I hear the rain pounding against the window; in some ways, it might seem as if they want to get in, to run away from the clouds; their pursuers... But the rain doesn't control itself. It gets pushed by the wind, and the clouds put them wherever they want to put them. The clouds don't care if you are having a picnic outside; they don't care if you are having the best day of your life. They're doing their jobs, and reminding me that I need to do mine.

I rub the stream of tears off of my face and begin to focus on the ceiling, my thoughts enveloping me once more. I start to close my eyes, and soon, I'm sleeping soundly in my bed, waiting for morning to come. Though, when I awaken, I see something. I'm in a white room that looks like the inside of a cube. I don't see any lights, windows, or doors, but there is something in the distance. It seems to have an impenetrable darkness around it… I begin taking steps toward it in a tentative manner. The closer I get, the more the form starts to take shape, but the more I step, the farther I seem. It's almost as if whatever is there is telling me "I'll let you see me, but don't come near me." Mixed emotions fill my heart, and I begin to walk more quickly. Soon, it takes the shape of a… tree? The tree is simply sitting there. There aren't any roots, at least that I can see, but it still looks sturdy. I know for sure it's a tree, but the leaves are charcoal black and… living? They look living, but dead. The leaves have a sharp pattern on them. It looks as if I touch the leaves, I will get charcoal on me, my hand will be cut, and the leaf will turn into ashes.

"Confidence and patience, Paula," I say aloud.

Taking one step forward, this time the tree doesn't move away. I take another, and another, until it seems I'm eight feet away from the tree. Even though I'm getting closer, I don't feel accomplished. Something seems to be missing. One more step, and it doesn't move. There's not much space separating me from the tree now. I take one more, unsure of myself, and I wake up. My heart is racing and I have no idea why.

That wasn't a scary dream.

When I think about the dream, I notice that the tree gets bigger and bigger as I get closer to it. I mean the tree literally looked like it grew… More branches sprouted and the leaves were multiplying. It seems like the tree was a reflection of me… but that couldn't be… could it? I try to fall back asleep, but when I awake, the dream still hasn't left my mind.

I can't be doing this to myself. This dream was just forced upon me by my subconscious mind. Today is a day that I must cherish. It's the last day I will spend with my best friend. Who knows the next time I will see her?

When I get out of bed, my head begins to feel dizzy and I fall back onto my bed. I get back up and look at myself in the mirror. My face is very pale and I look like I haven't slept in ages; however, I shake the feeling off. By the time I'm on my way to Katelyn's house, I barely even know where I'm going. She doesn't live too far, so my mom suggested we walk. Maybe I shouldn't have agreed.

I see Katelyn's small, quaint house. When I'm ready to knock, (which is after minutes of intense preparation), it barely makes a sound. Though, they must've heard it, because Katelyn's mom answers the door.

"Hello Paula, please come in," says Katelyn's mom.

I see a girl my age in the hallway, brown hair, green eyes, but it takes me awhile to register who she is. No, Katelyn doesn't look any different. The hesitation is all on me. She rushes over to hug me, and after a moment, I hug her back. There's no tension, but as far as I can tell, there is some awkwardness. My mind still isn't focusing. Maybe it's because when I enter the house, everything is packed up. It is no longer a home once you get rid of all the memories; it is simply a place of shelter. The walls are dreadfully bland, and my face seems to be matching my emotions. No one seems to notice, though.

"I'm not getting on the plane until later, so we can go up to my room and talk for a bit," Katelyn tells me.

"Ok," I respond, but to be honest, I didn't really hear what she said.

Katelyn's room is large and pink. Even though it shows a part of Katelyn's personality, it just seems like a room. It's no longer *her* bedroom. The thought makes me uncomfortable. It's like being in a stranger's house. There is no life.

"Look, I'm really sorry I didn't tell you. I was just scared I would lose my best friend," she quickly said.

"You wouldn't have lost me anyway. I started planning to keep in touch."

She stood a bit quiet after this. "So, you were going to keep in touch?"

"Yeah, of course I would! What else did you expect? I've known you since we were little, Katelyn. We practically grew up together. With that thought, I'd like to wish you a happy early birthday." A smile spreads across my face, but I know that I'm faking it. How could I smile at a time like this? All I can do is encourage her, right? Some part of me still wishes she would see past the façade… but I know she won't. We're both denying the truth, which is why we won't be able to understand each other right now. Maybe in the future, but it's nearly impossible to contain the dread enveloping me now.

"Aw, thanks so much! I can't believe you remembered after I sprung this on you yesterday!"

"Of course I would remember. Although I am a bit upset, you're still my best friend."

When I said this, I couldn't seem to swallow. I felt paralyzed… but I heard the pure happiness in Katelyn's voice. She's happy to leave… But I still wonder if she'll miss me. That's the thing with people. Even if you know them well, you still might be insecure about how they think of you *because* you care about them so much. Tears form in the corners of my eyes, but I blink them away. Not now. Not when Katelyn is leaving.

"If you didn't I would understand why."

I bite my tongue by accident. Next month, my birthday arrives on November 4th.

"It's too bad you have to miss Halloween," I say.

The words coming out don't sound right to me. It feels as if my heart is telling me to stop before I face drowning in my tears, but what choice do I have? This wasn't supposed to happen! Goosebumps appear on my arms, but I ignore them. Calming down my anxiety and the anger within me, I face Katelyn again, and she begins to speak.

"Yeah, but we'll probably celebrate it in North Carolina this year," She says with a smile.

"I'll make sure to call you," I respond.

Katelyn and I usually go to all of the houses on our block together, but that won't happen now…

"So, sorry I didn't really notice what was going on until later," I said, stifling a groan.

"No, it's fine. I mean, it's not your fault. You couldn't guess that I was moving away," she mumbles.

Katelyn then turns around to go downstairs. I try to move, but my body feels stiff.

"Hey, Paula, are you coming?" Katelyn asks.

"Um… Yeah," I reply weakly.

Sometimes I wonder why life is like this; why everyone pretends everything is fine, when it really isn't. How we want to ask someone for help, but don't have the bravery to ask; and before you know it, everything comes crashing down. I nearly trip over something on our way down, but I catch myself. How ironic.

"Hey girls, would you like some brownies? It's our last batch," asks Katelyn's mom.

My throat becomes tight, but we both take a few brownies. I can't bring myself to eat them, however. Katelyn doesn't seem to be hungry, either. We walk onto the front porch and sit down on the step closest to the ground. The sun is shining and the leaves are swaying in the cool breeze. The leaves on the trees are a beautiful shade of yellow, red, and orange. Some are a beautiful green, and still live on, but others are a dark brown. What happens when all of the leaves fall off? Is that the end? Or is it a new beginning? Just like the seasons, fall, winter, summer, and spring, it just seems to go around in circles. However, what happens when it all ends? What happens when you're left to figure out where everything all started? What if it's impossible? Sure, it seemed like nothing could be more picturesque than this. But when you have the thought that your best friend is moving away, everything comes to a halt. We aren't in the "perfect world," anymore. Time has frozen. I see my best friend smiling, but I can't help feeling horrible. What's going to happen now?

* * *

As we bid farewell at the airport, I hug Katelyn. I wait for her to board the plane, and then I fall back into my seat. I will not cry yet; not until I'm at home. At least home has distant memories of the past. Many people surround me with memories of their own, saying farewell to those they care about. This is an airport, and while I have been here before, this is not where my most important memories took place. Well… I guess… Not until now.

Secrets

Jeremiah's Point of View

I make my way to my guardian's office and take a seat. He quickly turns around and takes a breath. He looks nervous, as if he doesn't want to say whatever he needs to say.

"Listen, there's something I need to tell you."

"What is it, Mr. Switz?"

"Someone important is going to enter our school. Life might change as we know it."

"And how would you know this?"

"Her name is Katelyn-" He says, completely ignoring my question, "and she comes from Maryland."

I take a deep breath and a tear nearly escapes my eye.

"That's where…"

"Yes."

"Why is this so important?"

"There's something I haven't told you, Jeremiah." He says, with an intense glare. He takes out a small book, leaving me to wonder exactly what he's thinking.

When he opens it, however…

Dreaming and Darkness
Paula's Point of View

Today I had a lot on my mind. My head feels like a sponge, soaking everything up, but it doesn't seem to be letting it out. For once, I don't want to remember. I want everything to go back to the way it was, but will it? The odds are crashing against one another. Almost as if they are rocks on the beach during a storm. The waves are trying to push the rock, but the rock won't budge... Perhaps that rock is me. I want to stay in the life I have now, but life is pushing me somewhere else. Eventually, I will have to succumb to the force of the waves. Just... not right now. I'm being as strong as I can, yet I feel myself being tilted. Back to the shore or into the sea... I don't know.

When I arrive at home, I run up to my room and slam my door shut. As I walk into my room, I sit on the floor. There's no manual telling me how I should be feeling right now, but I wish there was. My heart and my mind seem to be fighting. If I keep locking my feelings up, I'll end up forcing my anger out on someone who doesn't deserve it! I pull on the carpet on my floor as if that's going to let my anger out. My hands and my elbows burn from rubbing against the carpet, and tears form at the corners of my eyes; but these aren't the kind of tears I want. I don't want tears from pain or anger, I want tears from sadness. My hands envelop my face, trying to hide how pathetic I seem to feel. As if on cue, the tears begin to flow. Rubbing my eyes, I take my glasses off and look up to my ceiling. I crawl onto my bed, the pillow masking my feelings. Anger begins to take over again, and I immediately get up, going through my drawers. Where are they? They have to be around here somewhere…

Rushing as I look through everything, I feel my knees starting to give out. I can't relax yet… Now is not the time. As I go through the bottom drawer in my dresser, I find the one thing that I need-my photo album. I jump onto my bed and look through everything. I see photos of me and Katelyn when we were little. There's one where we both have ice cream on our faces. I start laughing. As I turn the pages, however, something changes. I see someone that I don't remember. There's a little boy with brown hair, green eyes, and a tan skin complexion. I shrug my shoulders.

"He's probably one of my old school friends," I say while shrugging my shoulders; however, I seem to doubt myself.

Turning the pages once more, I find more photos of me and Katelyn, while allowing tears to fall down my face. I fall asleep, thinking of my past.

When I wake up, my face is wet with my hair sticking to it. The photo album is on my bed. Quickly putting the album in the bottom drawer, I walk into the bathroom. My skin is really red and burns quite a bit. Perhaps the tears had too much salt in them? I quietly laugh at this thought, but soon notice that my head is pounding. Dizziness seems to surround me, and I nearly yell in pain. I calm myself down quickly and return to my bed, desperate to sleep once again, but my mind will never fall back asleep with these thoughts swirling around my mind. Heat begins to surround me, and I know that I need to get some fresh air… Quietly walking down the stairs, I grab a bowl of ice cream. It's almost as if I'm trying to force the ice cream to succumb to *me*. I keep punching the ice cream into the bowl, desperate for something that I can take my anger out on. Then again, I don't know what I'm feeling anymore. Hurt, anger, sadness, and so many feelings are inside of me, dying to break out. I'm locked in a never-ending infinity of wanting to scream and yell, yet wanting to be able to laugh at all of this. Why do the ones we care about the most leave us? Why do these things happen? For someone as normal as me, I don't have anything else to look forward to. I'm a nothing.

* * *

It feels as if my heart has become a thousand pounds heavier. My mind goes blank and my face becomes hot. "Would this be what a fire feels like?" I ask myself. As I fall, I notice drops of water hitting the ground. I'm crying, but for some reason I don't feel it. My mind has gone into a depressed state, and I don't know how to get out of it. My ice cream bowl is lying on the ground, nearly spilled. Will I be left to melt one day? If I left right here, right now, permanently, would that make things better? I've never felt this before… And I'm scared.

Time seems to stand still, yet my mother is in front of

me, in her white robe, asking if I'm fine. I can't speak. My throat feels as if it is closed. I feel as if I am choking, but my physical body is fine. Everything seems to move slowly, but that only happens in the movies, right? Wrong. When you're going through something like this, you stop breathing. Realizations slap you in the face, and you're left broken. This isn't just because my best friend is gone, it's because I'm gone. I don't know who I am anymore. My whole life has been spent being with people I love. Sure, I've lost distant family members before, so why is this happening? Everything begins to fade into darkness, with my heart still beating strong. How can my heart be so strong when I'm not? Maybe the better question is, "Why am I so weak?"

* * *

Waking up in my own bed, the room is spinning. The light is hurting my eyes, and I have to wait for them to adjust. I try sitting up, but I nearly fall over from my dizziness. I manage to look out of my bedroom window, however. The sky seems to be a bit dark. How long was I asleep? My whirlwind seems to have come to a stop, but now I'm facing a hurricane. The darkness creeps up on me once again and I can't see and I'm breathing heavily. The unsteady intervals of my breathing seem to lull me to sleep, and I quickly find the darkness once again.

* * *

I guess everyone dreams of something when they sleep, but for the next few days, whenever I try to draw the picture of the tree dream, all I find is a blank. This dream seemed to affect me, but how can it if I can't even remember it? Though, I did have a fever for a few days, so it's not like I could trust my mind at that point anyway. If you want to know whether I'm scared, I'll answer truthfully. Yes, I am. Am I confused? Yes, I am. Am I truly lost? If you haven't found your way back yet, but you might, is that a yes, or is it a no? Can it be an indefinite maybe? What is being lost? Does everyone find their way back at some point? Can there be an infinite maybe? Is it possible for anyone to be truly lost, whereas they are choosing not to remember their way back? There are so many questions floating around my mind, and every time I think of them, I feel dizzy. What if I'm trying to remember my dream, but I really am choosing not to? There's a problem that comes with choosing not to: it's nearly impossible to change your mind back.

* * *

I don't go to school for a full week, missing boat loads of work. As I go to my locker, I notice Cornelia and manage to stride over just as she is closing her locker.

"Hey," I say.

"You could've at least asked for my phone number so you could call me. I didn't really have anyone to talk to, you know," Cornelia said accusingly.

"I'm sorry, I've been really sick for the past week," I reply. I was a bit taken aback by what she said, but I tried to pretend like what she said hadn't bothered me. We don't really know each other. Plus, why wouldn't anyone talk to her? Most people in this school are pretty friendly...

"Yeah, I know, and I'm sorry. It's just I have no one to talk to without you here," She replies with a sigh.

"This is a school full of people. I'm sure you can find someone to talk to," I say with a laugh.

"I've only known you for maybe 2 weeks and I'm already acting as if we are best friends," She shakes her head and turns around to face me.

"So, how are classes going?"

"They're working." She says, focusing on the lock on her locker.

"That doesn't mean they're good. What happened?"

"It feels as if the teachers are always calling on me, and I never seem to know the answer," she groans, "Yes, I did the homework, and I am studying normally, but that doesn't seem to be enough. None of this information is sticking to my brain, and it's so difficult."

"Trust me, I've been there. It gets easier, you just need time to sleep and think things through."

"And I have, but it's still not working," She groans.

"Keep trying. Well, we are officially 1 minute late to school. I think we should get going."

"We have Spanish in the morning, and something tells me our teacher is going to be late," She says with a smirk.

"What tells you that?"

"Let's just say a few friends of mine planned a little something."

We stride down the hall, talking about random things as we go. She's right, the prank they pulled, or are going to pull, will keep the Spanish teacher waiting. Another part of me tells me it's going to have consequences, almost as if something bad were to happen. I just wish I knew what. For the rest of the conversation, I hear what Cornelia is saying, but I don't take it in. Every morning, Senor Augment walks into the teacher's room at 7:55 AM. The students put toilet paper on the counters, so it shouldn't be that big of a deal. Cornelia said they're going to cover all the table tops in the room with toilet paper, or, at least, behind all the kitchen appliances. I have been in the teacher's room a few times for the teachers, but all I can remember is that there is a coffee pot, a fridge, and a microwave. I don't see anything wrong with... The microwave! If the paper is in or near the microwave, then a fire could start, and let's just say fires aren't the *best* thing for everyone to be around. I immediately come to a halt. Cornelia calls my name a few times, but I can't hear her over the sound of blood thumping in my ears. I immediately start running towards the teachers' room. This one action could kill me. Do I really want to risk it?

The Golden Fire

The teachers' room is covered in toilet paper when I get there. Senor Augment is in front of the sink, looking at what seems to be inside of it in shock. He tried to stop the fire with the water, but it was too late. The fire was spreading across the wooden countertops. Before I know what I'm doing, I yell "Get out! Now!" The teacher looks at me for a few seconds; a move that could be deadly in this situation. He's worried about me. Now is *not* the time. I run to him and push him out of the room, his heels scraping on the floor. My arms ache even though I didn't push him far. Though I know it's risky, I close the door. The fire grew in those few seconds that my back was turned, and I can feel sweat dripping down my face. The hot air is burning my face while the smoke invades my lungs, leaving me without a chance to take a breath. I take a few steps towards the fire, but it feels as if I am walking into an inferno. How can I continue like this? My heart beats very fast, and begins to feel as if it's trying to run out of my body and save itself. It begins to hurt more and more, but the only thing I focus on is the strong beats being created. It's almost like a pattern--a soft, then strong beat. The soft beats get softer, and the strong beats get stronger until I begin to lose consciousness. Thump! Everything turns white as my body burns into a crisp. There's a tree in my peripheral vision, and I make sure to look at it. At first it is blurry, but I focus on it, ignoring the prickling of my skin. As I take a step towards the tree, my legs nearly buckle. My vision returns back to normal for a second, and I see the fire about to crash down on me. Any sounds that I make won't help me. I'm about to die. "There's not... enough... time," I whisper while choking on the black mist that surrounds my reality. I black out for a second, and my vision becomes blurry. My heart beats hard once more and I see the darkness; the shadow of the tree that I've been so curious about. Without knowing what I'm doing or why, I run to the tree, each step taking a toll on my body. This can't be my reality, and yet, I feel such a connection; much like a surging fire within my hand, urging me to reach out. My hand, with full grace and tentativeness, tries to lie on top of it, but the tree backs away. My head feels heavy, and I fall onto the roots of the tree. I raise my hand and try to touch the center... trying to find the source... But before I know what's happening, my vision blurs for the last time, and my breathing seems to fade away. My heart seems to give out. Who knows if or when I'll wake up?

* * *

I try opening my eyes, but all I see are bright lights. The beeping that I hear in the corners of the room brings pain to my ears. My eyes begin to adjust shortly after, and the sounds hurt less, but all I see is a white ceiling. Trying to raise my arm up, it feels as if I some of the muscles tore, causing me to react. My whole body seems to cry out, leaving me in even more pain. Lifting my other arm, I notice that there is a white, translucent bracelet circling it. As I look around, I notice the room is a full off-shade of white. The walls are not quite a yellow, but are not yet white. There seems to be a fog around the place, which I assume are my own eyes continuously adjusting to the light. I can't describe what I feel. It's a feeling of violation, but also a feeling of curiosity; one of bravery, yet one of cowardice. There isn't one feeling that can fully grasp what I feel now.

"I'm your nurse. You had a pretty bad hit to the head and have been sleeping for around 2-3 days," said the nurse.

I jump at the sound of another person's voice and a low ringing sound in my ears. I slowly try to get up, ignoring the ripping feeling in my arm.

2-3 days? Could I have been imagining what had happened, then? Was what I saw even real? Or what I thought I saw...

The nurse gives me medicine through an IV. My whole body is sore and I can barely move a muscle. Through all of this, though, the thing I notice the most is that I feel... depleted; almost as if some part of me has been taken. It's a very uncomfortable feeling. I can't think straight, and it annoys me that it takes me forever to work out a basic math problem.

"Your mother said she'll try to pick you up today or tomorrow. She stayed with you in the hospital until late last night, so I imagine she might be sleeping right now. Then again, what happened desperately worried her. It's a possibility she didn't get a wink of sleep, so that's why we have to make sure you're fine, alright? We gave you necessary vitamins through an IV, and we might need to do further tests to see if everything is fine. Just be careful. Sometimes an act of bravery costs more than what it's worth," she says with a small, knowing smile.

Although I heard the nurse's words, they don't register with me. Confusion ripples throughout me, and as I think back, I can't remember doing anything special; in fact, if anything, what I did was dumb. If I did manage to put the fire out, then my school is fine, though, so I assume that's good. I was sleeping for 3 days, meaning I missed a lot of school work. As I internally groan, I remember that I also missed Halloween. Katelyn is definitely going to be angry with me. Calling her became of great importance to me, which means it also led to a great amount of nervousness. I was scared of how she would react. Would she let me explain, or just ignore me the second I began calling? I suppose I should relish the time left in the hospital because I don't have to call her yet, but unfortunately I am not filled with great zest. How will she react? Will she get rid of our friendship for good? Though, I doubt you can just throw away a friendship like that unless something seriously is seriously wrong. Making friends can be scary, but it can also teach you lessons you need in life. Friendship is never easy, and even when things go wrong, you can't stay mad at the people you care about forever. As I lay back down, I can see my vision starting to blur once more until I'm fast asleep.

Unlike my expectations, no nightmare was included in my sleep. When I woke up, I felt somewhat rejuvenated. I knew a bit more sleep would do me good, but I also knew it wouldn't completely heal me. Now, when I think back to times when Katelyn and I used to play, it almost feels like some of them are missing. Perhaps the feeling comes from not having her here to comfort me anymore, or perhaps I just forgot… But that doesn't seem to be very likely. Whenever I think back to my old memories, I just remember that Katelyn left. It makes me wonder if she took some of the memories with her. I laugh at this thought, but it makes me nervous. I hear the door creak open, and my mom enters, interrupting my thoughts. The nurses take the IV out of my arm quickly and I notice for the first time that I have a few stitches. *Great, that's going to leave a scar.*

We walk through the parking lot with my mother holding onto my good arm. Lying in the back seat of the car, thoughts of what I should do fill my mind. Yes, I could tell my mother about what I saw, but what good would that do? She might just make me see a psychiatrist, and I know that in this situation, that won't help me whatsoever. Depression seems to overcome me at the thought of not being able to know what's going on. Maybe if I knew what was going on, I could get passed it; but a part of me screams that is just the beginning. It seems as if my mom is noticing the dust of my emotions rising in the air. She doesn't seem to be as calm as usual. Did anyone else die from trying to save people after they saw such a thing? Did they begin to have a dull life like this one seems to feel? Or did they have a much worse fate? If this has happened before, I need to find out how they dealt with it, because if you don't know your history, then you are bound to repeat it.

* * *

I open my search browser and begin to type in "tree dreams". It may seem a bit funny, or maybe a bit weird, but I don't have much of a place to start. These dreams may vary among people, and different types of people may see different forms or shapes. Through each person, I would imagine, however, everyone has the same idea of a dream. Somehow they touch the object in their dream and it creates a memory out of the old ones. Almost as if they are recycling dreams… I search this topic up, and many things appear during my search. Mostly names of songs, or poems, but I come across an article, dated 20 years ago. The website is quite old, and you can tell it hasn't been updated in awhile. Unlike many other websites, ads don't pop up everywhere. The title is in bold with a pretty, calligraphic font. I scroll through the article, checking for something important.

"The girl said to have felt a void after the flood, despite the fact that she saved many people by swimming them to a dry piece of land. The water then just disappeared. No one knows how the water miraculously disappeared, but it saved hundreds of lives."

Somehow this incident seems more… special. Almost as if the girl really did complete a miracle, rather than just stopping a fire. I suppose both of the circumstances were dangerous, but even so… We felt something lost after we saved people. Maybe the article has the girl's name. I scroll, looking for some sort of description of her, but the name is blurred out. If she wanted to be in the article, why did they blur her name out? This took place North Carolina… I never received a name, but, for some reason, it says the girl died in a hospital when she was 15 after saving a man from a car crash. There was nothing wrong with her. The doctors couldn't find one single health problem aligned with her death. Looking up this incident further, it seems like the girl had died after saving 9 people from accidents. Then she died… I've only saved one so far. If I will have to save about

10 people, and then die from it, is it really worth the risk? Do I want to lose my life, and everything inside it?

She may have saved ten people, but she forgot to save herself.

On Monday, it feels as if everything has just started over again. The same old repeated weeks, days, and classes follow me around. Cornelia and her friends were suspended for a week. I feel bad for her, but she should've known better. I mean, you really can't be dumb enough to put paper in a microwave on purpose. Unfortunately, I never saw where exactly the paper was put because Senor Augment picked it up, which probably wasn't the best idea, for him and for me. What if they were trying to get a fire started? What if they really were trying to burn down the school? How would I fix this?

* * *

The next few days add more stress onto my nerves. The teachers are always smiling at me and it makes me feel as if I need to help them even more. *I need to risk my life even more.* Somehow, in their own little way, I know they're trying to thank me for saving the school, but it's not helping. We have an assembly on Friday about how people need to be careful with pranks, but the truth is everyone thinks that it's really about me. They really have no idea what went on in the teacher's room, and I want them to find out. The unfortunate part is that they will think I'm crazy or say something like "It seems like she's dealing with a little bit of head trauma, students." That would be *extremely* embarrassing. I have no other choice but to just keep quiet.

And so the week passes in what feels like a drag until we arrive at the assembly. There's a stage made by the students in the middle of the basketball court. Luckily, the stage has wheels so we can move it as we please. Sometimes we hold assemblies in the auditorium, but the drama club is performing a play, like most days. The basketball court can hold many people, so it's also good for the students. When the principal speaks, his voice creates an echo and his voice bounces around the walls, silencing students. "Good afternoon students. Today is a day we relish. Our lives and our school have been saved, thanks to Paula. If she hadn't been there to stop the prank that some other students made, we might not be here right now. Paula Berney will be remembered as the one who saved hundreds of students. We thank you formally, though I wish we could do more."

Sitting on the podium was nerve-wracking. It seems like every word, every letter of each word, slowed down time. And that's when the sound of the large court doors opening ruffled my vision. Cornelia strode in and began to yell, "You think you can suspend me? Well I hope you enjoy this week, because there won't be another like it. The only reason Paula saved you guys is because I told her about the prank. Without me, she couldn't have done anything! You all deserve this." Time slows, but I'm moving normally. I see Cornelia holding something... It's a lighter! This time she's really going to try to light the school on fire! Who would've known somebody I trusted this much could betray me? We've only known each other for a few weeks, but I thought she could be a real friend. Of course something was going on. That explains everything. My heart burns and aches with a sense of betrayal. Sprinting towards the lighter, I pay close attention to Cornelia. Although we didn't know each other that well, I trusted her! Tears start to form in the corners of my eyes, but I will myself to stop. Nothing can distract me now, or hundreds of children might die for it.

Why do bad things keep happening to me?

I look at my surroundings. There are students covering their heads. These children are innocent. How can you hurt someone that doesn't know how to defend themselves yet? I can feel my heart beating even faster, letting rage take over, but as soon as I think I know what to do, I question myself. This is another act of saving, meaning I only have 8 left if what that website said was true. I could die from this! Though I know it's wrong, I hesitate. Shivers get sent down my back as I let the selfish thoughts take over. Choices are what make a person, right? Well, now I need to make the right choice, but I don't know which one is. What do I do?

Time begins to move faster and I quickly grab the lighter, shutting it closed very tightly. Despite that I saved my friends from impending danger, I feel selfish inside. Other people were going to die, and yet I hesitated on protecting them! Just because I was worried about my own life, I put hundreds of others in danger. What happens when I really do need to make a decision between myself and other people? I still have 8 chances left, so it may seem like I have some time now, but when I only have 1, how drastically will my mind change? So many questions float around my mind, but have yet to be answered.

This time I don't faint, but I do sit down on the ground.

Taking deep breaths, I make sure that my pulse is still somewhat consistent.

The policemen check everyone while the principals and teachers come to me. They slowly take the lighter out of my hand and ask me if I'm doing alright. I didn't see where they took Cornelia, but I feel a wave of relief wash over me. I just want to fall asleep right now. This is way too much stress for a 12 year old in just 2 weeks.

* * *

I never wanted it to be this way. Why was I born so different from everyone else? I mean, I'm not special; instead I have powers which cause me pain. Sure, I've dreamed of being a superhero before, but not like this! Not having to choose between myself and others! Then again, isn't that what superheroes normally do? They risk their own lives for others... Thinking about how foolish I was to wish for things that I knew I couldn't handle, I feel silly. I miss the innocent times, where I could just be a child and play tag with my friends. The older I get, the more work I have, and that's without being a part-time superhero. I roll my eyes at this thought, but it causes pain in my head.

"How are you doing? Are you dizzy?" the principal asks.

I take a minute to gather my thoughts. As the principal waits in anticipation for my answer, I gather a straight face and do my best at pretending everything is fine.

"I'm fine, just no more assemblies for me please," I respond with a sigh.

Truthfully, I'm not dizzy or sick, and my head feels fine aside from the small amount of pain. The only thing I do feel is hurt; physical and emotional. The fire seemed to have licked the place near my stitches. That's not what really hurts, though. How can you have the audacity to betray someone like that? Can jealousy really drive people that mad? People have nothing to be jealous about from me. I'm 7th grader, Paula Berney, just a normal girl.

Reliving the Past

It's Saturday, the day after the assembly incident. It's also my birthday. Usually my mother and I go out to a restaurant and celebrate my birthday at home with Katelyn, but now things have changed. Although I am excited for whatever she has planned, I can't help but be wary. The past few weeks have been dangerous, especially with fire, and if she gets me a cake with candles on top of it, I could end up burning the whole house down. Although I'm the one putting out the fires, not starting them, bad things just seem to happen around me.

My mom called Katelyn to tell her everything that's going on. As her best friend, I already know how she reacted. Partially shocked and partially screaming out of excitement, but also filled with worry. Katelyn has always looked out for me and I've always looked after her. We're so much like sisters, sometimes I can barely tell us apart. Of course, I'm less bubbly and less girly. She's always been the one into wearing earrings and getting all dressed up for school. Well, as much as she can, anyway. I like wearing nail polish, but that's as far as you're going to get me. Wearing uncomfortable clothing is not on my bucket list, either. I wear dresses during special occasions now and then, but that doesn't mean I enjoy it. When I finally decide to get up, I notice that it's already ten o'clock, and I have five missed calls from Katelyn that are all within 2 minute intervals. "*Impressive,*" I say to myself while nodding my head. I call her back before my phone blows up.

"You finally picked up. Did-" Katelyn said, letting out a sigh.

"Yes, I'm alive and healthy. Yes, I am eating. No, I did not endure any head trauma," I reply, cutting her off.

"Ok, ok, I get it. I'm acting like a mom," Katelyn laughs.

"My mom was just happy I could talk normally. This way if anything happened…" I reply quietly.

"Yeah, I get it. You're mom really cares about you. She told me how worried she was."

"I know," I whisper knowingly.

When I think about all that has happened, it really seems unfair to my mother that I haven't told her anything about the dreams, but do I really have a choice? I can't worry anyone. It's not going to end up boding well for my conscience.

Katelyn questions, "How's school going?"

"I should be asking you that. You're the one that moved." I reply, stifling a laugh.

"School's good. The people here don't talk *too* much. The teachers here are really cool. My favorite ones are the math teacher, Mrs. Pellin, and the Language Arts teacher, Mr. Switz," she acknowledged.

"I'm happy that you like the new teachers!"

Although I truly am happy for Katelyn, I still miss her.

It's hard not having her around. Perhaps if she had been here, none of this would've happened, but that's not her fault. We can't control what other people want, and her parents *wanted* to move to North Carolina. I wish they didn't have to, but if they enjoy it better where they live now, then I suppose everything will turn out to be fine.

"Yeah… Well, I have to go eat breakfast. My mom's calling me. Bye!"

"Bye."

My back facing the windows, I can feel the warmth emanating from a planet that is so far away, and it makes me smile. No matter how far away the Sun may be, its light still manages to reach us. As I pay attention to the streams of light gathering into a small area of my room, I notice my laptop, and I begin to walk over to it. The light's reflection is strong on the laptop screen, but I can deal with it. Once I turn on the laptop, I turn it away from the sun and begin to search up the incident that happened with the girl 20 years ago again. This time, a new link pops up. It says:

"Margaret Livingston, daughter of Opal Livingston and best friend of Thomas Switzer."

Thomas Switzer… where have I heard that name before? Well, Katelyn said a guy named Mr. Switz was her favorite teacher… What if he really is one of the teachers at Katelyn's new school? If I can find him, maybe he can tell me about what's going on. This guy might be my only hope.

* * *

As a birthday present, I convinced my mom to travel to North Carolina for the winter break, which begins December 20th, on a Wednesday. We won't be going exactly when winter break starts, though. Two incidents have happened already, so I'm going to try to make sure there won't be another one any time soon, or at least, throughout this month. How I'm going to do this, I don't know, but I will do it. It's not like they'll keep happening everywhere I go, right? As I make my way downstairs, I notice the table has a few pancakes with ice cream on top of it. There are small flames lit near the pancakes and the ice cream is starting to melt. I become dazed for second, and I immediately know something is wrong.

I could feel the blood rushing towards my head; my vision was cut off for a few seconds, leaving me without sight; however, it returned, leaving my face pale and my lips a bright red.

"Are you ok?" asks my mom.

I blink, and respond with "Fine."

Walking to the table, I feel as if I'm a shell of myself. Every step feels awkward, and my mom's protective stare seems to be piercing my back. This isn't the same as before. Something has been changed; I just wish I knew what. Forgetting the feeling, I focus on what's right in front of me. Even if I don't have a lot of time left, I should enjoy the time that *is* left. Maybe I'm not technically dying right now, but as far as I know, I will. The thought of missing everyone, my mother, my friends, even the teachers from school, overwhelms me. They all have been such a big part of my life, and I'm going to have to lose them. Warm tears cascade down my face, and my mother becomes worrisome once again. "I'm fine, just thankful that you did all this for me. It's amazing, it really is," I whisper. Smiling when you want to cry is never easy. My life hasn't been anything special, at least without the life-threatening things that seem to keep happening. Why, when I suddenly gain something that makes me feel as if I'm special, it gets taken away from me? Nothing is fair! What did I do to deserve to die? Maybe that's the question everyone asks when their family member dies, except reversed, but... it's different when you're the one dying. You really don't notice how much you have to lose until you lose it all. Leaving my mother like that, after all she's done for me? It's not right. I need to be there for her, but now I can't. Anger courses through my veins, but I calm myself down. Do I want to spend the rest of my life like this? I'll be worrying about everything if I let the depressing thoughts take over. Inside of my head, though, where everything seems to take place, I can't help but think these thoughts.

My whole future is gone. Will people forget about me? I don't just want people to remember me for who I saved; I want them to remember me for who I really am. Then again, who am I? That's the one thing I have always questioned about myself. Who do I want to be? I've never tried to be anyone else. So, why is it, that I'm being forced to be someone I'm not? If I wasn't blessed, yet cursed, with these new "powers" of mine, would I really save anyone? Would I be a coward? Maybe that's something I wouldn't want to believe, but it's something I'm eventually going to have to come to terms with. Time passes quickly, leaving me with barely any time to really think about my birthday. Before I know it, I'm getting ready to sleep. Crawling into bed, my mother kisses my forehead, and I fall into the dark lullaby of sleep. The white room is back. I'm near the tree, but something is different. The tree grew. It didn't just grow a bit, either. Each branch extended and the ones that were already formed have another connected to it. Yet, still, the tree is charcoal. I watch my feet, and notice I'm trembling. I try to take a few steps, but none of them work. No matter what, I never make it to the tree. I'm always stuck in the same place until I wake up. A tear falls from my face, but I don't understand why. When I look, it seems that the tear didn't soak into the white ground. It's just sitting there. What does this tree feed upon, if not water? Without sunlight, how does it grow?

* * *

Once again, I am covered in sweat, but instead, it's 1 AM: one more hour than before. I quickly push the blankets off and let the cold air consume and devour me. I soon fall asleep to the howling of the wind outside my window… And wake up 7 hours later. Why was I so tired? My mother arrives in my doorway.

"We're going to the park, Paula. You need some fresh air."

* * *

As I walk outside, the birds are chirping and the sun is fully out. It's so different from last night… The howling outside of my window still lurks in my mind. How could I fall asleep to such a scary lullaby? As we are walking to the park, I notice things I never noticed before. People are outside, playing with their children and pets. They are the perfect picture of a family. Sometimes I wonder what it would be like to have a "perfect family". I don't have a father though, so what would I know. Yes, everyone has a father, but not one I grew up with. It's just my mother and me. Sometimes you need a dad to give you advice, which is something I never received. You can't give people what you don't get, I guess. This would be a great time for Katelyn to pop out of nowhere, saying she came for a visit, but I know that won't happen. I look at the sun and laugh at the thought. As we arrive at the park, some of my school friends are there. The trees are giving them shade, as well as the table they stand beside which holds food and drinks.

"Hey, Paula. The assembly didn't go too well, and we're some of your friends, so we decided to have our own little party. Happy late birthday, Paula," says Beatrice with a warm smile. Some of the other students near the food table are in the same class as me, but I haven't gotten a chance to talk to them within the past few weeks due to everything has happened.

"Guys, this is so sweet! Thank you so much!" I respond with a small squeal.

I run to Beatrice and hug her, then run to the food table. Everyone looks at me and follows my lead. There are salads, burgers, and cake, which I assume will be eaten last. I take a cheeseburger and some salad and find an empty seat.

"It's been a pretty busy few weeks, hasn't it?" asks Beatrice while sitting down next to me.

"Yeah, I just can't believe everything that happened," I respond. "Well, I'm about to put some music on. Everyone's going to dance, want to join?" Beatrice invites.

"Perhaps I'll dance in a bit. I'm just going to think a few things through," I respond softly.

While sitting down on the tree trunk, I watch everyone dance. They seem to be having fun. Soon, the colors of the iridescent lights they put out fade and my thoughts take over.

"Hey, seems like you're out of it today." says Bryan.

"Yeah, how could you tell?" I respond after a few minutes.

"We've known each other since pre-school. Didn't you think that I could tell?" he asks while laughing. "Let things cool down. It'll be ok. Come dance with everyone."

"Are you sure? It might be better if I just… Sit down…" I respond while stretching.

"Relax. No one is going to judge you. If anything, they will probably look sillier than you."

I sigh and put my food down. As I get up, I brush the dirt off of my clothes and begin to walk towards everyone. He's right; he's known me since pre-school. It seems crazy, huh? I have to admit, he probably does know me the best out of everyone. Arriving at the dance floor, I start laughing and dancing with everyone. There are no names for our weird dances, just us being us. Freestyle, I guess. I don't know when the party ended, or how, but I know I woke up in my bed with my nightgown on. My hair was messy and probably impossibly knotted. Looking in the mirror, I think about whether brushing my hair will hurt. Maybe I'll have to cut it. Though, that thought doesn't bother me too much. I'm just happy I had fun.

Walking downstairs, I see my mom making breakfast. It's Monday, November 6. Just the thought of being in school tires me. I want to fall back into my warm nest of blankets and pillows, even though the chances of that happening are pretty low. My mom would probably let me stay home, but I, for my mental state, need to go to school.

Without school, my brain might simply waste away. So, the day begins and I travel to school.

"Will things ever go back to the way they were before?" I ask myself, though I already know the answer. My life is encircled in a fate which I cannot control. Is there a way to change my fate? If so, I have no idea how to do that. My mind begins wandering off into the depths of my curiosity, and it begins to take over. Is life something physical, or spiritual? What gives our brain the spark to just begin living? Maybe science can explain how everything in our body connects, but I doubt it can explain how I'm feeling right now. Sometimes I think science can explain everything, but for me, at least, it really can't. Where do I travel to when I'm in that dream? Do I travel to an alternate universe? Am I stronger than what I originally perceived myself out to be? What am I, really?

I begin walking into the school where I will spend the next 8 months living my life. Will I be dead by then? One thing the articles did not mention is when exactly it all started, or what age the girl was. How can I possibly change what's going to happen to me if vital clues like that are missing? I want to know when my life will end, so I can plan everything out. I'll spend more time with my mother and my friends, and try to strengthen the bond between us. But won't that just make everything harder for me? What if I'm not supposed to know when I'm going to die? This way, I'll be able to live a normal life. Though, I'll die with regrets, and there's nothing else that can be said. No matter what I do, I won't feel fulfilled. At this moment, I can't control myself. As I enter, I feel everyone's staring eyes; everyone's hard, but meaningful glances. Some mean, some thankful, and some curious. Hot tears run down my face and I can't seem to control myself. Before I know what I'm doing, I'm outside, running. I don't know where I'm going, or why my feet are leading me there, but I'm going.

Old Memories

A few blocks down from my school, there's an abandoned building. It's burned down, and there's a lot of ash lying on its remains. I don't know why it hasn't been torn down yet, but I don't question it, either. Sitting on the side of the building, masked by the shadows, I curl myself into a ball. Crying into my shirt, deep feelings of sadness and emptiness fill me. I walk into the building through a side door which was cracked open. For some reason, the first question that pops into my mind isn't "Why is this door open?", but instead "Who lived here?" I walk through the corridors, fingers scraping the walls, covering myself in ash. As I slowly travel up the stairs, I begin to question more and more what I'm doing here. I come across a room that seems to be different than the others. Is it more... cheerful? The door is decorated in things that a little girl may enjoy. Pink, frilly, things that would make life feel more... is there a word to describe it? It makes the apartment seem real, but almost too good to be true. I slowly open the door. It won't budge at first, as there's ash all around the doorknob, bunched together like little rocks. Though, once I do manage to get the door open,

I see the fragile home which had been slowly deteriorated by time and the fire. The only intact thing that I see is a photo lying on the ground. It's also covered in ash, but it's one more form of life to look forward to. As I walk through a small, narrow hallway, I enter a room which seems to be a child's. I pick up the photo and brush the ash off. There's a two year old in a dress, and a man also there. For some reason, I feel a connection to this photo. As I look closer at the photo, I notice this man looks like the man my mother has in her photos: my father. I knew my father died when I was little, and occasionally asked questions, but there wasn't a time where I was really enveloped into getting to know a lot about him. He seemed like a jolly man. My question is: Why is there a photo, seemingly of *my* father, lying in the middle of the ground? Well, I suppose my mother can explain this, but I'm afraid I already know what she's going to say. By now, my school would've called my mother, and my mother will come looking for me. Something tells me she knows where I am. Something also tells me she's going to follow me up. My instincts tell me to run, but my mind tells me it's too late.

We're 3 stories up and my mother just fell; or, is falling, rather. Everything slows down as my heart pounds as quickly and as powerful as ever. The staircase she tried to walk up is circular, but there are no railings protecting us from falling, as they were destroyed. She must've slipped on something and fell. I could try to catch my mother, but I'm afraid that would only get us both hurt. Tears start streaming down my face and I yell something incoherent. I know I don't have long until I will start to faint. My vision is already starting to become blurry. My heart begins to beat extremely fast, and I can hear my mother's screams echoing throughout the air. I know I have to try something, and before I know what I'm doing, I'm floating. Time begins to slow down even more, and her hair waves slowly, as if it were a flag caught by the wind, in certain places. I quickly rush to catch her before she falls, and make it just in time. Time begins to speed up, but luckily, I'm already on the ground, pushing my mother onto her feet. She catches her breath, and immediately starts the interrogation.

"Paula, what is happening? I was falling one minute and now..." she questions suspiciously.

"I'll explain everything later, just, please, let's go home."

My mother nods. I think about the photograph and want to go back to get it, but I know that my mother won't let me. I sigh and we get into the car. I'm tired, but the fatigue is easier to deal with than last time. The last few times I saved people, I may have been around hundreds of students, but I wasn't doing anything crazy; just moving fast. This time might be a bit more... noticeable. After all, I was *technically* flying. For some reason, instead of worrying about explaining things to my mother, I think about my father. What would my life have been like if he was here? Would I still be cursed to live a fate that I don't want so early in my life, or would my life be normal? Though, normal can get pretty boring, I guess.

* * *

When we open the door, my mother walks past the living room and sits down on the kitchen table. I also sit in a seat, assuming she'll want answers.

"Are you ok? Well, first of all, thank you for saving me,

though I don't quite know how. Second of all, are you ok?" My mother asks.

"Yes, I'm fine. As you were falling I managed to catch you and push you onto your feet," I reply dryly.

"That seems almost impossible, but I suppose it's the only explanation," she says, though I know she's not quite done thinking this over.

There's an inquisitive look on her face, almost as if she doesn't believe that I saved her; like some miracle had occurred, but she doesn't know what.

"I don't blame you for running, but you will eventually have to learn to contain your feelings. To survive the rest of the 7th grade, you're going to have to. Not to mention you still have to get through the 8th," my mother warns me with a sigh.

My mother says so many words, but I don't register them. Instead I pay attention to the pattern on the table. The lines are intertwining and looping around in a wooden square. At each end, it doesn't seem like the lines bump into a solid wall, though. There's an infinite curve to the design, though it doesn't seem to make too much sense. Then again, nothing seems to make too much sense now.

"Mom, I'm going to go upstairs, ok? I need to clear my head," I respond.

She nods, but the curiosity still lingers. Her eyes aren't focused on me, almost as if they are going through me. Not a good sign. Before I go upstairs, I quickly and softly rub my mom's arm for reassurance. Walking through the hallway to my bedroom, I feel as if I'm not thinking. My mind is scattered, but it doesn't seem to bother me. As I sit down on my bed, I feel lost. Then it comes back. I look at the reflection of the sunlight from the bathroom mirror and begin walking toward it, unsure. As I look at myself, I see the same facial features as before. Brown hair, light skin, but as I go to look at my eyes I notice the sunlight is on them. For some reason, in the mirror it looks like amethyst is circling around the corners of my eyes, but I know it's not real. Though, it's nice to notice something different. For the next few minutes, I keep looking and do notice *something* different. My facial features are the same. Maybe they're dirty, but they haven't changed. It almost seems as if my demeanor changed. There's something in my eyes that wasn't there before. Perhaps it is fear or confidence. Neither of those really fit, however. I think the feeling is one of… readiness.

As time goes on, I report to school normally, as if nothing had ever happened, though that's just a façade. Or perhaps we all just want to forget. Either way, it's nice to pretend that everything isn't completely going wrong in my life right now. On the last day of school before break, I say goodbye to all my friends. I'm going to visit my best friend Katelyn in North Carolina within the next few days! I'm also going to find out about the mysterious Thomas Switzer. Before I exit the school, though, I hear someone calling my name.

"Paula! Paula! Over here!" Bryan shouts.

"Hey Bryan, what's up?" I ask.

"I was wondering if you're leaving during break."

"I'm leaving tomorrow to North Carolina."

"Want to go somewhere?"

"Sure. When is it?"

"We're meeting up tonight at five o'clock. There's this

really cool juice place 3 blocks from here. I think Beatrice and a few other people are going too."

"Ok, I'll ask my mom. See you later!"

"Bye Paula!"

"Bye!"

Opening my school's glass doors, a smile can't help but hint its way on my lips. As soon as I get into the car, my face is filled with full-out excitement. My mother opens the door and asks why my face seems so red. I tell her why and ask her if I can go. I look at the trees swaying in the breeze. For once, I feel like a completely normal girl. Now, this is the life I wish I had. This thought doesn't seem to bother me too much, but it's sitting at the back of my mind, waiting to strike. It's funny how much I wanted to be different before, and now I'd do anything to be normal again. Things really do change, don't they?

Getting Ready

When I get home, I quickly rush to my room and put on a navy blue dress with black tights underneath. The dress is made out of cotton, nearly fitting like a long shirt, except the cotton is covered with a lot of lace. It is somewhat itchy, but I cut the uncomfortable parts off. The tights are just fine and are more comfortable than any of my jeans. My black flats cover my feet and my hair is gathered in a pony tail. As I look in the mirror, there's one thing missing: my headband. I look everywhere for my headband, but I can't seem to find it. I look at the time. 4:30 PM. I still have about 15 minutes and then we have to leave. I search the bathroom drawers, emptying them out, but find nothing of the sort. I look in my bedroom drawers, but find an unfortunate revelation. My headband is not there. I walk down the stairs and ask my mother if she knows where it is. After 5 minutes of searching, I find it within the kitchen drawer. Without the headband, my outfit would seem dull and boring in comparison. It's funny how little things like that can change the look of a person drastically, isn't it?

Chapter 8

The Raytown Diner

I look at the building where I am supposed to be meeting Bryan and my friends. I quickly take in every detail. The red and silver going around the building in stripes that look surprisingly good, I can see a caricature reflection throughout the walls. The sunset is shown in a rather tall manner, which may seem humorous but yet still finds a way to remain beautiful. The land surrounding the building is a beige sidewalk maybe about 2 feet wide, and then the parking lot's asphalt floor, black but somewhat dirty with oil and other things that cars manage to leave behind. A shiny railing leads into a door. The building is somewhat tall for a 1 story, but nothing is as compared to the light breeze floating throughout me. The wind picks up my hair, letting me fly in a way that I never have before. Time seems to slow, but not in the same way that it would when my "extraordinary abilities" show. It's a happier, more exciting, and drastically less scary feeling. It is a feeling of peace and tranquility, yet one of excitement and anxiety. My mother drops me off at the diner and I walk through, slowly looking for Bryan. The tables are red with silver curves around the edges. They seem… soothing.

"Hey Paula."

"Hey. Where's Beatrice?"

"She called me and she couldn't make it."

I hear a ding on my phone and look at the text I receive.

Beatrice: Good luck on your date!

Me: It's not a date! You were supposed to be here!

Beatrice: Oh please! Like I believe that!

I blush for a few seconds.

"What happened?" Bryan asked.

I show him the texts and his face turns red.

"Anyway, do you want a milkshake? I'm not too hungry," he says.

"Yes, that would be nice. I'm not that hungry either."

"That's cool. Well, take a seat. Do you like the way the building is designed?" he asks, trying to cover the silence.

"I do. It's modern yet reminds me of old movies."

Bryan never brings up what had happened during the incidents, and we talk like regular people. We continue laughing about things that happened at school, how we're doing, and talk about what we want to do when we get older. Questions kept popping up in my mind that I wanted to ask, but couldn't. Sometimes I would get so distracted by my own curiosity, and forget what we were talking about in whole. Sure, it was nice to talk to someone, but it's even nicer to be able to show your weird side to that person; like what faults you have, your personal feelings, and whether you have had the same experiences or not. Though I was talking within the lengths of a normal friendship, it didn't feel real to me. These are times when I wish I had someone I could tell everything to; someone who wouldn't get jealous, mad, or judgmental before I have something to say. My best friend, Katelyn, was that person. But talking over the phone isn't the same thing as seeing a person face to face. Will I ever be able to live my life to the fullest if I have so much to hide?

The sky is a dark shade of blue by the time I leave, but it is only 6:45 p.m. I guess that's how it works in the winter. As I stare up at the sky, waiting for my mother to come pick me up, I see bright, white stars. In some ways, I'm almost like a star now. Stars eventually explode, and may leave a black hole in their path. Will I leave a black hole, or will other stars be created from my demise? All stars die eventually, though. I don't want to create more stars that may die themselves. I'm leaving them with either a good or a horrible future. There is no in-between living in this sky of wonders. You are left with two fates, but unlike flipping a coin, you truly do control yours. What will my decision be?

* * *

When I get home, I go upstairs and pick out my pajamas. I didn't really pay attention to what I picked out and instead began thinking about what it means to get older. I'm only 13, and I'm going to the 8th grade next year. It hasn't hit me that I'll be going to high school soon and that I'll make so many memories with new people. As I sit down on my bed, a smile forms on my face. If I make some new friends, I might be able to create a new life, right? It's a nice thought, but one that won't happen for me. The thought hits me, and a tear forms in my eyes, but I will myself not to cry. I've had enough crying for one year. A thirteen year old shouldn't have to deal with this. Not yet. Couldn't any of this have waited until I got older? I knew that if I didn't get in the shower within the next five minutes, I would be crying, my salty tears falling down my face, with my runny nose and angry thoughts consuming me. I want to be sad. I want to miss the time I have, but I'm instead angry. Why did this happen to me? My tears begin falling down in bushels. Just because my life isn't completely normal, it doesn't mean it's not worth living. At this thought, the tears stop. Shivers are sent down my spine.

"Maybe that means that everything truly is over; that I'm done for," I think, but I know that's not the truth.

Margaret Livingston died when she was 15. I wonder what she was like. Before I ask any more questions, I run into the shower, and let the water hitting my face wash off the salty remnants of my tears. My tears began stinging, but the stinging was put out. I didn't notice until now. I guess it's interesting, how sometimes you don't notice you had pain until you lose it. Maybe it's the same way with my life. I never noticed I actually was living one, and now I'm losing it. There's so much I wanted to be; so much that I wanted to do. And now none of that will happen because of my own selfishness. I'm causing my own demise, and now I need to fix it.

Walking out of the shower, I put on my pajamas that I just picked out. Looking out of the window in my bedroom, I stare at the moon that won't fully show itself. Sometimes people think that when clouds cover the moon, it's covering its true beauty, but I see it as if the moon is just showing another part of itself that we don't see often. Just because we aren't accustomed to something, it doesn't make it ugly. Sometimes new things are more beautiful than the old, until the new becomes old. That's the thing with beauty. On the outside, it may be superficial. Everyone likes different physical aspects, but when you begin to like the person for who they are, that's when you know you've met someone who you might be able to rely on. Of course, people change, but maybe they aren't changing at all. Maybe they're just showing their true selves. Am I the one that's changing, or is the world changing around me? It depends on everyone's point of view, I guess. In my point of view, I'm falling down, but in others' points of view, I may be getting stronger. What do I believe in? What I think or what other people believe?

I lay down, pulling the blankets over my head. For some reason, that comforts me, yet I leave the light on. Tonight is a night where I don't want to be alone in the dark. I need the light to protect me from what's lurking in the corners of the room. I'm not afraid of the dark, I'm afraid of losing my way. You can get easily lost when you're in the dark.

News for Mr. Switz

I walk down the hallways of my school, watching children dashing out of the doors and see a few staying after school for their extracurricular activities. As my heels click on the granite floor, I walk into my office and welcome Jeremiah.

"Hello, Jeremiah. How has your day been?" I question.

"It was normal. I was talking to Katelyn today," Jeremiah responds, "and she doesn't seem to be acting suspicious. Why are you so worried about this? Listen, uncle, all you've ever told me is that I'm stuck with some disease and just told me that this girl could fix it. What else do you want me to do?"

I look down at him with a warm smile.

"Jeremiah, I care about you as my nephew, I really do, but this isn't something to be taken lightly."

"Uncle, you never actually told me what the disease is, so how can I worry about it? Katelyn is a nice girl, but I don't really see us becoming friends," he says in a small voice.

"Jeremiah… There's no one else who can fix this. You understand that, don't you? There's only one girl, and that has to be Katelyn. Her timing is perfect. Just keep trying, my boy," I say the last part in a whisper, "I can't risk losing you too."

North Carolina

I get up bright and early, dressing for our plane ride. Excitement and nervousness course throughout me. This may be a mission, but I'm still going to see my best friend. Throughout all of this time of waiting to go to North Carolina, I never figured out a plan to meet Thomas Switzer. I didn't even look him up. With the last hour I have until we leave, I quickly open my laptop and search his name. I also put the state in which he lives right next to it so that I may be able to find out more information.

"Thomas Switzer is a 25 year old man who is a teacher at Pinehurst Middle School." I read.

If he works there, he must live somewhere near Katelyn, which means I might have a greater chance of seeing him. Soon, I hear my mother calling my name. I close my laptop but keep the page saved in case I need to go over some information. Bringing my laptop and its charger downstairs, I place it inside my bag and we leave for the airport. Our flight is at 8 o'clock. We leave our house at 6 AM, so our flight is in two hours. The airport isn't far from our house, so we make it there pretty quickly.

We make it to our gate 45 minutes early, but do a thorough check to make sure we brought everything. Once everything is checked to make sure we have it, I text Katelyn and tell her we're going to board soon. The airport is a bit cold and I'm tired, but adrenaline courses through my veins. We quickly grab something to eat and when we get back, they begin boarding everyone. Taking off at 8:15 a.m., the flight lasts approximately an hour and we get picked up by Katelyn's mother at 9:30 AM. We arrive at their house soon later, and Katelyn welcomes me by giving me a hug. She begins talking really fast and I have a hard time understanding what she's saying.

"So I have camp during the break and we go from Monday to Friday from 8 to 3 o'clock and one of my teachers is in charge. Thomas Switzer is his name. He's the language arts teacher at my school among other things and I was wondering if you would want to come with me."

"Sure. It starts on Monday?" I ask.

"Yeah, and it is Thursday, so in 5 days basically."

"Cool."

"Anyway, let's go paint our nails! You can tell me what happened while I was gone."

I follow Katelyn upstairs to her bedroom. It's light blue, which is different from her old room, but I suppose she would want a change of color. This room looks similar to her old room. The only real differences are just that things are rearranged differently and some things are new. She opens a white, small dresser and pulls out varying shades of nail polish.

"So, what color do you want?" she asks while picking out her own color.

I'm visiting a new place, so I should use a different color, right? "I'll choose green."

She begins painting my nails, and at first she is silent, but then she strikes up a conversation.

"How have things been going since the incidents? Are you healthy? Do you have any new friends? Specifically, do you have any new *guy* friends?"

"Well, after the incidents I felt I had a full change of demeanor in some ways, but I suppose that's just growing up. My health is fine, but it took me awhile to calm down about what happened. Same old friends, I guess; ones that I've known for awhile. I guess Bryan is a guy friend, but we've known each other since we were little so I don't know if he counts."

"Well, you're basically like a superhero now, right? Aren't you excited?" Katelyn asks while squealing.

"Not really. I guess once I lost my normal life I kind of missed it." I respond quietly.

"Maybe I can't really grasp what you're saying there. My point of view on this situation is a lot different than yours. If I were you, I'd be ecstatic."

I bit my lip when she said that. Part of me was scared she wouldn't understand, but another part of me didn't want her to understand. There's pain that comes along with this, and that's something that no one should have to go through. I think about people who have it much worse than me, though, and try to be grateful for where I am now.

"Have you heard of Margaret Livingston before?" I ask.

Katelyn pauses while painting my nails and then starts again.

"I mean, Mr. Switzer, my teacher, has talked about how

she was an amazing human being. She saved people and gave them a chance at living. He said he guessed she gave them her life until she passed away. She risked her life just to save other people. This girl reminds me of you, even though I know so little about her."

"Are we going to meet him?"

"I believe so. Why?"

"I just have an important question to ask him."

As the night goes on, Katelyn and I talked to each other as if nothing had changed. We laughed, we shared secrets, and we built a fort. It felt as if we were kids again. Instead of Katelyn sleeping in her bed, we got two sleeping bags and slept on the ground. It was fun because we could pretend to be sleeping when we were actually just hanging out. Somehow we got into a huge pillow fight which may or may not have been my fault. If you throw a pillow at someone, is that a declaration of war? We watched some of our favorite movies as kids and joked about how we were entertained so easily. We did each other's makeup and made mustaches on each other's faces. At 2 AM, after a long night of laughing, we both managed to fall asleep.

I woke up at 11 AM, but Katelyn was already out of her sleeping bag. I get dressed, wash my face, brush my teeth, and comb my hair. Running down the stairs, I see her on the porch of the house and follow her out.

"Hey."

"You finally woke up. I was wondering if you wanted to go to the park."

"Sure. Do they have a playground or something there?"

"They have a big lake and there's a playground a little bit further after that. There's also a tennis court."

"Do you have gloves?"

A smile spreads across her face.

"Do you have feet?"

We quickly grab our gloves and coats and rush to the park. The park is about 3 blocks from where Katelyn lives. Last night it snowed a bit, and now we can make snow angels. The snow kept on piling on, but only ended up equaling to 3 inches deep. Luckily, it's the sticky snow that's great for throwing snowballs, so when we enter the park, I attack Katelyn with the two snowballs I've been hiding while we were walking. Right when the snowball smacks her jacket, she turns around and throws one too. I throw my last one and dodge Katelyn's second snowball. Diving into the snow, I create 5 snowballs quickly as Katelyn is creating hers. I take 3 and begin throwing them at her, which buys me more time because she's still creating her second. Quickly, I create 3 more snowballs. When I look at Katelyn, she throws two at me and then continues making more, but I can tell she's keeping one in secret. Still only having 5, I decide to create 5 more. I've always been better at making snowballs. I'm not exactly sure why. As Katelyn is creating another snowball, I take a look at the trees. Time begins to slow down. The snow shines on the trees, and I get up to feel the tree bark, but I accidentally make snow fall down. The snow moves in slow motion, giving me a better look at the snowflakes. Each of the snowflakes is different. It's nice, isn't it?

I turn around and I notice a snowball being slowly hurled at me. Sliding into the snow, I dodge the snowball and time returns to normal. What was that? Was that an act of saving? I must have been mumbling, because Katelyn responded with "What?" I tell her it's nothing, and we go to take a better look at the park. Sitting near the park entrance, our multicolored coats don't blend in well with the snow. Anyone could probably see us clearly, but we sat near the trees anyway. Taking a look at the park, I notice there aren't as many trees as I originally thought. At the entrance of the park, maybe 20 were residing there, but as we look at the lake, the land around it is mostly clear. The trees near me, however, seem to be dead. Though, they are beautiful too. It seems like snow can make any scene beautiful. The lake is surprisingly frosted over, but definitely not frozen enough to support people ice skating on it. Soon after sitting down, though, we decide to take a walk through the park.

The only part of the park that isn't covered in snow is the sidewalk, which is a light shade of beige. It fits the snow, almost looking yellow, but not quite. We walk around the lake which is weirdly formed like an 8 and walk passed it. The trees are held back by a fence, presumably because there is a playground that children play on. They wouldn't want the children to get hurt. It's a quaint playground with swings that have snow on them.

"Let's go on the swings!" I squeal.

"Paula, we'll get wet," Katelyn responds while rolling her eyes.

"Who cares if we get wet? I'd be more worried about falling off."

"Fine, but we can't go too high. It's a bit dangerous."

I nod and we run to the swing set. I brush the snow off of the seat and sit down. The cold water seeps through my clothes within a few seconds, and a shiver is sent up my spine. It seems like it's been so long since I last felt or even saw snow. Even though it snowed last year, so much has changed. Not only the people I talk to, but I've changed too. My mind works in a way where I'm more thoughtful and meticulous about certain things, and I've also learned to be more grateful. For the life I've lived, and my present one here. Sometimes I wish things would go back to the way they were, but I know that everything that has happened so far is for a reason. If I didn't go through this, maybe I wouldn't see myself the way I do now. Sure, I'm not beautiful, I'm not exactly smart, and any extraordinary talents seem to evade me, but at least I'm kind and forthright. There's still a part of me that wishes to be someone else. To have talents that make up who I am. If I did have talents, who would I be? Someone conceited? Would I think of others more and be less grateful? Holding onto the life we have must be important, because who says we'll get another? And if we do get another, who says that life will be good? I believe in second chances, but I also believe nothing is truly ever whole after that first chance. People have already lost who they are. The person you knew then may not be the same person emerging now. Everything still leaves me with the same question: Who am I?

Katelyn and I walk home soon later and arrive to the sweet scent of brownies in the air. Instead of grabbing just a few brownies, this time Katelyn and I take the whole tray. We used to do this when we were younger, and after a while our parents became accustomed to it. We enter Katelyn's room, eat the brownies, and fall asleep even though it's still daylight out. Staying up so late on Friday tired us out. As I drift off into the land of sleep, thoughts about the snow play through my mind. Today was the sun during a hurricane.

It's always there to remind you that you'll be ok; that you are strong.

In the morning, Katelyn is still dozed off next to me with the TV still on and an empty tray of brownies. She must've stayed up later than me. As soon as I remember that soon I'm going to meet Thomas Switzer, my heart begins racing. I might just find some answers to my problem. I got ready slowly and peacefully, each movement full of thought. Planning everything was not going to be easy. I hardly knew anything about North Carolina. Sometimes I wonder why things happen. Why did Katelyn wait for me on the porch yesterday? She wanted to go to the park. Why do I want to sit down on the porch? I want to think things through. I need some time away from everyone to create a plan about not only this upcoming week, but what's to happen with my future. If I don't get the information I need, how will I manage on my own? The wind swirls around me, like a blanket. No, it doesn't make me cold. Even if it's in my imagination, it seems as if both the wind and the sun out right now are trying to comfort me. Yesterday was a day of snow, but today is a day of warmth and light. Sitting on this porch, alone, feels more peaceful than anything I have done since the dreams began appearing. Why can't I just stay here? Why did everything have to become so difficult? What's the point of questioning anything? Even if I do come up with an answer, I won't listen to myself. Then again, not listening to myself brought me into the warm sun. Maybe not listening to myself can also bring good. Within every decision, there are really only two choices, right? The colors are monotone, and may not make you happy either way. But they sure do affect your happiness in the future.

Monday

Katelyn and I both wake up at 6 AM on Monday and begin getting ready for camp. I suppose Katelyn already knew I was going to go, so she probably told her mom to sign up two people instead. Then again, maybe there wasn't even a signup sheet. Though, there would have to be, right? I need to learn to say questions out loud. Anyway, we leave at 7:15 and arrive there at 7:45. The name of the camp is "Camp Creative".

"That's a creative name," I think sarcastically.

As we walk inside the camp, there are different rooms made for different things. There's an arts and crafts room, a swimming pool, a sports room, and many other activity rooms. Within the middle of the camp there are a lot of tables and a stage set up in the front of the camp. There aren't many people here, but the people who are here wear t-shirts that say "Camp Creative" on them. They must be the ones that take care of the kids.

"Hello Katelyn. Who's your friend?" a boy with tan skin, brown hair, and green eyes asks.

"Hello Jeremiah. This is my friend Paula." Katelyn responds.

"It's nice to meet you." I cut in.

"It's nice to meet you too. I'm assuming you aren't from Katelyn's school because I haven't seen you around." Jeremiah says.

"Yeah, Katelyn is my best friend." I respond.

Maybe I was wrong. He wears the t-shirt and looks older than us, so was I right to assume he worked here? Then again, he doesn't quite look like an adult yet. He might be an 8th grader.

"Well, anyway, here are your t-shirts." Jeremiah informs.

Katelyn and I both put on the t-shirts, which are a bit big for us, and walk around.

"This is my first time here too, just remember that," Katelyn informs me.

"Yeah, it took me awhile to realize that. It just seems like you fit in here. So is Jeremiah an 8th grader?" I ask.

Katelyn smirks at me in a knowing way, and doesn't answer my question. She thinks I like Jeremiah.

"It's not that, I promise you," I cut into our silence quickly.

"Are you sure? We've only been here a few minutes, you just met him, and you're asking questions about him. Seems kind of suspicious, doesn't it?"

Katelyn had me there, but I didn't have a crush on someone I just met.

"Trust me, I don't. The t-shirts made me curious."

We both laugh at this, and how ridiculous this whole conversation is getting. My mind slips to Bryan for a minute, but I don't think I like him, either. Liking somebody would be a bit... complicated... at this point of time. My cheeks become hot for a second, but the feeling drifts away as soon as I realize. Even though I didn't see Katelyn's eyes move toward my face, I have a sneaking suspicion she saw it anyway. We walk around the whole camp, which is surprisingly large, and when we get back, some students have shown up. All of them wave to Katelyn and begin asking her questions and saying hello. The questions are hard to understand with so many people speaking. I manage to step away for a moment, but end up running into another conversation.

"Didn't get a chance to talk to your friend?"

I bump into Jeremiah and when he starts talking, I jump. His voice isn't too deep, but isn't high either. It's almost calming in a way.

"No, that's not what I-"

"It's fine. Everyone around here is usually friendly, so you won't have to worry about anything. I'm sure you'll be included just as the rest of us are, but you have to talk to them. Don't stay quiet."

I usually don't talk to people often. I mean, it's not like I'm shy or anything, but I just decide not to. In school I mostly read and anyone I do talk to usually hangs out with people that they know from the clubs that they are in. I hear footsteps and everyone begins to quiet down. The man that walks in has short, dark brown hair, green eyes, and stubs that show a hint of a mustache around his mouth. He walks up to the stage and begins talking. His voice is almost like Jeremiah's voice: not too deep, not too high. His voice is what you would call neutral.

"Hello everyone, and welcome to the first meet up of

Camp Creative. Usually everyone meets up during the summer, but we decided to open for a week to show you guys what we'll be doing if you decide to join later on. My name is Thomas Switzer, but you all can call me Mr. Switz. I am your caretaker at Camp Creative and will be leading all camp activities. Everyone please take a seat while I give you each an idea of what we'll be doing. The Arts and Crafts Committee works on the first door to your left. They work in the afternoon, from 12:30PM to 1:30PM. The Music Committee is the second door on your left, and they work from 11AM to 12PM. The Photography Committee is the third door on your left, and they work from 10AM to 11AM. The Jeopardy Committee is the first door on your right, and they work from 9AM to 10AM. The Sports Committee is the second door on your right, and they work from 8AM to 9AM. The swimming pool is the third door on your right, and during free time you may also take classes for that. The restroom is located in the door to the right of the stage, and you may enter backstage from the door on the left of the stage. You are not required to participate in all committees and may choose which ones you would like to go to. In your free time, though, you must remain with your caretaker, which I will introduce to you in groups. Now, everyone get to know each other and have fun!" The children were quiet for a few moments after this speech, but slowly they managed to create a roar of voices. I was surprised anyone could be heard over this noise, though it does seem like everyone is trying to out-scream everyone else. As I take a seat at the only quiet table in the room, I notice the children at this table are watching me with curious glances. It's funny how I refer to them as "children", when really they are near my age.

"Hello, my name is Paula. You guys seemed to be the most relaxed table, which is the main reason I came here," I say with a smile.

A boy spoke up.

"My name is Birdie. Well, that's just my nickname, but I never tell people my real name. You'll have to figure it out for yourself!"

I noticed he was smiling, and so were the others.

"How come you guys are the only quiet table?" I question.

"Well, we're new here. All the people sitting at this table are familiar with each other, but not with anyone else in this camp. For example, the orange-haired girl with brown eyes is Mila, the girl with the brown hair and blue eyes is Camilla, and the boy with the blonde hair and blue eyes is Chance. Camilla and Mila are actually cousins, but I originally met Chance at this place called Chimmy Checkers when we were 4. Oh, and I met Mila at school, who introduced me to Camilla. Not only are they cousins, but they've been best friends since they were 3. It's kind of cool, don't you think?"

"Yes. I've known my best friend Katelyn since we were very young. We've basically been best friends all of our lives."

"Wait, you're best friends with Katelyn? So I assume you've met Jeremiah?" Birdie asks.

"Yes. He's pretty cool."

"Jeremiah also hangs out with us, so you'll probably be seeing him often. As for Katelyn, she doesn't hang out with us too much. Katelyn is pretty good friends with Jeremiah. They live next to each other or something."

I think about the setup of friends that they have, but what strikes me the most is that Katelyn isn't hanging out with the... quiet people. She's someone who would be willing to talk to anyone, or, I guess, who *used* to be willing to talk to anyone. Perhaps my best friend is changing. It really has only been a month or two. How could someone that I thought I knew change so fast? I must be delusional. Of course Katelyn hasn't changed! Maybe she just met the... loud ones... first. Though, I thought I caught a small bit of a frown on Birdie's face as he said Katelyn doesn't hang out with them. Did something happen that no one is telling me about?

"Speaking of Jeremiah, here he comes."

As I turned towards the opposite direction, I noticed Jeremiah standing a few feet away. He hesitated when he saw me, but pretended it was nothing. What kind of reaction was that? His face showed that he was shy, but a form of confidence tried to overshadow the shy bit.

"Hey Birdie, I see you've met Paula," Jeremiah says with a smirk.

"Yeah, she's cool. Don't tell her my name," Birdie warns.

Jeremiah smirked as I looked at him.

It seemed as if I was trying to speak to him through my mind, *"You are telling me later."*

His smirk was a probable *"You wish."*

Mr. Switz sauntered over to our table and asked how everyone was doing. We all said "Good." at the same time. Jeremiah ended up speaking to Mr. Switz alone, and somehow I ended up in that conversation.

"How are you, Paula? Katelyn's told me a bit about you."

"I'm fine. Thank you. So all of the camp counselors teach at least one thing?"

"Yes. I teach Arts and Crafts and I also supervise the other counselors."

Good thing I was planning on joining Arts and Crafts. This shouldn't be too hard. I missed a bit of the conversation, and someone called Jeremiah's name.

"I have to go, Mr. Switz, but I'm sure Paula would like to know a bit more about the camp."

"Yes, I will explain a bit to her. Thank you, Jeremiah. Will you be helping me out in Arts and Crafts?"

"I definitely will."

Unfortunately I wasn't able to read his face when he said that, but I'm pretty sure there was another smirk.

"Well, Paula, any questions?" Mr. Switz asks awkwardly.

"I actually have one, but it's not that related to camp."

"What is it?" He said with a curious glance.

"Do you by any chance know Margaret Livingston?"

His face turned hollow for a minute before it regained its calm demeanor.

"Yes, she was my best friend in high school. What about her?"

"Well, this might sound a bit weird, but did she tell you what she was going through?"

His face turned thoughtful and then serious.

"Yes, but what would this be of use to you? She saved people with her remarkable "10 gifts"." He murmured, almost as if he didn't want me to hear the last sentence.

"My name is Paula Berney, and I have these "10 gifts" you speak about."

Truth and Trust

It seemed as if nothing in my life could compare to the one expression I received from Mr. Switz. The expression was one of agony, remembrance, curiosity, pain, and sorrow. I was happy that Mr. Switz hadn't pitied me. I may be just a child, but within the last 2 months, I've gained more experience than anyone could imagine. Feeling sorry for me wouldn't help anything, and may even ruin my chances of staying alive.

"Why did you come here, in reality?"

"I came to find answers and to possibly find a way to live."

"If you are speaking the truth, then you will need help. There is much more to this that you might not yet know. However, I do not know whether I can trust you. Remembering Margaret causes me great pain, and while I do speak about her occasionally, I never mention the ten gifts. I will need some sort of proof, like another incident."

"What if it doesn't come soon? What if the incident comes when I leave?"

"If you are meant to speak to me, you will. If you aren't,

you won't. I suppose the only thing I can do is hear your side of the story, this way I know every detail."

This came up a bit fishy to me, but Mr. Switz was the only person who could explain exactly what was going on. I didn't want to share details of my own encounters with these gifts, but I had to. Of course he wouldn't believe me. It's not something easily heard. But maybe that should give him more of a reason to believe me. How would anyone else come up with an idea that seems so impossible? Sure, we all dream of having powers, but having only 10 chances to use them *and then you die*? Well, then again, I don't know if I'll die. It's not the dying part I'm afraid of, it's the *how*. *I* would like to die peacefully in my sleep, but I'm assuming Margaret died in a very sad way. You're 10th chance to use your power must be something very important, mustn't it? But if it was so important, shouldn't she be thought of a bit more? Remembered happily instead of in a way that most people would like to forget? But perhaps... Perhaps that's the price you have to pay. But why? Why must someone die for something that they didn't ask for? Who is Margaret Livingston, and what connects us?

"Mr. Switz, one more thing. If I wasn't meant to speak to you, why did my best friend move down here? How would I know about Margaret Livingston?"

"It could've had been a coincidence."

"If I wasn't meant to talk to you, why would Katelyn join your camp?"

He bit his lip before answering.

"All right, I'll grant you certain answers to certain questions, but others will be kept a secret until you can prove to me you share the same abilities."

"How did Margaret Livingston die?"

For about a minute, he stood quiet. When he spoke, he spoke very softly.

"In the worst possible way. Suicide."

I stopped in my tracks. No one else caused her to die, she killed herself.

"Why?"

"She said she couldn't take it anymore, being a hero. It became too much for her. We got into arguments quite often. After one argument, I told her I could not be friends with someone who was hurting themselves. In reality, I thought it was my fault she was becoming angry, but it wasn't. Yes, she took her anger out on me. And I believe that's what caused me to declare our friendship over. That night, she was found dead by her own hands. She had only made it to her 9th gift, as you would call it. I don't know whether her gifts would've ended if she didn't destroy herself. I only speak of the 10th event as a gift because she was extremely unhappy and wanted everything to go away. I suppose she got what she wanted."

The last sentence was spoken with a hint of disgust, mostly sadness, and perhaps... admiration. For what, I would assume that she had the courage to save people. Not for sacrificing her own life.

"Did Margaret have any talents?"

"She did, but she wasn't one to notice them. Sure, she wasn't good as sports, and her artistic and musical talents were not very great either, but she had a personality that could light up the whole room. She always wanted to have something special about her."

So she was talentless too and wanted to be different. She got what she asked for. And so did I.

After he answered that last question, I don't think I needed anything more. That's how we were connected. How to save myself would be a whole other story, though. There's no possible way Mr. Switz could answer that because saving myself depends on... me. Something must happen that will cause me great emotional distress. Though, I don't think I would ever stoop as far as Margaret did.

Would I?

"Thank you, Mr. Switz. I think that's all I need."

"Paula, if you are speaking the truth... I will just tell you this. In the future, there may be someone who is involved. Don't worry about what happens. The truth always comes out eventually."

More Questions

I take my flight back to Maryland staring out of the plane window, thinking about how the rest of the week played out. Every day we had the normal classes we signed up for, and I got to meet a lot of new people. Every day we switched partners so one day I was partners with Birdie, and another day Jeremiah. It was really nice meeting the people that Katelyn hangs out with. They seem really nice. No incidents occurred, which boggled me quite a bit. Because of that, I never had any chances to ask any more questions, and during the time of camp, I couldn't think of any more anyway. Now I can.

Did you ever find out if anyone else was blessed with these 10 gifts?

Who did Margaret save? Was it random people, or people she knew?

Did she ever travel anywhere during the time she had these gifts?

Did she ever tell you about a figure she saw while she used these gifts? Like a car, a flower, etc.

The questions kept coming and coming. Why couldn't I

think of these before? They would've been extremely helpful. I suppose I'll have to research a bit more when I get home. Looking out of the plane window, I see clouds. There is no sun today, and the ground seems to be long gone. Perhaps we'll just keep traveling upwards and ignore our problems below us. But I know that if you ignore your problems, they will only get worse. My power may cause a new problem. Who really knows anything of the future, though? What's to come will come. I am not giving up on my life yet, but perhaps if I accept the fact I may die things will become easier. One pearl, shining and seemingly without color, touches the plane window. I watch as the strong push of the air around the plane drives it backwards, into the cloudy night. Will that be my fate? Being pushed through all of this just to fall once again? Life isn't really fair, is it? Throughout all of these questions, I still have something that resonates within me, however.

"In the future, there may be someone who is involved. Don't worry about what happens. The truth will come out eventually."

These sentences keep playing in my mind through a loop, and will keep playing until I find exactly what I'm looking for.

Home Sweet Home

As soon as I arrive home, I eat with my mother and go up to my room to sleep. While jumping on my bed, a bit of restlessness washes over me. It feels good arriving at home, almost as if I were separated from a family member. You may be able to leave, but you always feel better when you are near them. It is funny how home works. Maybe it's the smell, the look, or the people that you become accustomed to. Perhaps it's all of those things. Though, it's also funny, how you don't know how much you actually missed home until you leave. I've never moved, and if I did, I was too young to remember, but I've always wondered how people got used to a new home. Everything in this one room describes who I am: my bed, my walls, and my furniture. All of it has an essence of "Paula" that I wouldn't want to take away. My memories are what make me who I am, though. My living space may just be the backbone to my personality, enforcing it in every way possible. I *used* to be open to change, but I didn't think this much of a change would come to take place. My life wasn't just flipped upside down; it was twisted and turned in every way possible. No, it wasn't broken to pieces. I won't let that happen. But I need to find a way to restore my life back to normal; before I received these "10 gifts". Being a hero is nice, but not when you're a 7th grader and may just have to sacrifice your whole lifestyle for it! I was planning to get into a good high school, and go into college. How will any of that happen when bad things seem to pop up around me? Sure, I may save people, but when I'm around, more is lost then saved. If I wasn't around at all, most likely none of this would happen! I don't want to carry the burden of tens to hundreds of people on my back. Maybe this change is good though. Everyone needs a change of scenery at some point, right? Though it's not exactly *scenery* we're talking about. I wish I could remember how I felt two months ago, before any of this had happened. Not how the change felt, how living as a normal girl felt. Would I be thankful that I have these 10 gifts, or would I want my normal life back? I say I want life to go back to normal, but the truth is I don't know what I would like. My caricature of life is different from other people's viewpoints. I've always wondered what others thought of me, not because I rely on other people for my sense of "fashion", which I don't really have, but because I want to know what kind of people they are. Sometimes it's easy being "normal". People have nothing to be jealous of, and it's easier for them to accept who I am. Then again, having talents most likely means one day you'll rise to do something clearly special, doesn't it? Life can be so harsh yet rewarding at the same time. This thought floats like a cloud in my mind, but eventually fades away, leaving a path for drowsiness and peacefulness to lull me to bed. My eyes slowly begin to close, and I enter the world where everything is all but true; everything is all but a façade.

White comes into focus in front of me, and something grows: taller, and taller; larger than me. I try to scream, but I'm in my world of silence, but the silence is not silent either. No, it is louder than I ever will be, petrified and relaxed; not switching, all at the same time. A crescendo of fear trying to overlap the comfort, and a crescendo of comfort is laying its bed, trying to squash the fear, but, oh, it's still there. My vision clears in an instant, but that instant seems far too long. The tree is in front of me. My head slowly moves up, yet too fast for me to understand clearly what is going on. The arms grow and grow, overlapping each other, almost as if they are making weaves on a wicker basket. I cannot stop staring upwards at these fruitless arms, bare and dark, yet with an air of comfort. My feet cannot move. A magnet is holding my feet, yet nothing else. Though, I know there is no magnet; just the same white room which I visit quite a bit in my dreams. My head is stuck in place, but I can look around, well, as far as my vision will let me. I bring my arm up so that I may see what I am doing. Seconds, minutes, hours; no, days pass. I reach for the tree with an everlasting gentleness.

The room is dark. I can barely see anything. My heart still racing, I am afraid to get out of bed. My eyes start adjusting, but not before I think to try and move my head. Slowly turning, I realize I can move once again. I pull the covers off of me in one quick motion, and strive to get up. My feet are nearly on the floor. My heart begins racing again. I get up and look around the room to see if anyone is there, but I am by myself. That's before my eyes adjust. *"How silly of me, to be scared in my own room,"* I whisper, but I turn on my bedroom light anyway. I quickly slip back into bed with the light still on, drowsiness beginning to take over once again.

When I wake up, the birds are chirping and the sun is shining. It is now Sunday, December 31. I still have until January 3rd, the date that I must go back to school. I quietly open my door and walk down the stairs. Well, as quietly as humanly possible when I am not only jet lagged, but the stairs creak for every little movement you make. So, I forget the "quiet" plan and just rush down the stairs, hoping to get rid of the noises as soon as possible. Though, I hear my mother making coffee in the kitchen and know that this plan of mine was all for nothing. I walk in and my mother and I both say good morning to each other, though my voice sounds more like a croak. My mother instantly replies, checking my temperature.

"You feel a little hot, Paula. Go back in bed. I'll get the thermometer ready."

"Can I have food first?" I ask quietly.

"I'll bring you up something."

As soon as she says "something" I know it's not going to be good. It will most likely be medicine along with food that will give me a bad aftertaste. Before I go lay down, I stop off at the bathroom and look in the mirror. As soon as my foot touches the floor, a chill is sent throughout me. Why do we have to have tiles on the bathroom floor instead of carpet? I'm not saying I like carpet better, but at least carpet doesn't feel cold. I focus on my face in the mirror. My cheeks are a bit red, but nothing else seems to be wrong. My feet are beginning to get used to the temperature, and despite the fact it sent a chill throughout my body, the cold floor is beginning to feel nice. Every other place in my house is warm, but I never really took the time to notice this because it's natural for me. I step out of the bathroom with a hint of hesitation because I know the air outside of the bathroom may feel a bit hot. We aren't having a cold winter this year, which is abnormal. Though, it happens every once in awhile. Now that I think about it, isn't North Carolina supposed to be warm? I guess *they* were having a cold winter. The temperature outside doesn't seem to affect me much anyway, though. If it's raining I'd be fine with going outside, as long as I don't get soaked. If it's snowing, I would happily have a snowball fight. I'm pretty adaptable to certain circumstances, I guess. The creaking of the stairs sounds in my ears. I quickly run and jump into bed, pulling the covers over my head with a "Whoosh!"

"Paula, it's time to check your temperature," my mother informs me.

"Paula's not here right now. Please leave a message at the tone. Beep."

"Get up."

"I'm not sick."

"Now," my mother commands.

With a sigh, I pull my head from under the covers and look up at my mother. She hands me the thermometer and I take it willingly. We wait as the seconds pass by and we hear a "Beep." I take the thermometer out of my mouth and read "98.6" out loud.

"That's unusual. Normally, when your cheeks are red, you have a fever, or at least a cold. Have you been coughing or sneezing?" she eyes me suspiciously.

"No, I feel perfectly fine."

"Well, stay in bed anyway. I don't want to risk you getting sick."

My mother exits my room quietly, and I start getting out from under the blankets. I quickly turn my feet towards my door and begin to stand up.

"If you step one foot out of that bed I will spend my day making sure you stay downstairs on the couch. Anyway, I'm going to the grocery store. I'll be back in a bit," my mother warns sternly.

Quickly, I put my feet back under the blankets and close my eyes. I hear the door close loudly. A tingling feeling rises in my face and I force myself to look. Everything seems almost… pixilated, except the colors seem more abstract. My vision is blurry. I try getting up and find myself stumbling to the window. When I look out, I hear a car horn beep loudly. I can't see the license plate. Something clicks in my head. That car was going to crash into the one in front of it, and soon if I didn't stop it. The cars only were an inch or two apart, as far as I could tell. Perhaps I think of this because the honking doesn't seem to stop. It goes on endlessly. I run out of my room and down the stairs. My vision is still blurry, but I can make out a few figures. I run to my mother's red car and try to open the door, but it's locked. I can feel my energy draining. The colors begin to fade and my eyes begin to close. No! I wake myself up. Running back into the kitchen, I look for the extra pair of keys.

"Keys, keys… Where are the keys?" I say aloud, yet to myself.

I finally find them in a jar on a rack on our counter. My mom's car is remote-controlled, but there are key slots too. I run back outside. Things are moving slowly now, and time isn't frozen. I have to hurry. The lock is blurry and I can't see where I'm placing the key. After about 10 jabs, I feel the opening of the lock and force the key to turn. I open my mom's car and pull her out as fast as I can. Then, running to the other driver's car, I try opening the door. It doesn't work. Guess we'll have to do this the hard way. I run back inside the house as fast as I can and grab a pair of scissors. As soon as I make it back to the driver's car, I break the window and unlock it from the inside. The pieces of glass float slowly in the air. Despite what's going on, I am boggled by the look of it. Until you really pay attention, you never notice how the glass shines on the faint sun. But I don't have time for boggling. Opening the door, I pull the man out. Just in time, too. The cars crash into each other and a fire starts. How fast was this man driving? I fall onto the grass and the last thing I see is green... green... then black.

Glass Doesn't Hurt, the Cuts Do

I look around, waking up in my bedroom for once. I swear, every time something happens I never seem to be at home. My vision is clear and I can't move for a moment. When I do move, however, the stiffness of my joints surprises me. Not remembering anything I call out, "Mom!", and I see her face right over mine in an instant.

"What happened? Are you alright? Are you hurting? You finally woke up."

"I don't know. I just feel really uncomfortable."

"Do you remember what happened?"

Before I respond, flashes come into my mind. Blurry, but enough for me to understand what had happened. I groan.

"Are you alright?" my mom asks worriedly.

"Yes, I'm fine. What day is it?"

My mother pauses and answers, "Friday, January 5."

How can it be Friday? I was sleeping for 5 days? Nothing really happened, so why does it affect me so much? When I try to get up, my face and neck burns. My arms burn a bit and my legs burn a bit less than my arms, but the feeling is still there. No other part of me burns, and I just feel groggy.

"Why have I been sleeping so long?" I ask, even though I already know the answer.

"The doctors don't know. They thought it was probably shock, but you did perform an impossible task, so perhaps your body became tired from that."

I cringed at that sentence. I performed an impossible task? The chances are that this isn't going to be all over school is extremely low. The chance that this won't be all over the news is extremely low. Why did I have to make a big showing of myself? The next time I do something like this, I might just fall into a coma. Wait. What if I don't die? What if my body becomes so tired I fall into a *coma*? I try to get up, but my mother pushes me down. She's much stronger than me right now.

"No way are you getting up. Relax; your cuts are still healing."

I think for a minute. What would happen to me if I fell into a coma? I need to search the internet for information about this, but I know it's going to have to wait. Why does the future have to be so *complicated*? There are so many different ways my life could be going, and I have no clue as to what might happen. Margaret's death was caused by her own hands. Well, what if that's just a metaphor for something else? What if I don't mean to cause my end, but I do because of my own selfishness? Will I die happy, or sad? Can I make a choice? My future is bound to end in some way. That's it. No more Paula. But the least I can do is fight. Fight as hard as I can. Fight to be the best I can be; fight to be me. As I close my eyes, a single tear, alone and warm, falls down my face. The darkness surrounds me.

*** 1 Year Later ***

Nothing has happened since that last event. Maybe that was the finish line. Maybe that's what I had to notice. You had to fight for life. Whatever it was, I'm just happy it's gone. I've grown a bit in a year. I'm 5 foot 1 now. Also, I'm with my friends at the local mall. The mall is made up of about 5 sections: the food court, clothing shops, sports shops, a bookstore, and a library. We're in the food court right now, buying fruits and smoothies so we can drink them later. The mall is pretty large, but not so large where you would get lost in it. The tiles on the floor are white spotted with blue, and the walls are a mix of light blue and grey. There are many chairs and tables in the middle of the food court, all made of wood except for one in the corner which was just recently placed there. It's really a nice place to hang out if you just want to relax. I'm here with Bryan, Michelle (a girl who recently entered the school), and Beatrice. Michelle doesn't know about the past events because I told my friends not to talk about it. I'd like to keep it that way. No one treats me *too* different anymore, but I know that no matter what I do, I won't be the normal "Paula Berney" that no one talks about. I'll be the "Paula Berney" that *everyone* talks about. The events that happened last year aren't easily forgotten, especially in a small town like this.

I can't say I'm happy that everything is finally over. This whole event gave me a reason to feel special, and it made me think differently about the world. The last time I visited Katelyn was about a month ago, during winter break. Today is January 5, 2017, and I'm 14 years old. I wanted to spend today with my friends because I don't want to relive what had occurred with my mother almost dying; with my school being burnt. Remembering the lessons I had learned from all of it is different from remembering the feelings that went along with it. Though, some of those feelings were good. I don't think my friends know why I asked to meet up so suddenly this morning, but I'm certain they have a clue as to what the reason is. People always say "You know what you're feeling, but you don't want to admit it to yourself." What if that's a lie? I have no clue as to what my true feelings are right now because all of my feelings are mixed together. It's almost as if you mix food coloring together. After a while, chances are all traces of the colors you put in will fade and all you will see is a murky swamp color. You have the memories of the bright, beautiful colors, but that will soon be forgotten too. Nothing stays. You're forced to make good memories every so often so that they don't fade away, yet with the bad memories, they stay in your mind forever. Why is life like that? I can barely remember my 5th birthday! I can barely remember my 10th birthday! Everything good disappears, and you're left with the mistakes that are right in front of you. What kind of world is that? Am I angry, sad, lonely, joyful, excited, nervous, and confused at the same time? Whenever I try figuring out what my feelings are, I feel nothing! My feelings don't want to untangle themselves! The tree I saw in my dreams doesn't describe me at all! I'm basically a forest, and all I know is that when I entered the forest, everything was fine. I could always find my way back. After a long time of running, though, I become lost. The leaves close in on themselves and I'm nestled in a field of green with no feelings at all. Everything that I've been through hasn't helped me! It's only gotten me more confused!

I jump to the sound of a cart falling over. I guess I was too deep in my thoughts. We run to help the woman who toppled the cart by accident. After picking up everything she had dropped, we all received a quick thank you from the woman, and we replied with "You're welcome."

"Hey Paula, want to head to the clothing store so Bryan and Michelle can go run around the food court?" asks Beatrice.

"Sure."

Might as well let them have a little fun. Michelle doesn't like shopping for clothing, or for anything, for that matter. She hates trying things on. Beatrice and I walk to a nearby store, and look at some of the dresses they have.

"Soon we're going to be having the Spring Concert. We're going to need dresses," Beatrice says.

"The Spring Concert is more than 5 months away. We have plenty of time."

"Paula, what were you thinking of back there? You didn't seem to take notice of your surroundings like you usually do."

I might as well tell her the truth.

"I was thinking of last year and all of those events."

"Paula, you need to leave all of that behind. I understand

it affected you greatly, but I can tell you don't enjoy thinking about it."

"I can't just stop thinking about it, Beatrice. It's hard. Everyday things remind me of the events."

"We're shopping for clothing now. Are you going to say that this *clothing* reminds you of the clothes you were wearing then, as if you know exactly what color and what shirt you wore?"

"I don't remember things too clearly, but I know that I was most likely not wearing a dress or a skirt; so yes, it reminds me of the events."

Beatrice groans. "We're your friends, and we don't want you to feel like this, but you're forcing yourself to remember. At least try to forget Paula. Scold yourself for remembering certain things. It'll eventually fade away."

Perhaps Beatrice is right, but there's a part of me that *doesn't* want to forget. When I'm battling against myself, it's highly possible that neither side will win. Beatrice and I have gotten a lot closer since the events ended. I suppose I just had too much going on during that time to really think about making friends. Katelyn is still my best friend, but Beatrice is also a very good friend to me.

"We should start shopping for swimsuits!" Beatrice says.

"Beatrice! It's January! Not July!"

"Well by July all the good swimsuits will be gone."

"I doubt there's any store in this whole mall that will sell swimsuits."

"Is that a bet?"

"Beatrice, I will not run around the mall looking for swimsuits for you."

"Please Paula! Pleaseeeeeee!"

"Ok, fine. You search the clothing section, I'll search the bookstore."

"Ok!"

Sometimes Beatrice becomes so happy with the fact that she's getting new clothing, that she doesn't pay attention to what anyone says. I would help Beatrice, but I've been dying to get the next book of the series that I never finished reading last year. Though I suppose it would make sense to read the first book again since I don't remember most of it...

When I arrive at the bookstore, I inhale the fresh smell of paper and dive into different styles of literature. About 10 minutes later, I find the book that I want and purchase it.

"I suppose I had better check on Beatrice." I think to myself. Running back to the clothing store (though I must admit, I was more skipping than running), I thought about my excitement on finally getting the next book. Looking around the store, I try to find Beatrice, but it's extremely hard. When I finally find her, she's busy trying on swimsuits. I should've known she would find one. After all, she is Beatrice. She walks out of the fitting room and asks "What do you think?"

"I think it's too early and too cold to be trying on swimsuits. Put on a robe or something."

"Fine. You're like my mom," she grumbles.

I laugh at this because even I know it's true. She comes out of the fitting room in her old clothes, wearing a slight frown on her face.

"Frowning makes you age," I say.

She immediately puts on a smile and stalks out of the clothing store. I laugh and follow her. We find Bryan and Michelle at the Donut Stand with 2 donuts in each of their hands. I don't understand how they can eat that much, but I don't ask because it's just their personalities. Michelle and Bryan are very similar in some ways.

"Hey guys!"

Bryan and Michelle both say a muffled "Hello." with donuts in their mouths. At the sight of it, Beatrice cringes a bit, but I just laugh. Bryan has jelly on his face, and Michelle has sugar on her face. You can't win with either of them. They'll get messy somehow. I giggle at this thought.

"Hey Michelle, want to head to the pretzel stand?" Bryan asks.

She nods her head and they run to the stand.

"They have a funny friendship, don't they?" Beatrice asks.

I nod, and we follow them to the pretzel stand. We all get large pretzels, but Bryan and Michelle get their pretzels with mustard.

"Hey Bryan, I heard the video game shop is open. Want to go after we finish shopping at the mall?" Michelle asks.

"Sure, but what are Beatrice and Paula going to do?"

"It's fine!" Beatrice and I both shout at the same time.

"Are you guys sure?" Bryan questions suspiciously.

"Yes, we are completely sure. Paula and I don't play videogames so it wouldn't make much sense for us to go."

I smile brightly at Bryan and wave goodbye.

Bryan and Michelle walk away, leaving Beatrice and I in the food court. She starts walking, so I immediately follow her. I don't know where she's going, but she seems to have her mind set. I almost ask her, until I see her face. It's one of pure determination. What could she possibly be thinking of right now?

1 Month Ago

"Hey, Mr. Switz, remember how you were telling me about the solution to my disease?" I ask my uncle.

"Yes, Jeremiah. I remember completely. We both agreed that it was Katelyn and that we had to just wait," He replies.

"Well… That's the thing, uncle. I never agreed. You said that I would feel some sort of connection, and I did, but that was 11 months ago," I whisper.

"What are you saying, Jeremiah?"

"Katelyn isn't the person who can save me."

I had him the news article from Maryland and watch as his eyebrows knit together in confusion.

"She was… telling the truth," he whispers, almost making me miss it.

Almost.

He's Here!

I had shown Beatrice pictures of who I had met at Katelyn's camp, but I never thought she would remember any of the faces. I couldn't see anything, because I had put my glasses in my backpack when we arrived at the mall, afraid of losing them. Though, I could see that the person we were heading towards had almost tan skin. Who does that remind me of? It's on the tip of my tongue... Jeremiah! But he couldn't possibly be here. There's no reason for him to be here. Who is that sitting next to him, though?

We arrive at the table and immediately, Beatrice begins speaking.

"Hello, Thomas Switzer and Jeremiah. This is Paula, but you've already met her."

They both look up at Beatrice before their eyes flash to me. Jeremiah immediately gets up, a smile appearing on his face.

"Hello Paula. It is very nice to see you. You're probably wondering why we're here. Well, Mr. Switzer wanted to talk to you, and he needed someone to come along. Katelyn had been absent because she was sick, so she had to make up a few tests. That's the reason why she's not here. And I'm here because I volunteered like the good student I am."

Jeremiah smiled brightly after that speech. I rolled my eyes and he laughed. His laugh made me smile.

"Yes, Paula. I have something of major importance to talk to you about." Mr. Switzer said awkwardly.

"Well Paula, I'll be going. See you later!" Beatrice said.

She ran so fast out of the mall that I knew I would never be able to catch her.

"Paula, you're at the point where the incidents have stopped, aren't you?" Mr. Switzer asked.

"Yes, I am," I responded.

"I remembered something that I think may be of use to you. I know the first time I said I couldn't trust you, but… things change."

"What do you mean?" I asked.

I was wondering what Jeremiah was making of this conversation, since he doesn't know about anything that is happening. At least, I *think* he doesn't know about anything that is happening.

"There's going to be a catalyst to another event. No matter how much you try to stop it, it will happen. Margaret went through the same thing on her 5th incident."

So am I on my 5th? I can't seem to remember everything all too clearly. There was the fire, stopping Cornelia, saving my mother from falling, stopping the car crash, but what else? Perhaps the dream was one of the incidents, too?

"Wait. What was this catalyst?"

"Margaret's grandmother died," he said with a sigh.

"Wait… So someone had to… die… in order for her powers to erupt again?"

"Yes, and when they came back, it was as if the whole world had been torn apart. She was much stronger; not only mentally, but physically, too. It was quite amazing what she could do. I find it ironic how something so small could've taken her life. She didn't want it anymore. She was desperate. How could I possibly make amends for that; for treating her so terribly?" he asked with a deep look on his face. "Anyway, you must stay strong, Paula. I know me coming here is a weird occurrence, but I came here for quite a selfish reason, actually. I believe, even though she is dead, Margaret will finally forgive me if I manage to save your life in absence of hers. I must say, you are going through this younger than she did, though."

Wait. I'm younger than Margaret? What if I end up having more than 10 chances? No, that's impossible, Paula. I try to calm myself down, but I start to hyperventilate. What if this goes on for the rest of my life? Nothing will ever be normal, then. My life is just one big question mark that will never be answered, will it? I mean, you can't answer a question mark. So I suppose that thought doesn't make much sense, but even so. How can everything be so complicated? I love being able to make sure my friends and family are safe, but doing this for the rest of my life? Who else could've possibly experienced something like this? Margaret's life lasted an average of 16 years, and a lot of time has passed since she's died. A decade, if I am correct. Thomas Switzer would've been 15 a decade ago, and all of these incidents didn't occur all at once, either. If I were to find any other sources of a case like mine, it would be hard. These cases wouldn't be recent. If a decade passed between the time that my incidents started occurring and her life ended, then, if

I am correct, the incident before Margaret's death would've been before most people used the internet. The internet only really started becoming popular in the 1990s, I believe, and if that is so, then any newspaper articles might be hard to find. The incidents weren't all too common. It was probably sheer luck that I found Margaret's story when I did. Though, if luck did exist, I'm sure I don't have much. I mean look at the curse that's been put upon me.

"Um… hey, guys. I don't know what you're talking about, so could you please tell me what's happening, or…" Jeremiah asks awkwardly.

Mr. Switzer and I both look at Jeremiah immediately.

"We were just discussing certain events that happened in history. It's really nothing at all," Mr. Switzer said calmly.

He said that so smoothly, as if that sentence wasn't a straight-out lie. Technically, it wasn't though. Mr. Switzer and I *were* discussing events that happened in history. He just forgot to mention these are certain events that were happening in *Margaret's* history.

"Oh. All right then," Jeremiah says, but something escapes his mouth. He looks up, and it seemed as if all of the air was taken out of him. A small child was running over to the balcony, but there was something on the floor. The child tripped, but the bars weren't enough to stop the child from falling. He fell. Nothing happened. My powers didn't work. I rushed over to the floor nearest the balcony thinking "Come on powers! Work!" I did what I could and opened my arms. The child fell into my arms, saved from a dangerous fall. She was crying. Everyone rushed over to where I had caught her. My powers didn't work, but I saved the child anyway. How could this be possible? Maybe my powers reacted without me knowing it? Though, all I could think about was the child that fell in my arms; the one that I saved. Then I began thinking. "How was I able to catch the child without falling over myself?" The child felt like a feather in my arms. It wasn't me who saved the child, after all. It was my powers, once again. I become a bit deflated by the thought, but no less relieved that the child is safe. Paramedics rush over to the sight and check on the child. Even though she had a normal pulse, they wanted to find her mother and check the child for any signs of damage. So this was my 6th saving act. But what was the catalyst?

"Paula! I just got a call from a hospital in North Carolina. Katelyn was hit by a car."

No, no, no, no, no, no… Saving one but losing another? I truly, no doubt, hate this power. I will hate myself if Katelyn dies. How could this happen?

Another Plane Ride, Another Day

Katelyn was in a coma. The doctors had to perform surgery on her. They don't know when Katelyn will wake up; if she wakes up. Why is my life one big **if**? Nothing is set in stone, and I hate that. But what if that is the one thing that saves me? My mother couldn't come because of her job. They wouldn't allow her to go. What a cruel world... What a cruel world... Thomas Switzer and Jeremiah are in the room with me.

"Jeremiah, let's go get some food," Mr. Switzer says.

"But what about-"

"She'll be fine. Just come with me."

They leave the room. I think Mr. Switzer expects me to do something, but I don't know what. I put my hand on Katelyn's arm. Tears start streaming down my face. Sadness stares me right in the face. Where are you Katelyn? Please come back. Please. As soon as I think that, I feel a small movement in her arm. Was I just imagining that? Her eyes slowly open. I hug her.

"Paula... Be careful... Ow," Katelyn says.

"Be careful yourself. Did you look both ways while crossing the street? Everyone was worried about you!"

"Yes, but that car seemed to appear out of nowhere."

A sour look crosses Katelyn's face.

"Are you ok, Paula? You look a little… pale."

"Yeah, I'm fine."

But right after I say that, I start becoming dizzy.

"Katelyn, would you mind calling a nurse?"

And I black out.

* * *

When I wake up, the nurse says I've been out of it for a few days, but I know she's just trying to make me feel better. I should've been out for at least a week this time around. My mom enters the room quietly, happy that I'm awake.

"Hi sweetie," she says happily.

"What day is it?"

She hesitates.

"It's January 19th."

"It's been two weeks! I need to get up."

My mom makes me lay back down again.

"We're leaving the hospital tomorrow, so you're going to have to wait. Katelyn and Jeremiah are here to see you."

With that, my mom exits, obviously because she wanted to let me talk to my friends. Katelyn and Jeremiah walk in with smiles on their faces. Katelyn has crutches, and I can assume she either fractured or broke her leg.

"Hey Paula. How are you feeling? I'm fine, by the way," Katelyn says with a smile.

"As good as I can be doing while stuck in a hospital room."

"You've only been awake a few minutes. Don't start complaining," Jeremiah says with a smirk.

My face must show my fluster because Jeremiah's smile grows even wider.

"I heard that I woke up a few minutes after you entered the room. That's pretty cool," she says with a laugh. Jeremiah eyes me with a suspicious glance, as if I did something to cause her to wake up. Well, I did, so I guess his suspicion *is* on cue.

"I've been missing school so much; I might as well be homeschooled," I laugh a bit, but everyone else seems to look a little bit... guilty?

"Guys it's not your fault, you know that right?"

"But if I would've paid more attention-"

"There wouldn't have been anything you could've done, Katelyn," I know this is a fact.

It seems as if the universe is out to get the ones I love. Her smile fades a bit, and I know that she's blaming herself. Jeremiah, on the other hand, seems to look a little displeased with the situation.

"You should've stayed in Maryland, Paula. You would've been safe there," Jeremiah says. I couldn't have, though. Without me, Katelyn could've really died. I wasn't about to let that happen to my best friend.

"I don't think so. Bad things just seem to happen to me," I say. Katelyn responds with a gigantic nod. She knows what I've been through, but she doesn't know why. Jeremiah questions us about what happened. I suppose it's too late not to tell him. After we tell him everything that has happened to me, he looks as me in shock.

"How can one person possibly survive that many things?

How does all of that even happen to one person? Are you like a bad luck magnet?" He asks.

Katelyn tries to shush him, but I end up laughing.

"Jeremiah, I probably am. It might actually be safer if you stand a few feet closer to the door," I say. It's one minute before the nurse regularly checks in. Jeremiah puts his hands up and stands right in front of the door. The nurse comes in, hitting him in the head.

"Actually, maybe it's safer for you to disregard any of my advice."

Katelyn and I laugh at the same time, while Jeremiah grumbles. Though, even through his grumbling noises, I can hear hints of laughter escaping. This makes me laugh even harder, and Katelyn gives me a funny look. I keep laughing, and soon my laughter becomes contagious. Everyone in the room, except for the nurse, is laughing hysterically. The nurse looks at us all as if we are crazy, and we all giggle a bit at this. Though, Jeremiah's giggle sounds more like a chuckle, which, once again, sends us into hysterical laughter. This continues until the nurse pushes them out of the room. The nurse gives me the medicine, and allows the two back in, but warning them that visiting hours will be over soon.

"Hey, do you think I could hide and we could have a secret hospital sleepover?" Katelyn asks while laughing.

Jeremiah sends us both warning glances, but we ignore him. Sometimes Jeremiah takes what we say way too seriously.

Before we know it, visiting hours are over and Jeremiah and Katelyn must leave. I think of how boring it'll be without them. Then I begin thinking, *"What would happen if I had never met them."* Well, obviously I would be a different person. But if they had never met me, they would've been safe. Maybe if I hadn't met them, none of this would've happened. I'm not blaming them for it, but Katelyn helped me form my personality; my normality. I always look down on my normality because I wish I had something better, but Katelyn seems to like who I am, and so does Jeremiah. There's also Beatrice, Bryan, and Michelle. I can't forget about my mother either. If I hadn't met them, would I be the same Paula I am today? I think that I would have the same personality traits, but I would've found a way to develop them differently. Though, that doesn't really matter. I have a life right now, and I have to make the best of it. Especially since everything might be over soon. The thought saddens me, and my body seems to take advantage of that. I quickly fall asleep, suppressing depressing thoughts. I seem to have transported to the tree I used to see so often in my dreams. I am standing one foot away, but this time, when I go to touch it, I see the face of a girl. It is not mine, and it is not anybody I have met. There is no color, because her face is on the monochrome tree; the chalky dust tree; the dark tree. The death tree, it seems. She mimics my movements. When I go to touch the face, it wavers. The waves fade after a few moments, but every cell in my small body is screaming, and I can't stop moving. Waves begin forming around me: slowly at first, but more seem to form at a quicker pace. I spin around, causing more waves to be created. Soon, I'm laughing. The spinning is actually quite fun. I know I should be freaked out, but everything seems so... 3D; almost more than my own world itself. Slowly, I notice my feet are becoming deeper and deeper within the floor, rising from my hips, to my torso, in slow cascading movements.

I try moving my arms, but this is not something you can swim in. My face is almost under the water, when I begin to scream. The waves taste metallic against my tongue, but it soon turns to a chalky taste. I close my eyes and let the waves surround me. When I look up, I'm in my hospital room. I wasn't dreaming. My clothes are still wavering. How could this be? What was that place? I get up from my bed, even though I know I'm not supposed to. It seems as if, I, myself, am a hologram made of liquid, taking the place of matter, but also nonexistent at the same time. I look at my surroundings to see that the machinery has stopped. The machine that counts my heartbeat isn't working. Am I dead? When I go to touch the machine, it wavers, too. I try walking outside of the room, but the walls waver. Then the floor begins wavering below me once again. I try to scream, but this time I am left with a taste of decay in my mouth. This is even worse than before. I close my mouth, and I sink. When I open my eyes again, there's a tiled ceiling that I'm staring into. I slowly try to get up. Nothing wavers. The machinery is working. I hear the steady "beep" it makes. For some reason, I find that oddly comforting. My nurse enters with my mom and hands me my clothes.

"Rise and shine. We have to take a flight back home," my mother says.

"Why do we keep taking flights when North Carolina really isn't that far away? Isn't it expensive?"

"Would you rather be in a car for a few hours? And it's not too costly, so we should be able to afford it."

When my mother says that, I see a falter in her face, but it quickly returns back to normal. If you hadn't paid attention, you may have missed it. She's lying to me. Maybe the flights aren't that expensive, but surely the doctor's bills are. I sigh and quickly get dressed. Truthfully, I'd rather take a car. It gives me more time to think. Then again, when I think of my own bed, I realize how much of Maryland I'll really be missing. My mother and I walk out of the hospital, hand in hand. Katelyn and Jeremiah come to the airport to wish me goodbye. I hug each of them, and a small tear falls down my face when they aren't looking. Even though I miss Maryland, I will miss them too. We get on the plane and take our seats. I'm happy I get the window seat so I can watch the land fly by. It makes me think of how fast my life is going. A pungent stab of disappointment rumbles in my stomach, but I ignore it. I shouldn't be feeling these feelings. There are only 3 incidents left. My time is limited. Though I push the thought away, it lays in the back of my mind, bothering me 24/7. It also causes me to become restless when I get home. I guess I won't get much sleep tonight. Today is January 20, 2017, a Sunday, and I'll have school tomorrow. Is school another distraction or another problem? I grab a book that I have already read from a small bookshelf in the corner of my room. I make it to 98 before I fall asleep. Or was it 150…

8th Grade Year

When I enter the school, everything seems to be normal. Well, that's most likely because no one has found out about the North Carolina incident or the mall incident yet. Things will become weird again, and I will be a stranger among many. Beatrice finds me and hugs me when I walk inside the school.

"We heard about the incident. Are you ok?" Beatrice asks.

"Yes, I'm fine. Katelyn's fine too."

"That's good. No one here has heard about the mall incident yet, but I imagine in a few hours they might."

"What do you mean?"

"We weren't the only students from our school there, Paula. It's a popular location. Everything will be ok, though. And we don't have to throw a party if you don't want to. I know we did it last year, but now that I know you better, I would picture you as someone who would rather go to a bookstore than to a party."

"Yes. I really like reading."

Beatrice smiles and leads me towards Bryan and Michelle. Do they know about it? I forgot that they left, but then again, Beatrice left too. Knowing Beatrice, though, she was probably just around the corner watching to make sure everything was ok.

"Hello Paula. Hello Beatrice. What's up?" Bryan asks.

"Everything is great. Did you guys buy any games as the video game store?" I ask.

"We only bought two because most of the games cost fifty dollars. It was pretty expensive," he replies.

"That's too bad. Did you get a chance to play them this weekend?" Beatrice asks.

"Yes. Michelle and I headed over to my older brother's house and played the games there."

"Well, I have to go to Spanish, so I'll see you guys later!" I yell.

I almost run into someone on my way to Spanish.

"Oh, sorry. I knocked your books over," he says.

He helps me with my books, and I immediately recognize his face.

"Jeremiah? Why are you here?"

"Not even a hello. That's disappointing,"

He gave me a sour look.

"Hello. Now, why are you here?"

"I was actually planning to go to a high school in Maryland, so when Mr. Switzer offered me a transfer, I immediately took it."

"And what about Katelyn and your friends?"

"I don't have many friends. She's a good friend to me, and she doesn't mind me moving. She said to tell you in a few years she might be moving back here."

This had me a bit confused. He must've seen the confused look on my face, so he began to explain.

"Katelyn will move back here for college when she's 18. She wanted to go to a college here, and I looked at the same college to see how good it was. I liked what they had to offer here better so my family let me move in with my... uncle... to accommodate my wishes. Obviously I have to fill out paperwork and other things first, but in about a week I should be a full student here."

"So you're parents don't mind you moving here by yourself. Isn't that kind of life change serious?"

"Yeah, but they understand why I would want to do it. Plus, I would be with you two in college if we decided to go to the same one. I couldn't miss out on that opportunity. You guys are the first good friends I've had in awhile."

I smiled at Jeremiah and we walked through the hallway, talking, until we parted for our next class. I suppose this isn't a weird situation. A lot of children move so that they can go to better schools. I should consider myself lucky that I'll be seeing one of my good friends every day. It's kind of sad that Katelyn isn't here, though. The three of us being together is what makes our friendship work. If it wasn't for that, I don't know how we'd act around each other. Guess I'll just have to wait and see.

In Spanish Class I copy down some of the notes that they received while I was gone from the other students. After that, I took a quick quiz. The quiz was 10 questions, meaning each of the questions was worth 10 points, so I needed to be careful not to get any wrong. The test asked simple questions, but there was one that reminded me of everything I went through. Usually I'm so focused on the test, I don't notice specific things, but the word "chocolate" was on the test, and it made me think of last year. I answered a question in Spanish Class. That was also the day I found out Katelyn was leaving. Thinking back, I realize how frivolous certain things were back then. Although Katelyn was leaving, a flight to North Carolina from Maryland doesn't take that long. I just thought of not being able to see Katelyn every day. Was that selfish of me? The past version of me couldn't possibly realize what problems would erupt in my life. And I know, even if I could travel back in time, the past me most likely wouldn't listen to what I had to say. In fact, the past version of me might be quite stubborn even if we look nearly exactly the same. Since last year, my face has matured a bit, but not much. I quickly finish my test and watch Senor Augment clean the white board. Everyone exits the classroom while I put my test on the teacher's desk. Now I'm off to my next class, math. When I found out the schedule for this year, I was surprised to find out that it was the same one from last year. Sure, it makes everything easier to remember, but I still have the same thoughts about our schedule. It's all over the place. Having Spanish before math *still* doesn't make much sense in my mind.

When we get to the math classroom, there are cubes laid out across the table. It's supposed to help us understand algebra a bit better.

"Let's say y was this yellow block and r was this red block. I want you to arrange a math problem with y and r in it, using all of the digits 1-9. Then, put this into a word problem and hand it in so I can check it. By 9:30 I want two word problems completed, and then we'll discuss everything. As for you, Paula, we didn't take any tests and you handed in the project that was due a week early, so you're only about 5 lessons behind. Just go over a few things in your textbook and you should be totally back on track in a few days."

Writing word problems isn't hard for me, but everyone else in the class seems to groan. I'm the first one done with 5 minutes extra, so my teacher tells me what homework we have and says I can start it if I want to. I finish about 30% of the page before our teacher tells us to discuss the word problems. We go up and down the row, sharing one of our two word problems. Some are a bit funny, so the class ends up laughing. There are 14 of us in this classroom this year, so we only get through half of the word problems by the time it's 9:45. I did one of mine first since I finished first, and then the rest of the kids did theirs. Only one child didn't finish, but even so, he managed to finish his first word problem, and he was almost done with his second one anyway. The teacher gave us page 313 for homework in the textbook, and then she gave me everything that I missed. She wants it all handed in by Monday next week. There are 7 pages I have to do for homework. 4 of them are in the workbook, but the last three are worksheets that she had to give me. When we leave, everybody says goodbye to our teacher, and I head off to my next class.

"Everyone please take your seats and open your textbook to page 445. We will be reading a short story from there, and I would like you to answer the questions I have written on the board afterwards. Paula, you have a quiz on the last story we read tomorrow. You can go over the story, since I doubt you got a chance to read it."

Did the teachers know about the two incidents? I suppose it would make sense for them to know, but I'd rather not have anyone remind me of them anymore. A chill gets sent up my spine as quick as a lightning bolt. I do the work she assigned for us today, and begin doing the work that I missed. It's a relief to know I didn't have to ask a few of my teachers whether I missed work or not, to spare the rest of the class looking at me. Time passes quickly as I'm rushing to finish reading the last story that we read. It's a bit long, and I don't want to have to read it at home. Unfortunately, time runs out before I can finish reading. I still have 10 pages left in the story. The story was 25 pages long and I managed to read 15 of them, at the very least. The next class would be Science, except our teacher is absent.

"Hello class. I am Mrs. Sedery and I am your teacher for today. Your normal teacher is absent, so I will be giving you the work. She told me to tell Paula Berney to read the chapter for Friday. She says you missed a test. Also, there are some questions that the whole class must do. Turn to page 350 and start doing numbers 1 to 22. She wants full sentences for 20 to 22 and this must be done on a sheet of lined paper."

I read and take notes on the chapter for the whole period because I can't complete the homework without first reading the chapter. It wouldn't make sense. Something seems to distract me, though, and I can't keep my eyes on the textbook. I look around the room with words stapled across the walls. 'Memorize the work; you'll do well on tests. Understand the work; you'll do well in life.' There are pictures of complex math problems taped across the walls. There's also a reading list of books that our principal would recommend us to read. Then, of course, there's a picture of an atom and a diagram explaining which parts do what. The room has open windows, letting the fresh air consume us. It creates a good working environment. I believe I read somewhere that minds think better in cold air. If you go into any of the other rooms, they will most likely be around 70 degrees, and with people in it, the temperature rises a bit. This place might be my favorite room in the school just because it feels so open. Though, I'd much rather have classes outside, even though it's still wintertime and it may just be freezing. The air begins to have a damp smell to it, showing that it will probably rain soon. It is turning into spring, after all. What more can you expect?

I walk into the lunchroom and notice Jeremiah sitting by himself. As 8th graders, we can pick where we sit, so I walk over to him and take a seat.

"Hello Jeremiah. What's up? Do you have any new friends yet?" I ask.

"I doubt it." he says with a laugh, "I barely talk to anyone during class. Focused on my grades, you know?"

"Yeah, I got it. So are you going to Raytown High School?"

"Yes. I was going to try to get into a private high school, but I don't want my guardians to spend too much money on me, either."

"So you said Katelyn is moving back here for college when she's 18?"

"Yes. She said she might move into the dorm, though. So her parents don't have to move."

"That would make sense. I understand you wanted to move here because you like the college, but why so soon?"

"I didn't want to move to Maryland when I got older because it would be more difficult for me. I moved to North Carolina when I was 7, so I've been there about 7 years.

When I start high school, it'll be difficult not only to move in with my uncle, but also to know what kind of curriculum the school follows."

"That makes sense, I guess. Sorry for making you explain it so much. I'm just a bit surprised. I would've thought someone like you would be able to make a lot of friends in North Carolina."

"No, not really. With my good looks, most people shied away from me." he said with a smirk.

I rolled my eyes at this, but continued talking. For some reason, I just feel as if Jeremiah didn't feel a need to talk to anyone.

"So, what is this mysterious college?"

"Johnny Meyer University."

I immediately started choking when he said that. Johnny Meyer University, last time I checked, was ranked 39 nationally. I just had plans on going to the University of Raytown.

"I don't think I'm smart enough to go there."

"Paula, you just need to be a hard worker to get into John Hopkins University. And get good grades. It's not totally based on intelligence."

"If you want to move to go to such a great school, why didn't you go to Hortatory? It's ranked second nationally, I believe."

"Not everything is based on rankings. Plus, I have no one to live with in Massachusetts. I'm living with my closest relative right now."

"Then go to Docile in North Carolina."

"Now that, I don't think I'm smart enough to get in. It is ranked 5th nationally."

"What happened to 'Not everything is based on rankings.'?"

"Well, some things are. Anyway, it seems as if you're not happy that I'm here."

"I am, it's just the situation is a bit confusing."

"I can understand that. So, how's your first day back after the two incidents?"

"It's ok I guess. Just came back to a lot of work. I just have one question. Last year when I visited, you were a counselor? Aren't you supposed to be in the 9th grade then?"

"Didn't I tell you? Maybe I forgot. Either way, the reason I was a counselor was because Mr. Switzer needed help, and since I'm his nephew, I just happened to be there. I was training for awhile, but no. I am meant to be in the 8th grade *this* year."

Jeremiah laughs at this. We continue talking for the rest of lunch and then head to our next classes. When I enter the history classroom, I see different posters. I guess they put up new ones while I was gone for two weeks.

"Everyone read the next section in your history textbook and take notes. Paula, you're going to have to read the first 2 sections. After that, you can continue with the class. I would prefer for you to be done taking notes by Wednesday or Thursday, but if you can't read the sections tonight, that's fine. I understand what happened and I wouldn't want to put too much pressure on you. Just make sure that you get the notes you missed."

The history lesson goes by quietly, and I sigh because it seems as if the homework is just piling on. I guess I can't talk to my friends tonight. English passes the same way, reading rules for grammar and taking the vocabulary words down.

Luckily, I don't have too much homework for English. It's just a take home test due on Wednesday.

I gather everything I need to do to complete my homework and nearly exit the school building when I hear someone calling my name.

"Paula! Want to study for History together?" asks Jeremiah.

"I have a lot of other homework, so I don't think I can. I have a take home test due Wednesday, to finish the chapter in history, a reading quiz tomorrow, the science questions, and studying the 5 lessons for math."

"Going over the reading story should take you about 20 minutes, and everything else isn't due tomorrow. For math you can't really study, you can only really practice. Just go over a few questions and you'll be fine. Do the take home test we received. Everything might take you an hour to an hour and a half, so you'll be done quickly. Plus, I live right across the street from you so that's not a problem either. If I didn't, then I probably wouldn't be going to your school."

I hate to admit it, but Jeremiah was right. This homework wouldn't take me a long time. After what happened this past weekend, though, I really just want to relax and sleep a bit. Technically I slept for two weeks, so I shouldn't need to sleep any longer, but I'd feel better if I did. It would feel like I'm back on track.

"Sorry, Jeremiah. I can't. Not today. If I manage to not be busy, then I'll text you."

"Ok, but you don't have my phone number."

"Can I have your phone number?"

"Nope."

"Why?"

"It forces us to meet in person. I don't like talking over a phone."

I groan.

"So will we meet, or not?"

I mumble a quick "Humph." and walk outside. If he won't give me his phone number, then I won't give him my answer.

I ran to the car and got inside. My mother said hello and asked me about my day. I answered her, saying everything was good, Jeremiah was here, and that I needed to start my homework as soon as I got home. The ride was quiet as we drove home. My mother opened up my window a little bit, and the cool breeze from the winter air came in. I guess we haven't found the spring season yet. When I got home, I immediately ran upstairs to my room to start doing my homework. I studied for reading for about 30 minutes, *practiced* for math for about 15 minutes, and completed the take-home test about 45 minutes later. It's true; I really do want to see Jeremiah. I'd be really happy if I could, but I don't want to get too close to anyone anymore. Though, isn't it too late already?

"Paula, he basically just moved for you," I tell myself.

The thought is nice, but not true, and even I know that. He really did move here because he liked what Maryland was offering, and having someone that lives near me was really just an added bonus. Though, I didn't think that he'd live right across the street from me. Even though Jeremiah knew I lived in Maryland, he didn't know my exact address, so it's funny to think he lives so close. I hear someone knocking on our door, and I know who it is before my mother says anything.

"Hello Jeremiah," I say, rushing down the stairs to open the door.

"Hello Paula. You never told me whether we would meet or not, so here I am. Let's go to the park."

"Man, this guy is persistent," I think with a groan.

"So... Are we going or not?"

"Mom, I'll be back. I'm going outside with Jeremiah."

"Don't be out too long. Oh, and don't go too far away." my mother says.

"So are we allowed to go to the park?" Jeremiah asks.

"You think my mom would let me walk to the park with a boy? No. Let's just talk in the front yard."

"Maybe another day, then."

Jeremiah walked back to his house, leaving me with a blank stare. What's so important about the park that he wants to show me? I mean, they do have a new addition to the park, but I never got to see it. How could Jeremiah have known about it, anyway? He's only been here for a few days... I think. The truth is, I know nothing about Jeremiah, so he could've actually visited a few times, and I never noticed. Though, I don't know how I couldn't notice. I walk over to his house because he is *not* leaving me with a sentence like that. I've had too much mystery for one lifetime, and I'm not taking anymore. I knock on his door, but no one answers. I saw him walk back into the house. Someone finally opens the door, and it's not Jeremiah. It's Thomas Switzer. He tries to close the door, but I push the door open with all of my might.

"Well, hello Paula. What are you doing here?"

"The question is what are you doing here?

"Come in Paula, it seems we need to have a bit of a chat."

I sit down on the couch in their living room and demand they tell me what's going on.

"The amount you heard about Jeremiah moving in with his uncle is true, but you didn't hear the rest of the story," he says awkwardly.

"Tell me," I respond, giving him a sharp stare.

"Jeremiah's parents didn't let him come here. His parents died in a fire awhile back. Remember how I told you Margaret had 10 gifts? Well, there's another part to it. There's something called the "Unlucky Ones" who need the "Blessed Ones" to save them. Jeremiah, like you was bestowed upon 10… things. But, everyday Jeremiah is in danger because of the curse put upon him. He is one of the unlucky ones. Margaret committed suicide because we got into an argument, that's true, but she also wanted my bad luck to go away. There are two paths the Blessed Ones can take. They can either fight the "bad luck" as you would call it, with only their partner to help, or they can commit suicide, and their partner will be saved. Also, the 'Unlucky Ones' can cast a protective shield around the 'Blessed Ones' unintentionally, as long as they know a lot about each other. His parents dying in a fire was just one of the 10 things that had happened for him."

Maybe I run out because I don't want to hear the rest. I don't want to hear about Jeremiah being hurt. Maybe it's because these fights are nothing in comparison to my last one. Maybe it's because I'm scared. No one has ever faced the… the… I need to give it a new name. Bad luck doesn't describe its evil. Whatever that's controlling this bad luck must be no good. I truly am blessed in ways such as this. I really didn't have to worry about dying. Well, that is, until now.

Homeschooling

"You are getting homeschooled by Mr. Switzer from now on, Paula. There's nothing else I can say. You never told me any of this before, and then this popped up. This has been happening for a year. I can't believe I didn't notice. When your daughter almost dies 7 times, you think something would be off. But I guess not."

She's going to be like this all day, and she's going to blame herself. It's not her fault this was put upon me.

"Why homeschooling, though?"

"Because I'd rather have you safe. And every time you and Jeremiah walk into that school, you put other children in danger. I know it's hard to think about, but try putting yourself in the other kids' shoes. They have no idea what's going on, and then they're gone. You, on the other hand would know what's going on and would feel responsible for all of their deaths."

The universe is bringing Jeremiah and me together. How great. And now, I have to be homeschooled.

"I never chose any of this."

"Well now you have it, so it's time to take responsibility."

I groan, grab my book bag, and walk over to Thomas Switzer's house.

I knock, Mr. Switzer let's me in, and he begins talking.

"All right Jeremiah and Paula; this is not a normal class. Of course, you still have your normal schoolwork to do, but this is a class so that you can use your powers with more experience." Mr. Switzer says.

"Wait, so our powers don't just… work? Mr. Switzer, they've been working fine so far."

"No, they don't just work, Paula. And like I said a while back, call me Mr. Switz. So our first lesson will be controlling how to slow down time."

"Mr. Switz, I thought Jeremiah doesn't have powers."

"He doesn't, other than the shield, but if he wanted to, he could free himself from any of your powers. For instance, if you slowed down time, he could move normally, just as you can. So, basically you're going to be only slowing down time in a certain area."

"I thought our powers are only supposed to be used for the 10 gifts."

"Haven't you ever had a time when you accidentally used your powers?"

I stayed quiet because I did. One time when Katelyn and I were throwing snowballs at each other. I accidentally slowed down time and dodged the snowball. Jeremiah has not been talking so far. I suppose he wants to focus.

"Now, here is a small snow globe, Paula. I want you to shake the globe, and then try to slow down the snow in it."

I do as he tells me. When I try to slow it down, my powers branch out to everyone in the room, but I don't know how to stop it. A few minutes later, after intense panicking, they return to normal.

"Perhaps learning how to stop your powers would be more useful…" Mr. Switz says.

Throughout the day, we practice various different areas of my power. The Cursed One practiced trying to stop my powers from affecting him, and it was actually going pretty well. Apparently, bad things had been happening to Jeremiah since he was a baby. His parents died in the fire, when Jeremiah had lived with Mr. Switz there had been a house flood, he almost got pulled into the ocean by a riptide, when he was walking to school he almost got hit by a car, and I still don't know what the 6th and 7th events are.

"Mr. Switz, what are the 6th and 7th events?" I ask.

"The 5th is… when Katelyn fell into the coma. And the 6th is when you saved Katelyn, but ended up falling into one yourself."

This surprised me so much that I became as stiff as a board. Does Jeremiah really care about us that much? How can that be possible? We've only known each other for a year. When I look over at Jeremiah, his face is red, but he too, is as stiff as a board. I don't think he expected Mr. Switz to say that.

"Uncle… Did you have to give off every little piece of my history to her?" Jeremiah asked, obviously embarrassed.

"Yes, Jeremiah. It's important she knows that you truly do care about Katelyn and herself."

"I'm going to go outside for a bit."

I don't know why he took it all so seriously, I mean I understand that he cares about us as good friends. But then again, he's never had good friends before. Is the curse the reason for that? He doesn't want to put anyone in danger? How long ago did he find out about this?

"Mr. Switz, can I-"

"Go. If you don't go get him I don't know where he'll run off to."

I go outside and look around. I don't see him until I notice him on *my porch*, sitting in *my seat*.

"If you didn't want to be found why would you hide somewhere so visible?"

"Sometimes when you're out in the open, people tend to notice you less."

"Why on *my* porch?"

"Technically it's not *your* porch. It's your mom's porch."

"That doesn't answer the question."

"Can you ask Mr. Switz if he can take us to the park?"

"No, you do it. I don't know why you're so obsessive over-"

Jeremiah grabs my arm and leads me back to our "classroom". He also tells Mr. Switz to come with us, and he begins running to the park. Unlike me, I notice Jeremiah has a knack for running, and he's nearly dragging me on the ground to the park. When we first enter the park, I don't notice anything unusual, but then I notice he's not taking me to the park. He's taking me to the neighborhood surrounding it. He stopped at the front porch of one house, ashes and wood everywhere.

"This is where my parents died. I used to live in Maryland. I moved to North Carolina when I was a small child, as I told you before, so I don't remember having to leave everything behind. After you came was the first time I was told what happened to my parents. I always knew my parents had gone missing, but I didn't know what had happened. When I found out about my parents, I wanted to move back. It also gave me an excuse to actually have some friends around me for once. Being around me is what caused Katelyn to get into the car accident."

"It's not your fault. You weren't even around when Katelyn had been hurt."

"But I saw you saving the small child. That must've triggered something. Even knowing me isn't safe. You guys are my best friends, and I don't want to put you in danger."

"First of all, you can't put me in danger. I'm too stubborn and I have whatever these gifts are. Katelyn may be another story, but remember, this will all end soon. You can't possibly put her in danger now. Then, after everything's said and done, we will be able to have a normal friendship; a friendship without all of the danger. Are you ok with that?"

"I suppose that makes me feel better."

"Remember, we're partners in… good, I guess?"

"Yeah, we're not partners in crime because we're saving lives."

The wind blows down upon us, and we walk side by side back to our neighborhood. In the corner of my eye, I see a tear fall from Jeremiah's face, but I don't mention anything. Sometimes you need times where you can cry without anyone interrupting you. It helps you calm down and gives you a greater sense of peace. Jeremiah has been through a lot more than me, and I wasn't around to help him back then; but I'm here now. Even before, when we didn't know each other, we were connected by this curse, but now we are connected by friendship and trust. Everything is ok now. Jeremiah wants me to know about his past, which makes me trust everything that is going on a little more. Though, it doesn't fix it. When I get home, I have about 200 texts from Beatrice, Bryan, Michelle, and Katelyn. 2 hours pass before someone knocks on my bedroom door.

"Come in."

"Hey sweetie, Jeremiah's here to see you."

"I'll be down in a second."

I walk down the stairs and see Jeremiah in the doorway.

"Hello Paula. Mr. Switz wanted me to ask you whether you have any questions. He understands that it's been a long day, and he wants to know how you're doing. Let's go out on the porch."

"Ok."

We walk onto the porch and I see Mr. Switz sitting down with two other seats beside him. Jeremiah and I both sit down.

"So, any questions?" Mr. Switz asks.

Everyone is quiet for a few seconds.

"Why, if I was supposed to be protecting Jeremiah, did it take you guys so long to find me?"

"Jeremiah is cursed, so obviously the curse wouldn't want us to find you. The curse would make certain things happen so that you two wouldn't meet. That's probably why I doubted you in the beginning. Though, my senses eventually won over. The curse is something quite complex, and everything that happens, every incident, is caused by it. It was already destined that Jeremiah was born to have the Curse. When his parents died, he was meant to die too. It's a miracle that he's alive. Though, I like to believe that *because* you two hadn't met, he had extra protection. The Curse needed to make a decision. Without you, he would have a better chance of dying, but he would also be granted extra protection, too. My guess is that the Curse chose to keep you away from him because the protection would fade, and you are much stronger. If Jeremiah had met you, and he did, there's a smaller chance that the Curse will take over."

"I guess that makes sense. So basically, the reason we weren't near each other is because the curse didn't want us to be. Now that we are, will bad things happen to me more often?"

"They might, though nothing will be as bad as the last event. During the last 3 events, you two will need to become much closer. There isn't a lot of time left and you don't have much time to prepare. It seems like there is so much time, but there isn't. Your powers have increased greatly since the first event, but I don't know whether it's enough to fight off the curse. I've never been through this sort of thing fully, as you know."

"Why did Jeremiah lie about it in the first place?"

"Jeremiah didn't have the ability to tell you what was happening. He kept lying about it because he had to. Otherwise, he would've told you the truth."

"He didn't have the ability? As in… the curse wasn't letting him?"

"Yes. The curse is something very… weird. We don't know *what* it is, but we know it brings misfortune to whoever has it. And, somehow, every person that had to go through this is connected. For all we know, it could be a family curse. Maybe our ancestors did something bad."

"Hold on. Although I couldn't tell you the real reason, everything that I said was something I meant. I just didn't mention wanting to come back for my parents, also," Jeremiah says with a tight smile.

I smile back at him reassuringly, and keep asking questions.

"I thought I was supposed to protect people. Am I only supposed to protect Jeremiah?"

"Well, here's the thing. You were supposed to meet by destiny, and he is essential because he offers extra protection, but you can choose to continue on without him."

"Wait, so I'm not supposed to help you?"

"You are, but your main job is protecting normal people. People that don't know anything about this sort of... What am I supposed to call it? You have supernatural powers. You have to protect people, but you also have to protect Jeremiah. I don't understand why the world wants to do this, and why it would happen now, but apparently you two are stuck together and you're just going to have to deal with it. The first 4 incidents you didn't deal with together, but after the 5th incident, that all changed. In reality, you two were already bound together after you first met, so technically, the question isn't 'Why now?' The question is when."

Of course my teacher was right. So technically we've always been together even though we didn't know it. How peachy.

Concerts and Quiet

The weeks were passing quickly. I decided it would be safer for Beatrice if I didn't talk to her. That's where I ended with our friendship because I can't trust myself. It'll probably be safer for everyone if I wasn't here. No, I still don't love myself. Yes, I'm forced to be close with Jeremiah. My personality isn't the same as it was when this first started this. Lately, I noticed I haven't been paying attention to my own feelings. I've become so far away that even my mother is having a hard time connecting with me. I'm not some mystical being, and I think I've begun to forget that. Just because I have to work with Jeremiah, it doesn't change anything; just my friendships. Though, can friendships change you? Sometimes I forget that my personality isn't just created by me, it has been formed by all the connections I've made. The paths are still there, but the choice isn't presenting itself yet. Soon, I'll see it. I'll see my future; but now? I still have time. And I'll make the most of that.

When I look up, I see Jeremiah smiling at me. We're on our way to a concert. Time Flying By is performing their latest album. As we turn the corner, I see T-Shirts being sold near the front gate, and there are many fans lined up to get inside. Luckily, we're early, so we managed to get in without any confusion. In about 15 minutes, though, it begins to become extremely crowded, and the band comes out.

"Thanks for coming everyone! We're really excited to play for you guys!" Andy, the drummer, says.

The guitarists and singers are in the front, and Andy is in the back. You can see him, but it's hard to see behind the drums. The guitar starts playing low at first, but then the sounds grow into a roar. The crowd begins screaming out of excitement. Jeremiah and I enjoy the music and sing along whenever they ask us to. My mother is outside getting some food. She doesn't like loud music. Two hours pass by quickly, and even my eardrums are tired. Jeremiah is in his seat, looking like he's about to fall asleep. I shake him and make him stand up.

"It's time to go home," I say.

"But I'm tired," he whines.

"You can be tired in the car. Come on."

When we get out, I see my mother looking at the t-shirts.

"Sweetie, do you think this would fit me?" my mom asks me.

She holds up a black shirt with the name of the band on it and a picture of them.

"I'm not sure. Jeremiah's really tired, though. I think we need to go home."

My mother looked at Jeremiah and nodded.

"He practically has bats under his eyes. We'll return him to Mr. Switz. He's probably going to fall asleep as soon as he gets home."

"I wouldn't be surprised if he fell asleep in the car."

When we walk back to the car, Jeremiah gets into the back seat and begins to snore. My mom and I both laugh as we begin our journey to our home. The city passes by quickly, each second allowing the sky to become darker and darker. Night is approaching.

We arrive at home, Jeremiah fast asleep in his house. I, however, need something to eat before I go to bed. Today was a long day, and this will give me time to relive each moment of the concert. As I take out the cereal, I stare at the wall for a bit and remember how Jeremiah and I could barely hear each other during the concert. We tried talking, but our voices would be covered with the sound of screaming fans. I laugh a bit at it, not because it's really funny, but because it brings back old memories that we had gone through together. I remember when I was at the hospital with Katelyn and Jeremiah, and despite Katelyn's bad state, they would both try to make me laugh. They are both really good friends, and I wonder what I would do without them. Life really did take a turn, didn't it? During this time of being able to talk to one of my best friends, Jeremiah, I actually managed to have a lot of laughs throughout this whole messed up thing. It's incredible how much other people really can change the bad times into good ones. I'm supposed to protect Jeremiah with my life, but I'm only 14, so how can I possibly have the bravery to do such a thing? Every incident wasn't me, it was instinct. I don't have that kind of bravery... Do I? Sooner or later the 7th event is going to happen, then the 8th, and then the 9th. How will I ever be really to-?

I hear a loud crash and wonder what is going on. When I look outside the window, I see that a quarter of Jeremiah's house has fallen. If one part of the house is falling on another, it's only so long until the whole house collapses. I run onto the porch, and see a light coming from the back of the house. Something... someone... is holding a torch, and it is lit on fire. Why is it that I'm always fighting against fire? I run, and time slows down once again, but I become quick. A part of the house is falling. I catch it before it falls, and jump into the nearly collapsed second floor of the house. Jeremiah is still lying on his bed, sound asleep. How can he be sleeping at a time like this? I run and grab Jeremiah's arm, then jump down to the ground. Jumping back onto the second floor, I look for Mr. Switz.

"Mr. Switz?"

"Over here. She's downstairs. I don't know if the house has collapsed on her, but please save her!"

I grab Mr. Switz's arm and try to get through the demolished pieces of the house. There's a fire about 8 feet away from her, and I run to her. She's on the dresser. Trying to lift her, I notice my strength fading away. I try to run with her, but I trip, and she falls onto the cold, hard ground. Part of the house has collapsed on my body. I can't breathe. The fire spreads. The room spins, and it all becomes grey. That is, until everything fades into black.

The She, the Who?

I don't know when I wake up, but this time I'm not in a hospital. My eyes open, and even though the room is quite dark, it all seems too bright to me. I use my hand to shield my eyes, and soft sounds penetrate my ears. My hearing is very weak, but I can somewhat make out what the words are. Then, I begin to feel; feel the ache surrounding my body; the pounding of my head and the grime, the ashes, the small pieces of wood lodged underneath my skin. I don't feel clean, and I feel an urge to want to take a shower. I can't stay like this.

"Don't move, Paula. You're covered in wounds. Your back must ache from everything landing on you."

I heard them, whoever it was, but I couldn't agree with them. My back wasn't hurting at all, when that should be the part of me that hurts the most. I try getting up, but someone's hands stop me.

"My back doesn't hurt; just get me a warm towel please," I manage to croak out.

Someone rushes away. I can't comprehend what's happening yet.

"Don't worry Paula. You saved the box. You saved Margaret."

Everything comes back to me. I remember the saving, I remember trying to grab Margaret's ashes, and I remember tripping and falling. Margaret did die long ago, but Mr. Switz still holds onto the ashes. They're the only things left of her.

Someone hands me a warm towel, and I begin to wash my face. I already begin feeling cleaner.

"While you were asleep, we tried taking out some of the splinters you had. Most of them are gone, but there are still about 7 left, I believe," my mother informs me with a soft look on her face.

"Please just take them out while my senses are dulled," I say, stifling a graon.

I feel barely anything, sometimes small pinches, but besides that, it's a relief to know that is the extent of my injuries.

"Does your back hurt?" my mother questions.

"No, but can I take a shower?"

"I'll help you," my mother states.

I go upstairs and look at my face in the mirror. It's clean in comparison to my body, which looks as if I jumped into a pile of dust. As I get in the shower, my mother helps me and makes sure I don't have any big bruises.

"That's weird. You seem to be fine, but that wouldn't be normal," she whispers, mainly to herself.

I take a shower and quickly get dressed. Yes, my body does ache a bit, mostly from being tired, but I still want to see who's waiting for me downstairs. I see Mr. Switz, my mother, and the nurse. Where's Jeremiah? I begin to worry, as I don't yet know whether he got hurt or not.

"He's outside," says Mr. Switz.

My heart relaxes at an instant and the pain becomes prominent again.

"Thank you for your help. We very much appreciate it," my mother sighs.

"Well, it looks like I'll be going. I hope the injuries you received heal quickly. Please call me if you need any more help," says the nurse.

My mother nods and takes me outside to see Jeremiah. She leaves, but I can see her watching from the living room window.

"Hello Jeremiah," I utter quickly.

"Hi Paula," he whispers.

Watching him carefully, I can see that he was crying, as the tears left streaks down his face where there should've been dirt. My heart aches in sadness and I look away. He just lost his home, and not to mention that this has happened before. His parents died because of the fire, and he must blame it on himself.

"So, what are you doing out here?" I question.

"I'm just getting some fresh air."

Jeremiah doesn't lie very well. The smoke is puncturing our nostrils and our lungs, leaving us without much oxygen to breathe in. It's already hard to breathe when you look at their house, and this just makes it much worse.

"You seem upset. Why?" I question.

"It's my fault this is happening, Paula. Without me you'd still have a normal life."

As he says this, his eyebrows furrow together. I can take

pity on Jeremiah, but I don't want to. Rather than take pity, I want to understand, because the only way he will heal right now, is if I'm there for him.

"It's funny," I respond quietly.

"What?"

"I think the same exact thing sometimes. Things seem to happen around me that are bad, and other people get hurt. If I were to be truly honest, you could say I hate myself for it. There's a reason I haven't been talking to Beatrice or Bryan or even Katelyn as much, and that's because I don't want to put them in danger."

As I look away from Jeremiah once more, I can see my neighbors in the distance, watching the house carefully.

"They would be in danger because of me. I'm the cursed one. I'm the reason you're stuck in this mess."

Anger flares throughout me with a need to protect everything that we've worked for so far. I'm not angry at Jeremiah, per say, but I'm angry with how he's seeing things. Jeremiah should be the optimist, but he's here acting as if this is tearing his whole life down.

I can't let him stay this way. If anyone needs to be happy, it's him, because we're in this together. I've shouldered the guilt for a long time, and I know that letting someone else take some of it might make it easier on me, but I can't watch Jeremiah suffer as I stand idly by. It's my turn to be the optimist, and act as if I know everything will be alright. Maybe if I pretend long enough, I'll start to see it that way.

"Well maybe some of these things would still happen even if you weren't around. Car accidents happen every day, Jeremiah. And fires? They happen too. No matter what we do, we are at risk to die every single second of our lives, which is why we have to make it count. Am I being a hypocrite? Sure. I'm telling you to be happy when I can't be happy with this situation myself, but guess what? I'm being a hypocrite for the right reasons. I'm not scolding you, I'm telling you to be happier than I am with this situation. I wasn't happy with my life before any of this happened. And guess what? I'm still not happy with it. Nothing has changed. So stop thinking it's your fault when it's my fault for wanting to be someone I'm not. I don't like putting people in danger, Jeremiah, but remember that you have no control over any of this. You think I'm the hero? If anything, I'm the villain. I'm not life, I'm death itself. If I don't do my job right, I have someone's death on my hands. This is who I was meant to be, Jeremiah. I'm meant to make mistakes. People will die because of me, even with so little time left. Katelyn almost died because of me! Nothing that is happening right now is your fault, and it will never be. You're the one who doesn't have the choice. I have a choice, and if I make the wrong one, it's my own fault. I am death itself, no matter how you look at it. I may save people, but I'm the reason they need to be saved!" I yell at him.

"And you think you're the reason? The child fell when I was near you! Katelyn got into a car accident when I was near you!" he screams.

"You weren't near me for Cornelia. That's not your fault. It's not my job to save you. It's not something I must do. It's something I want to do. So stop being a baby about it and just accept the facts. I will risk my life because you're my best friend. I will risk my life because if I don't save you, I'll die anyway. And I'd rather choose a life with my best friends, than no life at all. Got it?"

Jeremiah started crying. My heart nearly stopped beating again, and I immediately regretted how harsh I had been. Everything I said was right, but maybe I just should've calmed down a bit more.

"I'm... sorry. Was that too harsh? Should I get Mr. Switz?"

"It is fine, it's just no one should have to risk their life for me. My parents died because of me, Paula. I already did cause death. Don't you see? You're the lucky one. You don't have death on your hands," he cries, whimpering.

"Listen, Jeremiah. We could sit here arguing all day about this, or we could go inside and eat some food. Personally, I'd rather eat food while arguing, so let's go," I say, trying to drastically lighten the situation that we're in.

"Thanks Paula... for trying to cheer me up."

I look out of the window as we get inside, seeing construction men working on the part of the house that fell. Half of the house was still intact, but the roof is what caved in. Some of the windows are broken too. I sigh and turn back to the table, eating my food.

I smile at Jeremiah. A little while ago we had 3 more events. Now we have 2.

Better or Worse

I wake up on Monday, February 18th, to a chilly breeze coming in through my window. It is still winter, but it is changing into spring. Winter is a beautiful palace of ice, but only at first is it pristine. Dirt gets on it, and it loses that perfect look, yet we can't help but admire it for what it once was. Isn't it still beautiful, though? I see the children laughing, snowflakes in their hair, cheeks pink and noses red, all beautiful in their own way. A soft blanket seems to cover the land, hiding warmth under it. Of course, the warmth eventually wins the battle, but winter will come again. Right now we are in the middle of the battle between spring and winter. Though, spring must be like winter, with so many raindrops falling from the sky. Of course, raindrops are practically melted versions of the pristine snowflakes. Maybe snowflakes are frozen versions of the raindrops. It depends on how you see it. And just like the comparison between raindrops and snowflakes, I, Paula Berney am neither a raindrop nor a snowflake. I am a cloud waiting to be blown away. Forgotten by many, but remembered by those who cared to look. My problems are neither raindrop nor snowflake, and resemble the drowning grass afterwards. You might say that the raindrops provide water for the plants, or the snowflakes melt to help encourage spring, but just like any side of any story, there are different perceptions. It doesn't seem like neither Jeremiah's nor my perception is good, though. Who is right? It depends on who you ask. Jeremiah has nothing to defend himself from these events, whereas I have to learn to control my defenses. Of course I would perceive that I am right, but I must also pay attention to Jeremiah's point of view, otherwise I will never fully understand him. I make my way downstairs to sit on the porch in the front of our house.

Today we're supposed to have homeschooling, but Mr. Switz gave us a break because of what happened yesterday. Jeremiah is out somewhere, so it looks like I'm left with my mother today. Still in my nightgown, the wind blows it to the side. My hair blows on top of my face, but I don't move it. I don't want to go inside, but my face is cold, and the warmth of my house provides some shelter from the wind. I know it's a weird thought, but I prefer to be outside now. I realize I haven't sat down yet, and have instead been standing in one place for a few minutes. You lose track of time when you focus on the smallest details in life. The seat in which I am sitting is filled with feathers, and you can see a few sticking out from one of the corners. Finally pushing the hair out of my face, I look up to see the sky over Jeremiah's house. There are some clouds, but the sun is making its way out. There is no one out here, and I feel a bit lonely; however, the loneliness gives me comfort, as I can think about things clearly now. I've been spending so much time with other people that I'm not used to being alone. It rejuvenates me to think by myself. Even though I might get sick out here, I can't help but feel a longing to stay. This moment is so different from the rest of my life. My father died, my mother was always there, and I always had Katelyn. There was a time I was alone, but it wasn't the same as this. I know that if I fall, I have someone to fall back on; someone to trust.

Anyway, I can't believe I'm 14 already. Sometimes I forget that life is passing by so quickly. Will I miss these times? I mean, after all, Jeremiah will probably go to North Carolina again after all of this is over. Katelyn will be there too. Will things return to normal? Do I want things to return to normal? When I had my friend back for just a few hours, I realized how much I was missing. Then, when I made a new friend, I realized what life could be like. What could happen and what I'm missing are two completely opposite thoughts. I've never had more than one best friend before, but now I do. There are still 2 more events, but who knows when they will occur? I'm just riding along with life, waiting for something to finally stop me, or at least, halt my journey. Everything about this situation is so confusing.

The dream hasn't happened in awhile. Usually it happens before the event or right after it. Where could it have gone? What if the tree represents what I am: dark, depressed, and scary? Death *would* be a word that would suit me then. Jeremiah dying sounds like something that would automatically be my fault. What if everyone gets hurt because of me? Life and death are things not to be toyed with, yet somehow I manage to be right in the middle. What is the middle of life and death? You're either living or you're not, right? Well, what if I'm neither?

Good to Be Back

Jeremiah enters my house with a smile on his face. He just got back from the movies and seems to have enjoyed it. Though, I don't yet want to ask him how his day went because I'm still thinking about how everything works. What is happening after this? There are so many different paths. Will I be saying goodbye to my best friend again? Do I really have to go through that? I just want to go to my bedroom, curl up in my blankets, and think about life. I already thought about what's to happen, but I didn't give myself enough time to comprehend the information. Who was my father, anyway? My mother never told me. Is he possibly connected to all of this? He's obviously was not the cursed one because Mr. Switz was, but could there be more than one cursed one? Well, it does have *one* in the name, so I kind of doubt it. Like that has anything to do with it, though.

"So, how was your day without the fabulous me?" Jeremiah asked with a smirk.

"Are we reverting to the conceited Jeremiah?" I ask.

"Hey, a little self confidence doesn't hurt."

"You confuse me so much," I say with a laugh.

"Yes, one day arguing about who's the worst out of the two of us, and the next day I'm saying that I'm the best. What can I say? I'm just a weird person."

"Weird doesn't even describe you."

"Well, I'm a good-looking weirdo."

"You took that out of context."

"You didn't deny it."

"I didn't say it was true, either."

"So, looks like we're hopelessly bound together for eternity. How's our friendship treating you?" Jeremiah asks with a smirk.

"Well you're annoying, so pretty well I guess."

"I'm annoying? Well at least I'm not down all the time."

"How am I down? See, I can smile," I say while showing my teeth.

"All right, all right. You can fake a smile. Come on, let's go to the park."

"Will you stop with the park? It's like that's the place you always want to be."

"Well, my parents did die near there," he responds with a small smile.

"Jeremiah?"

"Yes?"

"How can you say that as if it's nothing? You've been without parents your whole life, and you act like it is normal."

"As sad as it is, I can't act like I know them, either. They were my biological parents, but to be honest, Mr. Switz has been more of a father to me. I don't know what I'd do without him. Paula, he's my only family, and you're a part of that now. Even if we aren't related by blood, you're like a sister to me. I think."

"So you *think* I'm like a sister to you. Why?"

"That doesn't matter. Anyway, please just ask your mom if we can go to the park," he says with a groan.

"Fine," I say with a smile.

Surprisingly enough, my mom says yes, and Jeremiah and I travel to the park, racing to see who can get to the entrance first. I win, and Jeremiah starts laughing. We walk around and he talks about his family.

"I don't have any sisters and brothers to rely on, and I don't know my aunts and uncles. It's a sad story, but I can't seem to hold onto it. Every day I wonder what life would have been like if my parents had been there to teach me things that I had to learn the hard way. I love Mr. Switz as my father, but nothing quite fills the need to really call someone 'dad'."

"I don't have a father, either, Jeremiah. My father died in a fire too," I respond warily.

"He did? Why didn't you tell me?"

"I figured it wouldn't really matter. You lost both of your parents. My case is nothing compared to that."

"Well, both of our fathers died in fires. I guess that's another way we're connected."

"Yes. I guess so," I say with a smile.

"It's starting to get dark. We should probably get back."

"Are we really that different from other kids?"

"I mean, it depends on what you mean."

"Well, because of losing our parents, we've had to mature faster, but we still make the same mistakes. You lost your childhood, but I didn't. You never got to experience what being a kid feels like."

"And?"

"Tomorrow we're going to get hula hoops, and we're going to ride bikes, and just... do whatever kids do."

"But... We have school tomorrow."

"Mr. Switz called it off again. He got sick, and not to mention they're still repairing your house."

"You would think because he's living with me I would know he's sick..."

"Just come on. You need energy for tomorrow."

"That's not good," he responds with a smirk.

"The hula hoops will be in the bushes tomorrow, or at least they should be. When I was younger I used to hide them there, this way I would never forget them at home," I inform Jeremiah.

"Alright, but how do you know that they're still there?" he questions.

"I've kept them there for years and no one has taken them. The chance that someone will just magically appear and decide to take them is probably very low."

"With me around they probably will. Anyway, let's go home. I'm starting to get tired."

We both run back home, yelling out ideas for tomorrow. Jeremiah wins the race this time, and we said goodbye on my porch. Mr. Switz and Jeremiah are still sleeping in the same house, but they have to rebuild Jeremiah's bedroom and clean up a bit. I step into the living room, and my mother immediately starts pelting me with questions.

"So how was it?" my mom asks.

"Nice, why do you ask?"

"Well, you like him right?" she whispers with a knowing smile.

I become a bit flustered, but I hope that she doesn't

notice. Personally, I don't think I like Jeremiah, as we're just good friends. Throughout my middle school life, I haven't really had any major crushes.

"No one ever said that…"

"You're blushing. Spill the beans."

"He's just a friend, I promise."

"I completely believe that," she says while rolling her eyes.

"Mom, I promise."

"Well, just so you know, I think that boy likes you."

"Well, I don't plan on dating until I'm older."

"We'll see."

My mom is totally off of it today. Jeremiah is *just* a friend. And besides, we're basically stuck together. That's it. If we weren't bound together for eternity, we probably wouldn't have met, and even if we did meet, we wouldn't be talking that much. He would still live in North Carolina, and I'd be here in Maryland going to a normal school while having normal friends. Besides, I'm not even 15 yet. Plus, I thought moms were supposed to discourage you from dating! Is it opposite day? I think I'm hyperventilating. I quickly run upstairs and begin getting ready to go to bed.

"I don't like Jeremiah, do I?"

There's no possible way that I like him. Jeremiah liking me is nearly impossible, anyway. Though, I can't help but wonder. It might be hours before I fall asleep, thinking of the possibility that he might just have a tiny crush on me, but I eventually succumb to my exhaustion.

"Yeah, there is no possible way we like each other. We're just friends, after all."

Cloudy Dreams

The same white room appears before me, along with the same dark figure. But this time… it's blurry. I try walking, but my body looks like it's spreading out in different ways. My legs and my arms are spreading out as if I was food coloring in water, and the tree seems to have clouds in front of it. I can't move at all, and although I can look around, all I see is a blur. Soon, I wake up, sweating, and I look at the time. How can it be morning already? My other dreams only took maybe 3 hours and they had more of a purpose than this dream. Why did this dream last longer? The time is 7 AM. Getting dressed very slowly, I contemplate everything that just happened, before I hear knocking on the door. My mother answers and I hear Jeremiah's name being mentioned. I quickly finish getting dressed and run down the stairs.

"Hello Jeremiah," I say with a smile.

"Hello Paula. What's first on the list?"

"Hula hooping is first. Let's go to the park."

"Now who's obsessed with the park?" Jeremiah says with a laugh.

"Santa Clause. Come on."

"Where's the reindeer?"

"They are right over there."

I point to the bikes and we run to them.

"Can I make a confession?" Jeremiah asks, "I don't know how to ride a bike."

"Guess this will be an interesting day, then," I say, giggling.

"If I fall off of the bike you won't leave me behind, right?"

"No one said I was good at riding bikes, either."

"Why don't we just run there, then?"

"Yeah, that might be a better idea," I respond, stifling a laugh.

Jeremiah beats me to the park this time, and I look in the bushes for the hula hoops that I leave here; however, when I finally find a hula hoop, the other one is missing.

"Seriously, bad stuff happens when I'm around." Jeremiah says.

"It's not your fault. Guess we'll just have to use the one. What I don't get is why someone would take one hula hoop, but not the other."

"Well, you did try to hide them in the bushes, so maybe they saw one and took it."

"Yeah… Probably not the best hiding place."

"Paula, instead of having planned all these things, why don't we just hang out? Sure, I didn't get to hula hoop or ride a bike, but the main purpose of being a kid is just hanging out with your friends, right?"

"Yeah, I guess. So what's the plan?"

"Well, we could use the sprinklers."

"It's like 50 degrees out, Jeremiah."

"Exactly," he squeals with a smirk.

When we get home, we wait until 2 PM for the sprinklers to automatically turn on. Then we run outside, and play a game where whoever gets sprinkled with the water first loses. Jeremiah loses, but I'm pretty sure he let me win. Surprisingly enough, our clothes managed to get soaked with water. After the sprinklers turn off, Jeremiah goes to his house to change his clothes, and I go watch TV.

"Paula, you should change too," my mother tells me sternly.

"But it's hot in here," I whine.

"I don't want you to get sick. Now go change."

I end up going upstairs and changing into my pajamas. Even though it's only 3 or 4 o'clock, I'm tired. We did a lot of running today because of the fact that Jeremiah didn't know how to ride a bike. Then again, if I were to try to ride one, I would probably fall over too. My balance isn't the greatest. I wonder if Jeremiah got to see what it's like to be a kid. With everything that he had to deal with, it's dismal that he had to be responsible all of his life. Sometimes you just need to have fun, and I don't think Jeremiah was able to have much fun throughout his life because he could never make any friends. He's a really nice person, but if he shied away from people, I would understand why. Yes, I became friends with Beatrice, but that's only because I thought everything was over. Apparently something bigger was just starting. Beatrice has been a good friend to me for the past year, which is why I have to stop talking to her. It's the only way to keep her safe.

"Hi Mrs. Berney. Is Paula there?" a familiar voice questions.

"Oh… She's taking a shower," my mother responds warily.

"May I wait until she's done?"

"She's really tired, Beatrice. She's had a long day. I don't think it's a good idea to-"

"Sorry Mrs. Berney!" Beatrice shouts.

I hear someone coming up the stairs and instantly think to hide, but my mom already gave away that I'm here. I quickly turn invisible just before my door opens.

"Paula, are you in here?"

I stay quiet because she may not be able to see me, but she can hear me. I don't move from my place, either, because if I step on something, I will make it move. Beatrice comes towards me, and it causes me to fall backwards. I slow down time because I need to get out of here. After falling, I walk around Beatrice and resume time while I am on the staircase. When I see her looking around my room, I run downstairs and out of the door.

"Paula, what's wrong?" Jeremiah asks.

I take his hand and lead him to the park.

"Beatrice is here. We need to hide right now," I whisper.

"Where?"

"I have invisibility, Jeremiah. The park will shield us for now. My mom saw me leaving so we don't have to worry about that. Just hold my hand and you'll become invisible too."

"You're explaining this to me later."

"There's not much to explain. I willed myself to turn

invisible, so I did. Did I know I could turn invisible? No I did not. Got it?"

He nods his head and we continue trying to hide.

Jeremiah and I sweep through the park looking for signs of another old classmate. We don't see anyone except small children and mothers, so Jeremiah and I walk back home, but are careful to stay invisible.

"So, if we're invisible, can they still hear us?"

"Yes."

"Do you have a power against that yet?"

"No."

"I wonder why you received certain powers, but not others. I mean, all of the powers you received help in saving lives. It seems like that is all they are for. Well, and possibly keeping your identity a secret Mrs. Spy."

"Please don't call me Mrs. Spy. I'm just a normal girl. There is no need to rub in the fact that I have supernatural powers," I groan.

"Yes, there is, Paula. You just hid from Beatrice with *invisibility*. Not to mention the fact that you saved a lot of people."

Shivers are sent up my back quickly, and I think about what he just said. Are my powers what make me special? A sinking feeling grows in my chest, and I start feeling depressed again.

"Just because I saved a lot of people it doesn't make me a spy. It makes me a hero, which is even worse. I want to be normal, not someone with supernatural powers that's supposed to defeat the only foe she has, which is the curse."

"What if I'm the bad guy, or the villain?"

"You're not, Jeremiah. Like I've said before, you were placed upon with a curse that you can't control."

"Well, what if I make bad things happen when I'm happy? Think about it. When we came to visit you, I was *happy* to see you, and the baby fell. Then Katelyn fell into a coma. The house collapsed after the concert, which I was *happy* to go see."

"So what if bad things happen when you're happy? I'm here. I saved Katelyn. Everything will be alright."

"You say that, but you don't know. Stop trying to make me feel better, Paula. We're in this situation because of me. There's no doubt about it."

"Let's just go home, Jeremiah."

"I put people I love in danger at home."

"So what are you planning to do, Jeremiah!" I shout while turning around and ripping my hand out of Jeremiah's.

"They'll hurt even more without you around, so stop complaining! Don't you see that they would all risk their lives for you?"

"I don't want anyone to risk their lives for me! I'm a 14 year old boy that has no idea what he's doing with his life! I only put people in danger! Please, understand this Paula," he says, tears streaming down his face.

"I won't because you don't understand the fact that everyone back there loves you, and without you, they'll be depressed for the rest of their lives. You'll affect them greatly," I quickly mutter.

"Yeah, but they'll be living."

"You know what Jeremiah, do what you want. I'm going home back to my family. You can sit here and mope for all I care. Goodbye Jeremiah."

I walk away with Jeremiah looking shocked. I will not be around someone who is always making themselves feel bad. The second I get home, though, I feel bad about what I said. Why am I always so harsh? We're both in a troublesome situation, and we need to learn to work together.

Running Off

Paula was right. I can't face anything, and I don't want to. The ache in my heart keeps growing and growing. Tears stream down my face as I run to the old house that I used to live in when I was younger. My parents, the people that loved me and relied on me, were killed by their only son. My whole life is one big mistake waiting to happen. And even though I know that Paula doesn't like the fact that she's recognized only for her powers, I keep pushing it. Why do I have to make such a big deal out of it? She cares about me, and I care about her. She's my best friend, and I don't want to see her hurt. Everyone that I care about, I push away because I'm afraid. If I stay away… she will be safe.

Paula doesn't really know much about what happened in North Carolina, and she hasn't asked me yet. I want to tell her, but is it too soon? Katelyn and I were never actually close. We started hanging out, but the only reason for that was because Mr. Switz wanted to save my life. I know that the reason I'm here is for the wrong reason. Paula doesn't need to save me, but she's trying. She doesn't need to care about me, but she does. The hardest part about this, though, is that I care about her, but I'm too afraid to really do anything to stop this. Margaret... killed herself to save Mr. Switz. Sometimes I often wonder why I can't do the same thing. To protect those I love, I can end it all, and it will be alright. Everyone will be safe. I'm a coward, and everyone can see it. My internal battle is whether fear is stronger than love. I'm scared to end everything because of everyone that I love, and Paula just keeps making it harder for me. She told me that people would risk *their* lives to save me; that by killing myself, I'd be killing other people unintentionally. Why is Paula always there to stop me from making the wrong decisions? Why does she want me to try and fight?

She hates herself because of what she is and what she has, but she has not yet given up. She hasn't given up because of me.

When you truly care about someone, what are you willing to do? I care about Paula more than anyone would know, but how do I know that it isn't just the curse? How do I know what's real and what's not real anymore?

Someone, please, just tell me. Why, out of all times, do I have to feel this way about someone now?

Come Back

Waking up, I hear someone knocking on our door. Mr. Switz is there in his pajamas. He hasn't brushed his hair yet. He is very frantic, and asks whether either of us know where Jeremiah is, but all I can say is that I don't know. We all look in the front yard of our house. He's not in any of the bushes or in a tree, and this breaks my heart. What has he done? I run to the park, immediately looking for him. The park is nearly empty, and there aren't too many trees to look through, but even so, there isn't any sign of Jeremiah. Just when I was about to run back home, I think of Jeremiah's old house. I run as fast as I can, and see Jeremiah crying near the debris. He looks like a nervous wreck, not to mention he didn't sleep last night. I could tell from the bags under his eyes.

"Jeremiah! Jeremiah, it's time to go," I say while shaking him.

He looks at me for a few seconds, and then hugs me. He doesn't let go for awhile, and I think about everything that happened yesterday.

"I don't want to," he whispers.

"Jeremiah, I'm sorry about yesterday. Everyone cares about you, but we need to go," I respond while slowly getting out of his embrace. The look on his face breaks my heart, as I can tell he feels horrible.

I grab his hand and drag him a few inches away from the building when I hear a cracking sound. I look around, but see nothing out of the ordinary. Then I look up. A piece of debris is falling straight for Jeremiah. I jump up, slow down time, and push the piece of debris away. I take Jeremiah's hand and get him far away from the house in which his parents died.

"Thanks Paula," he says while sniffling.

"Come back home. Please," I whisper while looking at him.

"Why?"

"Mr. Switz was looking for you this morning and he was really nervous because you hadn't come home."

"He was worried?"

"Yeah. I told you he would be."

"I... sorry. I didn't think anyone would actually care."

"Of course they would! You're such a dunce, you know that?" I say with a laugh, "Let's go home."

We make it home just before Mr. Switz called the police. He embraces Jeremiah and messes up his hair. I can see tears forming at the corners of his eyes as he takes Jeremiah inside and begins to put him to bed. He sleeps for a really long time after that, waking up at 9PM. I'm still on the porch by that time, thinking about everything that happened. Jeremiah begins running to my porch and shouting "Paula!"

"What's up Jeremiah?"

"Thanks for saving me today."

"No problem, I mean, it is kind of my job."

"Yeah," he says nervously, "Mr. Switz wants to know if you and your mother would like to eat dinner at our place. As a thanks."

"Sure, just let me ask my mom. When are we having it?"

"He said it'll take place tomorrow and 5PM," Jeremiah states, "What if all of the incidents that happened today… What if they happened because of the curse?"

"My mini-detective is beginning to learn. They might just be. If we don't have class, that means I can't learn how to use my powers properly."

"Paula?"

"Yes?"

"Wasn't today the 8th event?"

I stay quiet because Jeremiah's right. I saved his life. That means…

"There's only one more event before we have to fight the curse," I whisper weakly.

"Well, maybe not, Paula. What if we were wrong and we don't end up fighting the curse?"

"You could be right, but something is telling me we will have to fight. I just have this feeling. Why would anyone go through all of this to just have it end sometime in our life? It wouldn't make much sense."

"Well, whatever happens, we have to stick together."

"Right," I say with a smile.

* * *

When I wake up, I notice the wind is cold and sends shivers down my back. I must have fallen asleep while talking to Jeremiah, because I'm on the porch with a blanket around me. As I go inside, I look in the mirror. My hair is a mess. I guess falling asleep on the porch wasn't the best idea I've ever had. Brushing my teeth and getting dressed, I begin walking over to Jeremiah's house. I knock, and Jeremiah answers. I smile when I see him, and we both nod at each other.

"Hello Paula. Come in. Don't forget to ask your mom about the dinner tonight."

"Thanks, and I won't."

When we sit down in the classroom, Mr. Switz begins telling us about how we have *so* little time left. I understand that we're going to die soon and everything, but it'd be nice not being reminded of it every single day.

"There's only one more event, and we don't know what's happening after that. The 10th event could be many things. None of it is set in stone yet, so we're going to have to prepare you in many different ways. Paula, your powers are mostly under control, so we're going to do exercises to make them stronger. As for you, Jeremiah, you're going to play games that will strengthen your mind. You need to be able to think in times like these. After an hour, Paula will play the games and Jeremiah, you will be learning physical defense. We don't know what we're going up against."

I practice different areas of my powers. For invisibility, I work on spreading it out to multiple people without touching them. For slowing down time, I practice pausing and playing with time. For my strength, I don't really need to practice. I just see how much I can carry. The hour passes quickly, and I switch places with Jeremiah. I spend 15 minutes of my time on memory, 30 minutes on comprehension, and the last 15 minutes on focusing on multiple tasks. Jeremiah spent his time punching and kicking. He also practiced moving out of the way in case someone was trying to attack him. When we switched places, I practice punching for 20 minutes, kicking for 15 minutes, blocking for 15 minutes, and moving out of the way for 10 minutes. The rest of the day passes by like this until 3 o'clock, when we stop for the day. We all relax because doing physical and mental work are both very tiring to our bodies. Surprisingly enough, after I walk home, I take a one hour nap. Later on, Jeremiah knocks on my door and we play tag outside. While I'm running, though, I fall and scrape my knee. It doesn't hurt too badly at first, but when I show my mom, she says she has to clean it. She disappears from the room, and I stare at the scrape. What I notice, though, is that it seems to be healing awfully fast. When I tell Jeremiah, he looks at the scrape and agrees with me.

"Why am I healing faster now?"

"Well, usually after each event you receive some power, so I guess this is what you got."

"Mom, never mind. I think my scrape is healed."

"Nonsense." she says, but when she looks at it, she seems to agree with me.

"Alright, seems like it wasn't as bad as I thought. Go play outside. Just try not to get hurt, Paula," my mom warns me.

"I will."

We walk onto the grass and sit down.

"So, now you have healing powers. You're basically invincible."

"I'm not invincible. Anything can kill me. I may heal faster than normal, but I imagine fatal wounds would take longer to heal; far too long for my body to actually be able to live afterwards. Besides, after all of this is over, I won't have any extraordinary healing powers."

"We don't know how long this will last, Paula," Jeremiah adds, giving me a side glance.

"Why are you holding onto the thought that this might last forever until we eventually die of old age?"

"This is the first time I've had any really good friends, Paula. Why would I want to lose that?"

"Jeremiah, Katelyn and I can't mean that much to you."

"Of course you do. I don't have parents, Paula, so whenever I get the chance to grab onto friends, I can't let them go that easily. You guys are probably the only thing keeping me sane. Obviously Mr. Switz would get tired of playing 'Duck Duck Goose' sometime in his life, and then I'd be alone again. And plus, with Katelyn, she's in danger too. You're the only friend I have because you're the only one that can't get hurt."

"Any of us can get hurt Jeremiah. If I die, what's going to be left for you to hold onto then?"

"You won't die, Paula. We've come too far," he says weakly.

"Jeremiah, it has only been a little over a year. Yes, a lot has happened in that year, but truth be told, we've only been really good friends since Katelyn got into the coma."

"Are you saying our friendship is purely based on Katelyn?"

"No, it's just, none of this would've happened if I didn't have to save you. You probably would've stayed in North Carolina, and I would've stayed in Maryland."

"You don't know that, Paula. We still could've become good friends."

"Wouldn't it have been more difficult, though?"

"I'm not really sure."

"Anyway, I totally forgot to ask my mom about the dinner," I say while getting up.

"Go ask her now. I'll just be waiting here."

Dinner Party

My mother and I travel to Jeremiah's house across the street and are welcomed by Mr. Switz. We all welcome one another and talk for a bit, then heading to the kitchen for dinner. The table is made out of granite and the chair legs are a dark wood. As for the cushion, it's also brown with several designs on it. The food is delicious, but our conversations seem too formal. Almost as if we have new neighbors and we are going to welcome them. While I pay attention to what my mother and Mr. Switz are talking about, someone kicks me.

"Paula! It's kind of boring. Want to go outside?" Jeremiah whispers.

"Jeremiah, you and Mr. Switz are the ones who invited us here," I whisper back with a stern glance.

"Well, it was mostly Mr. Switz who invited you here. Honestly, I would've been fine with a barbecue in the park. It's extremely awkward."

"Not awkward, just quiet."

"Mr. Switz, can Paula and I go outside?"

"Jeremiah!" I yell.

"Sure. You two must be bored in here," Mr. Switz answers.

Jeremiah runs ahead of me and I try to catch him in a game if what I believe is tag. He isn't that fast, but it's hard to see him in the dark. Before I know it, I've lost him, and I'm stuck in the middle of the street trying to look for him.

"Boo!" he yells from behind me. I scream and tell him not to do that.

"You're going to give me a heart attack one day," I half-heartedly laugh.

"From my charm," he says with a smirk

"You wish."

"Come on, Paula. Let's go home. We just finished having dinner," my mother shouts from across the street.

"Well, it looks like I have to go. Bye Jeremiah!"

"Bye, Paula!"

As we're walking across the street, I come to notice how our house seems very lonely without people to lighten up the porch or the windows. It's almost an eerie feeling. Though, I can't imagine how you can be in the dark and not have an eerie feeling; without anyone with you, at least. As we step on the porch, I notice how tired I really am. I guess because I was having fun earlier, I didn't realize what running around was taking from my body: energy. With everything going on, I should be focusing on making myself stronger instead of having fun. It would only make sense, right? But when I think about how nice it is to be a normal kid, the common sense is thrown out of my mind. The side of me that wants to have fun is battling the side of me that has responsibilities. Though, that's just a vague idea of what is going on inside of my mind. In my mind, there are so many more thoughts and feelings that want to be unleashed. Most of which might destroy the situation that I'm in. My thoughts are about how I don't want to have to deal with any of this. Another part of me is blaming Jeremiah and is saying that this is his fault; that Jeremiah is the one to blame. I disagree with this thought, but I can't help but think it. Then again, maybe everything about this situation is a blame game, and in the end, everyone will end up hurt from it, including me. Though, I suppose the worst that can happen is… Well… That I die. But, aside from that, everything will be ok, right?

* * *

On Friday, February 22, we have half-a-day. School passes by normally with brain games, self-defense, and power practice, as well as some normal classes. Jeremiah and I both use the 3 hours extra that we have to spend the day with our parents. Jeremiah spends the day with Mr. Switz, and I spend the day with my mother. We play board games and watch TV for a long time. It's comforting to know that I can have a normal family life once in awhile even with everything that is going on. I eat potato chips and think about everything that is to come. With my mother, I feel like I can finally have peace. My mother watched me grow into who I am now. Even though we don't talk as much as we used to, just having her around me prevents me from completely going insane. I know I can count on Jeremiah and Mr. Switz, but it isn't the same. My mother will always be there for me, but as for everyone else, they might just leave out of nowhere. What if Jeremiah just wants to get this curse off of him? Then he might leave and never return. As much as it hurts to say it, the only person I can fully trust during times like these is my mother. Then again, I'm the one putting my mother in danger. She almost died because of me before. Do I really want to risk her? But I know my mother herself would have a mental breakdown if I left, which is why I can't. Jeremiah did, and Mr. Switz went berserk. He became extremely nervous and worried. If my mother had to deal with that every day, then I'd feel just as guilty, because she wouldn't be living her life to the fullest. Even when she performs the simplest tasks, there might be things that remind her of me. I don't want her to go through that, which is why I have to live. I know she's happiest when I'm right there with her, and I shouldn't be the one to take that away. Crawling onto the couch with my mother, I look at her and she kisses me on the forehead. We continue to watch TV, but I feel so much safer in her arms. Almost as if everything will be fine… almost.

When I decide to take a break from sitting on the couch all day, I walk out onto the porch and take a few breaths of fresh air. The air fills my lungs, giving me energy to continue smiling about everything that's going on. Maybe Margaret had such a hard time because she didn't confide in anyone. I don't know what her family life is like, but maybe she forgot that her own feelings count too. She forgot how Mr. Switz would feel without her. Thinking about everything that's happening makes me feel a bit depressed, though. I shouldn't have to think about any of this right now. This is the time when I finally get a break from the stress. I think about how the problems that we had when we first started seemed so frivolous to the problems we have now and begin to laugh. My mother was always there to raise me, but no one can totally take my mind off of everything that is happening. And these are the times when I can only count on myself for guidance. Where does this guidance come from? It comes from my own personal experiences and mistakes. Throughout everything that has happened so far, I have made plenty of mistakes which I carry within me and those mistakes inspire me to do more. Though, my mistakes *have* caused me pain. Was it a mistake to trust Cornelia in the first place? I mean, at first she seemed like a trustworthy person. I suppose my intuition was shocked from Katelyn leaving. Either way, being friends with Cornelia taught me that you can't trust everyone you meet, and that you have to be careful when you do put your trust in someone. I trust Jeremiah and Mr. Switz. Will that end up being a mistake too? I don't want to be thrown away and I don't want to have to feel the pain of losing someone that I truly care about again. Most of this situation may not make sense, but I don't know whether I want it to change or not. Do I want my normal life? Yes. Will my life be normal after this? No. My friends will have memories of what has happened too, and I don't want to be reminded of this every single time I am with them; how I put them in danger so many times. How can happiness survive in my world when everything I love is being taken away from me? It's not like my friends are the only reminders, either. I will have pictures and memories of everything that has occurred, and certain things will bring those memories back. Now it isn't a choice of whether or not I want to live. It's a choice of whether or not I want to remember. If I choose not to remember, I'll die. If I choose to remember, I'll live, but I won't be happy. Is life really worth living if you aren't happy? And it can't be a question of whether I'll be happy or not, either, because I have no clue as to what the future is to bring. I have no clue as to what anyone's intentions are. Why can't I know for once? Why can't I know what is to come? My choice would be so much easier then. But then maybe, just maybe, to die, I would be sacrificing someone else's life. How am I supposed to know what to do? What to be? Is my choice really that important that it could affect so many people's lives? If I live, I'll meet plenty of people, and there's no doubt I'll leave an effect on those people. But what kind of effect will I leave? I don't want to be a bad person. I want to be able to encourage people to love themselves for who they are and use their talents to the best of their abilities. But how can I help others when I can't help myself? It's true; I see nothing special in me. Well, other than the gifts, that is. I'm just a host to a disease, a viral infection that will take out everyone I love. And I don't know how to stop it.

The Weeks Are Passing, But Not Living

I don't know where I should be right now. There's no guideline as to how strong I should be. Yet, everyday in school, my strength must be stronger and the weakness abolished. There will always be weakness, but apparently to Mr. Switz, he wants me to become stronger than *humanly possible*. I am a human, maybe he is forgetting that. I'm not some mythical being that can beat up 10 humans at a time. No, I am a 14 year old girl worrying about her best friend's birthday present when his birthday is only a week away. Every day passes by in the same way; every time we come home we are exhausted from all the work we put into training. I never knew what truly working was, but now I do. It is May 25 and Jeremiah is turning 15. He was held back a year because when he was younger, the incidents put him at risk for putting others in danger. What am I supposed to get him? In my mind there's a voice saying *"You're saving his life. That's his birthday present."*, but I know that as a real friend, I need to give him a birthday present. Can't I just get him a snow globe? That would make everything so much easier. Not to mention, every time I say Jeremiah's name my mom gives me weird looks that say to me *"I know you like him."*, but of course I don't. Jeremiah is one of my best friends. I'm starting to get sick of Mr. Switz trying to make us closer. He always says, *"In order to save each other's lives you need to become better friends."* We spend *every waking moment* of school together. What more does he want from me? Not to mention the last event that leads up to the 10th event hasn't happened yet, so we shouldn't be worrying, right? I shouldn't be freaking out right now, right? Well, of course I am. What else can I do? We happen to be in a very depressing situation and I have to somehow make Jeremiah *happy* about that? We are having a party for Jeremiah's birthday, which is extremely dangerous. There will be candles with fire on them, and for some reason, fires seem to just randomly pop out of nowhere around me. I wouldn't be surprised if I burst into flames myself. Is that too gory? I think not. Any of these things could happen and everyone is just sitting down and expecting things to go well. Maybe I'm just trying to prolong the fact that I actually have to get Jeremiah a present and that I have no clue as to what he would want. We spend so much time talking about everything that is going on, that I don't know what Jeremiah likes and dislikes. I mean, come on, what else are we supposed to talk about? Plus, asking him about it now would make it obvious as to what I'm going to get him. It wouldn't be a proper birthday present if he knew what it was, right? Right now, a birthday present is the last thing I should be worrying about. Now that the pressure for getting him a birthday present is laid down upon my oh-so-fragile mind, I am becoming dizzy with thoughts. I have to worry about *breathing*, and they expect to put the pressure on *me* to get a birthday present? That's just not fair. Maybe I sound like a small child throwing a tantrum, but why do I have to figure out what Jeremiah likes and dislikes? Plus, lying isn't my best area. I only lied when I had to hide my powers, because I needed to, but even then, I was a bad liar. My mother almost saw through them. With my lying skills, you had better expect for Jeremiah to find out about the whole party. While Mr. Switz and my mother are setting up for it, I apparently have to walk him to the park and distract him. How am I supposed to do that? I mean, I could take him to the house where his parents died, but isn't that a bit *cruel?* Even Mr. Switz suggested it. Why is this party so important? Is it important because it might just be our last?

"Great job, Paula. You managed to make a birthday party sound depressing." I say to myself.

It's not my fault that we're in this situation right now, right? Now all my thoughts are getting mixed up. I really don't want to have to deal with this. I see Jeremiah outside of my bedroom window on our lawn and I run downstairs to greet him.

"Hello Jeremiah. What do you want for your birthday p- never mind? Anyway, what gift?"

See, I'm really bad at lying.

"I want nothing Paula. Hello to you too. Do I seriously have to get birthday presents?"

You have no idea.

"Jeremiah, it's a custom. Just give me an idea of what you would like."

"Fine. I want a bag of oxygen. Will you stop now?"

I pouted and Jeremiah laughed.

"You're seriously like a little sister, you know that, Paula?"

"Yes. It's my job. And no, you can't have a bag of oxygen."

"Then draw something. I don't know. My birthday isn't my favorite holiday because it reminds me of my parents."

"Think about it this way then. Your parents were really happy when they gave birth to you. My mom says that having a child is the best thing that ever happened to her. So that's how they felt."

"Maybe that's how they felt, but I don't know that, Paula."

"No more maybes ok? Not this week. Just say whether it is a yes or a no."

"Fine. Then Paula, will you go out with me?"

"What?" I stood there, shocked.

"Just kidding. Geez, you take everything so literally. No dating at 14 for me."

"It's the same for me. That's why I was a bit confused when you asked me that question…"

"Yes. You're my best friend, Paula. Nothing could change that. Plus, I wanted to see how you would react. Have you gotten asked out before?"

"Sort of? It was with my friend Bryan. I wasn't really sure whether I liked him or not during the time. I kind of did, but at the same time I didn't want to date him. Also, other people were supposed to come anyway."

"I couldn't go out with anyone even if I wanted to, so…" he cuts off.

"I get it. When I think about how I was more than

a year ago, I realize how careless I actually was. I never thought that I could affect people this much."

"A year ago I didn't talk to a lot of people. People always thought I was an introvert and left me alone, but when I did start speaking to someone, it was hard to get me to stop."

"Yeah, when I met you I could see that. You also seemed kind of conceited during that time," I sigh, remembering the past.

"Am I still conceited?"

"*Somewhat*, but your condition has improved."

"Why do you have the extra emphasis on somewhat?"

"Just like the sentence said. Your condition improved somewhat."

Jeremiah tried to pout but it ended up looking like a frown.

"You can't pout," I laughed.

"You're kind of annoying, you know that?"

"Hey!"

"I'm just saying the truth, since I'm 'somewhat' conceited. Somewhat."

Jeremiah pokes me and runs away. I chase him around. Luckily, I've managed to become stronger and faster over the past few weeks, so chasing Jeremiah was not a problem. When I catch up to him, I grab him by the collar and he begins whining.

"That hurt!"

I mumble a quick sorry and poke him back.

"There. I win. Now I'm tired, so this is where I leave you. Good night Jeremiah."

"Goodbye Paula. See you tomorrow."

Running upstairs and crawling into my bed, I think

about how Jeremiah's birthday really isn't that far away. I mean, so much time has passed. It seems as if there were months that I really don't remember at all. Looking back at all of our school days, we basically did the same thing every day, but it just kept getting harder. Waiting for everything to finally come to an end wasn't easy, either. It's been a long time since the last event. Throughout these past few months, Jeremiah and I have been getting to know each other better and better, but it's funny how I *still* don't know what to get him. I remember the time Jeremiah told me that he was in the same grade as me but grew up learning to be a counselor. Recently, he told me that he was held back, but I didn't really pay much attention to that fact until now. The fact that he was held back doesn't bother me, but it makes me upset. Not only did the curse affect our lives at home, but also how we acted in school. We couldn't really be who we wanted to be, but even I was luckier than Jeremiah. I grab a small bouncy ball and throw it up in the air as I lay in bed, slowing down time and catching it once more. What do I do?

Another Long Day in Waiting

I wake up to the sunrise down pouring light upon my face, leaving a glow which doesn't last long. Perhaps only a few seconds, for the Earth would revolve on its axis, leaving the window in a shadow that is dark and bare. The room will turn cold and water will seep through the windows because spring is fast approaching. The last downpours of winter leave us in waiting for the next season. Yesterday was a Monday, and not only did I have to go to school and work out there but I also had to come home to expend more energy running around the lawn. I don't want to get out of bed, but I know I will have to. Except, when I try to get out of bed, I feel a sharp pain going up my leg. I have healing powers, so I shouldn't be hurting. Though, I guess waiting an hour might work. If I wait an hour then I might be able to check if it has healed. But what if it is something serious? Maybe my bone is cracked. Though, I think I would feel it if it was. Mr. Switz said Margaret had been having a hard time. Well, what if this is the beginning? What if the 9th event is coming soon and the curse is hurting me so I won't be able to fight it? Though, can the curse fight Mother Nature? Sure,

I have supernatural abilities, but if other people expect me to heal, then the curse has no control over that, right? The curse has control over the events and when they happen, but it doesn't have control of the people that are present during them. Therefore, if the curse didn't want people to find out about what was happening, then the curse would make the pain stop before I go to the doctor. The pain began to subside, and I knew I had won this battle. The curse didn't want to be known, and it would do anything to make sure no one found out about it. Brains over brawn, I suppose, but just how smart is this curse? Every time I'm about to have an event, the dreams begin happening again. Though, the last time, the dream was blurry. Why is that?

My leg is partially asleep as I walk. I know this is just an effect of the pain. Looking at the time, I see it is 9 AM. I go downstairs and see my mom making breakfast. It is a Tuesday and she must go to work. I don't know why she didn't leave already, actually. I mean, I woke up an hour late for school.

"Hello Paula. Mr. Switz called school off today because of Jeremiah's birthday. He needed to go shopping. Anyway, Jeremiah is with him so you won't be able to hang out today. Guess you're staying home with me."

"Mom, you should be able to go to work."

"Look Paula. It's only a part time job. I took it up to cover some extra expenses, but I don't need it. Staying home is really not serious."

"You quit your job because of what I was going through. How are we going to support ourselves for about 4 years? Not to mention you have the rest of your life to worry about."

"Relax Paula. I made a lot of money from my job, and your dad left me some money to take care of things. I should be fine, not to mention the house is paid off. So is the car, which is only used for me to go to work."

"You didn't make that much money, mom."

"I've been saving up for awhile. I knew that when I had a child I would have a lot of expenses, so I have a lot of money left over. I was planning to use some of that money for your high school and college anyway, but I can't send you to a private high school now. You're going to have to go to a public high school or still be homeschooled; depending on how lost this lasts."

"Are you sure everything will be ok?"

"Yes, Paula. The only real expense is food and that's about $200 every month or so. I like where I live and I don't plan on moving. Trust me; I've saved up enough money to last for a long time."

Despite what my mother says, I know that she is having a hard time. Even if she has enough money, which I'm almost sure she does, she loved her old job. I know she would've stayed if none of this had happened. This is purely my fault and I hate that I took her away from what she loved. I nod my head and walk out of the room, not completely trusting that she's fine. Every day this predicament puts stress on her, and I'm afraid one day her knees might give out on her. My mother has always been there for me. Now it is my turn to be there for her. Even though I have so much that I can do, such as saving people, I feel unable to help the ones I truly care about. How can I take some of the stress off of my mother's back? She knows I'm going through a hard time, which adds even more to her stress. Before I walk onto the porch, I walk back in the kitchen and give my mother a hug. She hugs me back, and we stay there for a few minutes. It feels comforting to be in my mother's arms; it feels like home. Unlike many other moments in my life, I am calm and composed right now. Someone that I can fully trust with my life is with me. I've never had a father, but I would like to know more about him.

"Mom?"

"Yes, sweetie?"

"What was my dad like?"

Back to the Baby Times

"Your father was someone who was optimistic but caring, and he brought happiness into my life when I felt down. He was a wonderful man and you would've adored him. When the fire happened, he sacrificed his life to save you. Paula, you meant the world to him and to me. Your father was brave, but also made mistakes. And quite a lot of them, I might add. When you were born there were many arguments between us. The bills were stacking up because taking care of a baby was no easy matter. Sometimes we would have to stay up to feed you and that often tired us out. We were exhausted quickly, and that is what leads to many arguments, but we sat down and worked everything out. Trust me, it took a lot of time, but by the time you were a toddler, everything seemed right again. Unfortunately, near the time of your birthday, a fire started. When he died I was broken, but I cared for you as best as I could. I know that now he still watches over you. You were his little girl, after all. Maybe we don't know exactly what is going on right now, but everything will be explained in the time to come. Just believe in yourself and remember that you have people that support you," my mother says, cupping my face in her hands.

"I will, mom. Do you have any other photos of him?"

"The photos were burned with the fire, so unfortunately, no. Well, at least none that I could find. I'm sure that you remember him a little, even if it's the tiniest bit."

Did I remember my father? No, not really. I suppose if I thought about it, I would remember something, but what if what I remembered was too difficult to handle? Though, after everything I've been through, nothing should be too difficult to handle. I've been through rough times before, and I understand what it's like to make mistakes that will affect you forever. I could've ended everything awhile ago, but I didn't. I still don't want to, but in the future, who knows what will happen? Life takes many turns, but you are the one that chooses which direction it may turn to, and eventually, you come to your destination. What is my destination, though? How do I plan on letting this experience affect me? Every word I say will affect my future. What have my words done so far? They've led me to Jeremiah, I suppose. They also led me to Katelyn. Can words really be that powerful? You can choose to hurt someone with just one word. Is that really the path you would want to take? People have died because of it. I wish words didn't matter as much, but if they didn't, then a lot of relationships may not be as strong as they are now. Though, along with words, comes actions. You can say something, but without the action to properly commit to your word, your word is a lie. Do I like to lie? No. Do I have to sometimes? Yes. Then again, I never really have to lie; I choose to do that too. I could choose to say the complete truth, but someone might get hurt. If you don't say the complete truth, though, someone might get hurt even more. I don't know which is better, but excessively lying isn't right. I want to scream to the world all of the problems I have on the inside, but I can't. I suppose screaming into my pillow will have to do for now. Writing down each moment into a diary so I will eventually have to live through it again isn't my style, so what if I write down only the good parts? Let's say my future self were to read about how good life was. Then, my future self might just lose the lessons learned from the mistakes I made. Diaries can be good to let out your emotions, but would I read my diary again? No, I wouldn't. I've already learned what I need to learn. For me, there's no need to go through it again. But if I did have a diary, I would ask my future self questions instead of telling her about my present life right now. My future self already knows what has happened in her life. I want to see if she achieved what she wanted in life. Most likely, not everything will be accomplished, but I hope she shoots for the stars anyway. What choices will I make? Is the future really set out for us already, or can we change it? Am I meant to think these thoughts? Will everything I think about teach me a lesson? If I were to gather a diary from my 7 year old self, what would I say? As for my 4 year old self, I'd write down every single moment. Most of the memories I had when I was 4 years old are gone, and I won't remember them when I get older, but if I was able to write at that age, I could remember the happy times I had, and maybe have a description of how I felt when my dad died. He must've meant a lot to me. I can imagine myself with a big smile on my face and red cheeks, getting ready to run outside and play. How carefree was I when I was younger?

Was my personality changed because of what happened to him? How can his death have affected my personality if I don't remember it?

Knowing my father was a kindhearted man does give me courage, though. Even though genes don't completely describe a person, it's nice to know I may have a bit of bravery and kindness in my blood, even if that amount is not great. I hug my mother once more before I leave and go out to sit on the porch. It seems like lately I've been going out to the porch a lot. Thinking about everything that is happening clearly and carefully may be another one of the few reasons why my sanity is being kept during times like these. Connections make us closer, but also give way to more conflicts. Though, if you are able to handle the conflicts that come your way, then having connections to many people may not be a problem. But if the conflicts overwhelm your life, stress will enter too, and times will become rough. Sometimes, instead of fuming out all of the anger and stress you have, you just need to think about everything calmly alone. Everything has changed so drastically in a matter of months. Now, however, things are beginning to slow down. I am anticipating my death. I suppose I shouldn't be so sure that I am ready to die. After all, I won't know until I'm really in the situation. Do I want to be in the situation? No, of course I don't. But will I have to be? Yes. Problems of different difficulties will arise, and there will be ways to deal with them, but my life isn't a video game. I don't get multiple lives to do something, I only get one. And if I mess that up, it's all over. Everything will be *all over*. No home to go to, no mother to see. No friends to meet, and no future to greet. For sure, I will be all alone. Is taking a risk really worth it? The thoughts in my life seem to be piling on my back, creating a burden that can never be lifted. Soon, I will be crushed by the thoughts, and I won't be able to take it anymore. I keep asking the same questions over and over, until those questions turn into something else and I'm left on a completely different thought. Why do my thoughts always cascade into more depressing, saddening thoughts that leave me breathless with each word; each syllable; each letter of each word? Why does every moment of my life make me more and more separated from the outside world? Why am I lost in this whirlwind of feeling and unknown? Why am I not human anymore? Why did I lose people that could've meant so much to me? Why didn't any of this go away? Do I deserve this?

"WHO PUT THIS ON ME? WHAT DID I DO TO DESERVE ANY OF THIS?" I scream out loud.

The hot tears cascade down my face. Each one feels like fire, and my face is left burning afterwards. My eyes turn into waterfalls, but instead they are made of fire, and connected through streams of oceans straight into the center of my heart, where I feel a great pain. I don't feel backstabbed; I don't feel jealous; I feel lost. What am I supposed to do from here? I'm only a child! Why can't anyone think about how I feel for once? Why don't they understand? I fall to the ground and hurl my fists at everything. I sob and sob again, waiting for all my anger and sadness to be released. My mother runs outside, but I don't hear her. All I feel is a gentle rub on my back as I wash my existence away.

Drained and Dehydrated

When I wake up, my eyes are sticky and sore. It hurts to open them and my vision is blurry. My hands and arms feel sore, and my knees feel like they have a bit of a burn. I don't remember what happened yesterday. I receive a flashback, and my heart begins hurting again. I lose my breath and another sharp pain runs through my heart.

"I'll be fine," I whisper to myself, even though I know that is not the truth.

I don't try to get out of bed. I don't want to see myself right now. Everything that has happened to me is leaving scars on me; maybe not physically, but emotionally. I'm being bullied by my own conscience, and fighting it just adds more stress to the wound. If things will never be the same, why do I try? I don't try for myself. I know that's not the answer now. I know that if I didn't have anyone I loved supporting me, I would fall victim to death the same way as Margaret. It makes sense, doesn't it? I'm working to save other people, not myself. The depression would've taken over a long time ago if it wasn't for them. Yesterday was just the beginning of what is going to happen to me. The next few days will be a difficult journey, not to mention the time before I actually reach the 10th event. How can I see Jeremiah like this? My eyes are probably red and puffy, and my hands might be bleeding. When I look closer at my hands, I see nothing is wrong with them, however. They must still be hurting because I have the thoughts of yesterday taking over my mind. It is like walking a mile just to open my eyes now. Why did I assume I wouldn't feel as bad as Margaret did? I had so much trust that I would be fine... But I suppose that I was wrong. When the tenth event does happen, will I be emotionally ready? It is a lot to go through, and I don't know if I can do it alone. But I do have Jeremiah with me, urging me to try my best no matter what. The same thought is replayed in my mind: What if he'll leave right afterwards? It kills me to know that no matter what I do, this thought will never leave my brain. Whether it is buried in the back of my mind or not, it is still there, lurking, waiting to jump at the chance to tear me down from the inside; waiting for me to crack; waiting for me to break. My confidence disappeared as of yesterday. But what if it was never really there? What if I was just pretending all along, when I knew that trusting myself was a mistake? I can't trust my own thoughts anymore. I can't trust myself. How do you build up your confidence? Do you build up a wall? Do you seclude people from your life? Well I can't do that right now. I will be forced to become lost in my own thoughts even more. I don't know who I am anymore. I always said I was Paula Berney, your average teenage girl, but now I'm not. Am I even Paula anymore? Because as far as I knew, Paula never gave up on those she loved, but most of all, she never gave up on herself. I'm a lost cause, aren't I? I still don't love who

I am. In fact, ever since this started, I think I hate myself even more. I don't like my old self, either. I admire her for a few things she had, but she was never anything special. It's the same way right now. These supernatural powers don't make me different because they aren't mine. After this is over, I'll go back to the boring Paula. How can I want to go back, but become disgusted at the very idea at the same time? How can I want to stay, but be disgusted at who I am right now? Depression is taking over. I hear a voice inside of my head; my voice.

"No, Paula. The curse is tricking you. You need to be strong, believe in yourself, and have confidence."

Confidence is something I never had, don't you get it? With these thoughts, I lay my head down on my pillow, waiting for sleep to come. Who knows when I'll wake up?

Back to my Normal Self! I Think...

Waking up, I try to clear all thoughts from the previous two days which were full of sleeping and crying. They are just another two days I don't want to remember. Even though I know those two days will affect me for a long time, it doesn't hurt trying to forget. I need to be happy for Jeremiah. His birthday is in 4 days, and I need to get him a present. What should I get him, though? I mean, he still doesn't know how to ride a bike, so I guess that would be the obvious present, but he's already seen it. It wouldn't make much sense to give him something that he already knows about, would it? Would a hula hoop be too cheap to give him? I really don't know what his gift should be, and I've had a mental breakdown for the past 2 days. Looking at the clock, it is 10 AM. I really am late today. For the past few days I was supposed to have school, but I haven't been in good enough shape to go. Now it is time for me to get up, so I take a shower. When I feel the hot water on my face, the muscles in my face tend to relax. It feels good to wash the tears off of my face, but it also hurts because my eyes are still swollen. The rest of my face is pink, and you can tell that either

I've been crying for a long time or I'm blushing. I come downstairs and my mom looks at my face. Nevertheless, she seems truly happy. I'm assuming it's because I finally got out of bed. It feels good to stretch out my legs and walk around again. My mother begins making breakfast and I walk into the living room where I sit down and yawn.

After that much sleep, I feel well rested, but my emotional side isn't getting too much better. I don't want to have another breakdown, but I think I might be able to keep control of my feelings for a little while at the very least until this is over. I'm not exactly sure. I don't want to walk outside yet, in case Jeremiah is there. I don't know if he knows that I've been crying, or whether he thinks I'm sick, but I want to postpone this meeting until I'm totally sure I won't break down, but I doubt that will happen. My mom puts oatmeal on the table and calls my name. I sit down at the table and begin to eat slowly. Wait, if it is 10 AM, then shouldn't Jeremiah be in school himself? The thought hits me like a truck. I don't have to worry about him for a few hours! No questions will be asked. I can let the cool breeze hit my face and feel my sore eyes return to normal. When I walk outside, the street is lonesome but perfect at a time like this. When a strong breeze hits my face, it hurts the soreness under my eyes. Though somehow, it feels nice. Like something I needed. I spin around as I walk onto the sidewalk, letting the air cool me down. It is like ice being put on a bruise. My eyes feel better and they may not look as bad later on. Taking in a long breath, I let the cold air fill my lungs and engulf my body. The shirt I am wearing waves in the wind, and the pants keep me from having goose bumps. In a few seconds, however, the air becomes too cold for me, and I decide to go back inside.

The temperature change feels good once again, as I become warmer. When I go to look in the mirror, I can already see that my face is returning to normal. I splash cold water on my face, hoping to bring down the soreness again. Careful not to touch it, I dab my eyes with a small towel with warm water on it to clean off any excess dirt. I then go back to putting cold water on my eyes. It is funny how even though hot water and cold water help you, using water that is too hot or too cold is not safe. You can hurt your skin by only using hot water, and using cold water might not clean everything off your face right. You need a mixture of both in order to get the job done right. I suppose that's how it is with the curse. I need both my happiness and sadness to inspire me to work my hardest so that I may protect the ones that I love, just like to defeat it, Jeremiah and I are both necessary. Even though both feelings hold opposite meanings, each means so much in your life. I don't like feeling sad, but we can't have too much happiness in our lives either. If you're happy all the time, then the best moments in your life won't shine as bright. It isn't that I don't love saving people; it's that I miss my old life. There's so much to worry about now, and controlling it all will not be easy. They say I need to master physical and mental skills, but they forgot about one important part: Emotional Skills. I don't know what environment I'll be put in during this last battle, but it could cause me emotional pain. If I lose my focus, I won't be able to fight as well as normal. Even if the curse is making me depressed, it's actually doing me a favor. I learned that even if you're sad, you can't stay in bed all day because that won't make things better. You'll be losing time in which you could be happy. If you get up out of that bed, you can find things that could make you happy. Maybe your friends will be there or you can go shopping or do something you like, but if you stay in bed, you're missing out on all of those things. Staying in bed may be a way to get away, but it's also a way to lose things you love. Maybe things aren't great right now, but you need to show the world that you are a fighter; that you are worth it, and I know that everyone is. Even though I may not like who I am, I have to believe I am worth something. Every person I meet I leave an effect on, so I am a cause to fight for. I am a person who needs to live to protect others. I will do what I can to help everyone, even if my own happiness is tainted. I know loving other people is hard when you don't love yourself. I've heard it before. But I also know caring for someone doesn't have to be done in grand gestures. It can be giving them a hug or comforting times in need. Did I make a mistake by staying in bed all day? Yes. Do I regret it? No. I have the aspiration to keep people safe, so that's just what I'll do. I can't promise everything will work out, but I can try. Trying is better than nothing, and at this point, the only thing I have to lose is myself.

The time passes quickly, and before I know it, Jeremiah is getting out of homeschooling in 5 minutes. I have nowhere to hide, and if I try to go to sleep I know I can't because I've been sleeping for nearly two days straight. Plus, Jeremiah's birthday will approach soon, and I will have to see him then. Facing him today will lift a burden off of me, which is why I must see him. I am emotionally unstable, and I have to regain my strength. Perhaps the only way to regain my strength is by having a few laughs or at least an ounce of happiness in my life. It'll make me forget about what's going on. It'll make me feel normal. Instead of walking back to my room, I walk onto the lawn and patiently wait for Jeremiah to come out of school. My anxiety level rises until I finally see him walking out of the house. It takes a few seconds, but when he sees me, he runs to greet me.

"Hello Paula! How are you feeling? Your mom said you got sick."

So that's all she said? Or maybe he just doesn't want to bring it up… It would be generous of him to do that. It's hard not knowing what's going on, because then you are unsure of what's fine to say.

"I'm doing fine. Anyway, how was school?"

"I guess it was fine, but without anyone to make fun of Mr. Switz with me, it's kind of boring," he says with a laugh.

I begin laughing too, and immediately feel better. Jeremiah and I keep talking until about 7 o'clock, and then we both return to our own homes. I find myself missing the time I had with Jeremiah because now I must return to my own depressing thoughts. Is Jeremiah just an escape from the pain? Is that a good, or a bad thing? Should I be afraid? There have been so many questions as to whether I can trust Jeremiah or not, but no matter what I think, we're stuck in this together. He doesn't have a choice but to stick by me until this is all over. Whatever happens afterwards… it'll come. But for now, I need to think about the present. There are so many conflicting emotions and my thoughts keep going back and forth, but I'll make it through this. All that's left is the 9th and 10th event. But now that I have to get Jeremiah off my mind, new thoughts will surface: thoughts about how I'm going to defeat the curse without actually knowing whether it is something that can be defeated. What's going to happen if I do defeat it? Will everyone else's lives change too, and if they do change… How drastically?

Back to School, Welcome the Dream?

My mindset is stronger now that I have the emotions temporarily out of my system. I can focus more in class, and the day goes by without a single hitch. I don't notice how quickly the time is passing, and before I know it, school is over. Mr. Switz invites us to have iced tea and loaf cake, which Jeremiah and I both agree to. Everything is quite pleasant until Mr. Switz begins speaking of Jeremiah's birthday again.

"Jeremiah, April 1ˢᵗ is your birthday, which means it is an especially dangerous day for you. There's no guarantee that something will happen, but just in case, Paula will be your guard for the whole day."

I put my food down and look at Mr. Switz.

"Mr. Switz! I cannot guard Jeremiah for hours upon hours on end. That'll be boring," I elbow Jeremiah, "Plus, no one ever told me it would be dangerous for him. You could've told me this earlier or gave me some warning that something is to happen."

"Please Paula. You were absent for 3 days. I could've told you in those three days if you were willing to come out of your house, but you stayed trapped inside, like a little bird in its cage. You closed the cage on yourself. You caused this to happen."

I felt a strong pulse go through me.

"I caused this to happen? Fine, blame me. I guess everything is my fault! Everyone here has been worrying about Jeremiah, but you don't understand the amount of trauma I'm going through either! Yes, I understand that Jeremiah could die, but so can I! Doesn't anyone understand that? You all are treating me as if I'll always be there, but my days are numbered and nobody seems to care! I feel bad enough having Jeremiah's life in my hands! I'm just a kid! I'm trying to be strong right now, and I'm being stronger than most kids could be, so don't you dare put this on me! I already know it's my fault! There's no need to add insult to injury!"

I storm out of the house, fuming. I know that what I did was disrespectful, but nonetheless, it feels good to finally get my emotions out. I'm angry, and I want to scream. I'm depressed, and I want to fall. But most of all, I'm stressed, and I want to run. So I do. I run as far as I can. Is this part of the curse? Am I meant to become this angry? Of course I am. But that doesn't stop me from pausing. Not even for one second. I breeze past the park; past Jeremiah's parents' house. I don't know where I'm going. And it feels good.

* * *

I end up in a neighborhood that is hard to recognize in the dark, but it still has an air of familiarity to it. Where am I, and why do I feel as if I've been here before? It isn't too far from my school; there's only so far a person can run. There are trees everywhere, and the houses here are similar to mine. When I try to look for details, though, it's too dark to see. I obviously wasn't running that long, but somehow it became dark. Is it possible that I... sped up time? That's not good then. I can slow down time, which helps a lot, but speeding up time? That is really bad. I can lose my life is a second. I hear a female person's voice. Who does that remind me of?

"Paula, is that you?"

"Um... who?"

"It's Beatrice. What are you doing out here?"

Oops.

"Playing hide and seek with my friend... you know... the normal."

"I came over to your house awhile ago to look for you. Paula, you never texted us, and I felt at a loss for that. Why? Why did you leave us alone?"

I sigh and look straight at her.

"Listen, Beatrice, there's a lot going on. I can't explain it right now, but I promise I'll explain it sometime in the future. It's too dangerous right now."

Beatrice must hear my tone of voice. I personally don't know how I said it. I was tired and lost. Perhaps that's why she didn't pry. However, she does hesitate to answer.

"A-Alright. Do you want my mom to drive you home?"

I weighed my options. I could either stay here; not knowing how to get home, wandering off into the cold darkness alone, or I could go with Beatrice's mom and make it home safely. I think I'll choose the latter. The drive was quiet, with Beatrice's mom asking questions every so often. When we arrived at my house, Beatrice sternly said to me,

"I'll let you off the hook this time, but you will explain everything to me. Bryan and Michelle are hurt too, you know."

Beatrice hugs me and lets me out of the car. As soon as my mother sees me, she takes me in her arms. She grabs a blanket from Mr. Switz and puts it on me. Immediately warmth is sent through my body. Though, I don't feel it right then and there. Jeremiah sees me, but he just stands there. He looks really worried. As for Mr. Switz, he looks… apologetic? Tears start forming in my eyes, but I quickly wipe them away before anyone has a chance to see them. Now I should be happy. So why do I feel as if I have a weight in my stomach? Mr. Switz looks at me in the eye, and asks if I'm ok. I answer honestly and he hugs me, but briefer than my mom. He walks away, and begins talking to my mom. Now Jeremiah comes over and grabs my shoulders.

"Never do that again," he says with tears in his eyes.

He also pulls me into a hug, and I hug him back. I don't think I have to worry about Jeremiah leaving me anymore. That action alone was enough to convince me he really does truly care about me. He looks at me once more, and tears begin forming in my eyes again. I follow Mr. Switz and my mom into our house, with Jeremiah nudging me lightly. I do have someone to help me get back up if I fall down. I do have someone to tell me what needs to be told in order for me to be ok. I do have someone who won't leave me. And that person is Jeremiah.

* * *

After awhile of talking, Mr. Switz and Jeremiah leave, and I'm left to go to bed. My room has been my safe haven for the past few days, hasn't it? My ceiling is the same purple color, but has a darker shade to it with the moon out. I can see it; the ceiling, and the emotions that are webbed within it. The ceiling is not bare here, it has life. It has life because I cried in here; because I've shared feelings like anger and anguish in here; because I've felt happiness. I've made mistakes that I recognize. I've been scared before. If you want to live, you need to have all of these feelings. There is no such thing as only bad or good feelings, because any of them can be felt. If you have mostly bad feelings, that's ok. If you have mostly good feelings, that's ok also. No feelings are better than another. All feelings are something you need. These feelings help you grow. Sometimes the saddest people are the wisest because they've gone through the most. And sometimes the happiest are actually the saddest because they're hiding everything to make others smile. No matter what you do, you'll be reminded of the sad times in your life, but that just makes the good times shine brighter. You need to learn to get through heartbreak, depression, sadness, or anger, just as you need to feel happiness and love. Without the bad times, you can't have the good times, and without the good times, you can't have the bad. The way I see myself is that I am changing for the better, even though I am hurt; even though I am broken. Whatever is broken can be repaired. Even if you can still see the cracks, those cracks are just reminders of how strong you have become. Sometimes they are reminders of how weak one has become. Your future is changed by the past decisions you have made, but your future can still take a different course. Each second, you have a chance to change the course of your life. So take that chance, and hold onto it. That chance is your energy which inspires you to go on. That chance is your motivation. I will keep fighting and I will stand tall. My chances have been renewed, and I'm not losing them that quickly. Maybe life isn't perfect right now, but doesn't that make it all the more beautiful?

Dreaming Once Again

A white veil has engulfed me, opaque and pure. When I look around, I see something masked in figure, rooted into the deepest parts of my mind; a living, yet non-living organism that has come to haunt me within these past few months. I face the same feelings of fear and mistrust as I see the world I was poured into, all at once, but for this one time, this one event… I feel a feeling of happiness deep within me. It leads to small giggles erupting from my throat. Why? It is almost over. Everything is almost over. As I walk towards the tree, my feelings of happiness take over. The tree begins to cower. Is this tree the root of all evil, or is it just scared of something new and unsought of? For me to feel happy in a time like this! What a curious thought. I remember how Jeremiah will have a horrible, terrible road ahead of him. My feelings of happiness vanish, and I am left with a depression that takes over. The tree returns to its normal state, but does not lean towards me. It is not attracted to my depression. This tree is not the root of all evil… it just found something it wasn't used to. As I come closer, I touch the bark of the tree. It feels so fragile, as if after one push, it might fall over.

But it doesn't. The tree is strong. When I remove my hand from the bark, dark residue is left on my hand. What is this residue? This tree lives in a place where nothing bad could seem to reach it. So why does it seem so sad? When I saved people, the tree flashes before me in an instant, though not every time do I think of it. I can sense the tree in the back of my mind, and I can sense myself finally being able to reach it, but I do not see it anymore. Is the tree becoming farther away, or is it just getting ready to become closer than ever? I let my mind wander, and soon become curious of the surroundings. I remember when I first saw the tree; it looked as if it were just placed there. Now, when I look down at the roots, it looks as if it is truly connecting to something. The roots have become larger, and the floor around it has grown to a sort of ground. The tree has sustenance, and it just doesn't seem as bare. It seems like it has a life. Hidden, possibly, but it does have a life. Only when you choose to truly look, can you see that. Only when you choose to truly look, can you see the truth. The tree has always had life; it was just my fault for never noticing it. When I sense that my eyes are awakening, and the dream soon vanishes, however, I am left with the thought: What does this all mean?

May 30, Saturday Has Arrived

Waking up at 6:30 AM isn't the most pleasant experience ever, especially when you don't have anyone to talk to. Though, Mr. Switz might be awake. I get dressed and walk over to their house, first checking the windows... just as I thought. He's drinking coffee while watching TV. I knock on the door and Mr. Switz answers.

"Hello Paula. Isn't it a bit early?"

"Yes, sorry about that. Is Jeremiah awake?"

"No, but you can go wake him up. I always try to get him up early but he always ignores me. Even though I know he can hear me," He says with a grumble.

"Thanks Mr. Switz."

He lets me in and I walk to Jeremiah's door. I knock on the door loudly and hear a grumble.

"Who is it?"

"Paula. Now get up."

"Why are you near my door? This is a no girl zone."

"Don't act like a 5 year old and get up."

"Why should I?"

"You should get up because I have powers. It seems

you're forgetting about my super strength and floating abilities. Not to mention I can stop and move time forward as I like."

"And I'm up. Wait. Did you say moving time *forward?*"

Well. Oops.

"Um… I'll explain later? Just meet me outside in 5 minutes; otherwise I will break your door down."

"Don't break my door down please. It took me forever to decorate."

"You have 5 minutes; I'll be waiting on my lawn."

I begin counting and quickly sit down. The time passes slowly when you count. It's a bit annoying. Though, I see Jeremiah running out at 4 minutes and 30 seconds. He looks a bit worn out, but I did force him to come out here at 6:30 AM.

"It took you 5 minutes and 10 seconds. Guess I'll have to break your door down," I say with a smile.

"You're kidding, right?" He says with a nervous laugh.

"Yes. It took you 30 seconds less than what I said."

"Ok, good. Now explain."

"When I ran away," I see Jeremiah cringing, "I noticed that it became dark fast. I realized that time couldn't have passed that fast with me going such a short distance, not to mention that we are approaching summer."

"You don't know for sure, though, right?"

"No."

"Then let's test it out!"

"No."

"Why can't we test it out?"

"We can't because I had the dream last night," I say with

a sigh, "The next event is coming soon, and I don't want to rush it."

"But then it'll be over sooner," He whines.

"Jeremiah, what if we end up not being prepared for the tenth event? That's why I've been hesitating to rush it so far. What if I rush time, and I accidentally make it go too far, and we are both dead? I can't go back, Jeremiah. It doesn't work that way. My best bet is to just leave time as it is, and if I accidentally rush it, then I'll have to deal with the consequences."

"Mr. Switz noticed the time was passing quickly. He was curious about it, but didn't ask any further questions. I doubt anyone else noticed it though. If someone did, they would've made a big deal about it."

"What if this means that everyone that I don't know goes about their daily lives, but everyone I do know will notice something is different?"

"You might be right. According to the clocks, you would've been gone a few hours, but according to us, we only thought you were gone an hour. If we had thought it was longer, we probably would've called the police. Though, we're going to have to tell Mr. Switz and your mother about this. It would make everything easier and probably make some of the suspicions disappear."

"But with each suspicion that disappears, a new one will take form. The questions will never disappear. Maybe we have to stop wondering, and just act."

"But if we just act, then there won't be much thought behind it," Jeremiah sighs, "Sometimes you need to correctly think things out."

"But sometimes too many thoughts can confuse you and just leave you more boggled."

After a moment of silence, I speak again.

"Jeremiah, this won't end, will it? We'll still have the memories."

"No, it won't, but we need to remember that those memories made us closer. That's the bright side, right? There's always one."

I sigh.

"Not always, Jeremiah."

We both sit in silence, knowing that danger lurks near. It may be hiding in the corners, but it is more dangerous than we ever could've imagined. Things that hide within the depths of the darkness have secrets that should not be found out. But of course, the darkness crawls up my back as if it was a tiny spider and sends me into a never-ending wasteland of discomfort and puts me at a loss of recognition. I can't seem to remember who I am anymore. Perhaps maybe it isn't that I don't remember it, but that I cannot recognize it. The image in the mirror hasn't changed, but the image of me in my mind lays an abstract thought waiting for someone to uncover its meaning. The cool morning air brushes my arms, sending goose bumps throughout my body. I hold my body away from the ground with the force of my arms; my arms touching the ground, yet somehow defying gravity. The very fact that I can stand somehow remains a mystery to me, so imagine the mystery of what this curse is! How I, out of all people, have supernatural abilities. How I manage to stay somewhat calm and composed throughout all of this, with only 2 breakdowns. Margaret committed suicide, so I must be handling this pretty well, right? Thinking of Margaret sends another wave of shivers up my spine, rubbing me the wrong way. I hesitate on moving, however, because I know that in the future I will miss these moments that I have with some of the people that I hold dear to me. When the fight begins, I may have to sacrifice myself for their sake. Is it good that I'm willing to do that, or does it show how ungrateful I am? It's funny how I can think these thoughts so nonchalantly now. How would I have treated these thoughts so, so long ago, when I was a normal girl waiting for life to take its course; to have a normal life with a normal family and just be happy? I didn't expect everything to be fantastic, but I expected to at least have a long-lasting, fulfilling life. Is my life fulfilling, or am I holding back based on my cowardice? Am I holding back based on my feelings or my thoughts? I act like I'm not afraid to lose anything at anytime, but I am. I am afraid to lose my life because that means I lose the ones I love. I know what it feels like to lose someone you care about, and I don't want anyone else to feel that. Just because I don't think my life is of importance, it doesn't mean other people don't. I mean the world to my mom, and she tells me that. Why do my emotions have to be so conflicting? With each choice, emotions are attached, and it makes everything so much more complicated. How does that make anything easier? How does that give me a chance to choose? I've been trying, but I can't seem to find more pros than cons in either decision. It seems like the choice is either 50/50, but I know that isn't possible. There will always be something to tip the balance off; something that will make a difference. There has to be, right? What if I'm undecided? What if I'm unsure? Do I not get a choice then? Will I be condemned to live a life of waiting for someone to finally see what I feel inside? For someone to answer the questions I've been asking for so long? I keep asking the same questions, but I never get an answer. What's the point? If no one will answer my questions, then I'll never feel fulfilled. My life will always feel meaningless. Everything will be in black and white. Everything will be Colorless.

24 Hours and at a Loss for Words

Sunday, May 31, is a morning that I wake up extremely tired for no apparent reason. It seems as if my energy has been taken, never to return. I can't shake off the feeling that I'm losing my strength as time goes on, and this later becomes even more apparent to me. I eat my breakfast and feel refreshed, but feel emptiness inside of me. Something is missing. Did I lose my motivation to fight? I don't understand how I couldn't have motivation considering that Jeremiah's life is on the line. If that isn't it, then what is? I feel hollow, and it seems as if my emotions have vanished. Shaking off the feeling becomes extremely hard to do, especially when reality starts to kick in. This is what is meant to happen. The curse will keep on draining me until I have nothing left. The curse may not kill me physically, it seems, but may drink every ounce of energy that I have. It feels as if I am a zombie living in a moving world. Well, everything is moving, except for me. I'm slowing down time, bringing it to my own pace, until time completely stops. And when that happens, I will be too frozen and too clueless to see the truth; the truth of what I brought about. A life without living is no life at all, but what about a life that moves slower than others? What if that life has more anxiety than the others? And the slowing of time is just so that person may be tortured and tortured until her last breath? So she remembers the feeling of terror that rests in her heart? So she can feel the pain of losing someone? So she can live out the rest of her life saddened and at a loss for words? The pain will be so great that, even she will not be able to speak. The woman or man, the thing that was able to speak so freely and flowingly will lose all inspiration to help others, and so others will end up losing their way, just as the ones before them. And before you know it, one woman not doing her job wrecks havoc on many other people. The world will be lost in a lazy turnout of events, creating a whirlwind of what seems to be doom. Why doesn't anyone see? Why doesn't anyone see what needs to be done to save our cursed souls? What happened to the kindness and prosperity we all shared once? Is it devoured by selfishness and cowardice? Going back to the way we were, a united country in all of its truth is not an option. But we can learn to rebuild. Fights have taken place that we all regret, hurt has been placed in the hearts of many, but we can instead fill these hearts with kindness and joy and remove hateful vengeance and thoughtless words. Hate will never be destroyed, no. We will always fight amongst one another. But is forgiveness so far away? Sometimes I become at a loss for words about what we have turned into. We turned, from something loving, into something that should be hated. Yet we still have people that stand by us. Let me tell you, these people are the only ones to be trusted. These people are the ones that you can count on. And these people are the ones that you should have around you during your worst, so that they may become closer to you; so that they may help you through this trial and error relationship that we are going through. These people will reconcile when you are at your best, and share the glory you proclaim from your successions. However, remember to keep a close eye on these people, so that they too, don't become one just like the others, so that they, in all beauty and mercy, remain someone who can be trusted. We must work together. For the sake of humanity becoming a one, united nation. We are the people of this generation, and we need to save the rest.

* * *

After eating breakfast, I go upstairs to take a shower. When I look in the mirror on the wall in my bathroom, I see that there are dark lines under my eyes. However, when I look at them from far away, you can't see them too much. I find relief that no one can tell how tired I am because that would put more stress on everyone else, and right now, the last thing we need is stress. We all need to work together, and we can't have biased thoughts clogging that. I want to close my eyes and sleep right here, but I know that even if I try, I won't be able to fall asleep. I groan at the thought and get into the shower, thinking that the warm water would wash my exhaustion away, but it doesn't. Normally I would feel awake by now. My desire to get back in bed is strong, but I know I will have to go about my day normally. Luckily, I don't have school today, so everything will be a bit calmer. Not to mention I won't have to partake in fighting classes today. What date is it again? May 31. That means... Jeremiah's birthday is tomorrow! Why do such important things have to bother me at a time like this? Maybe the idea of getting Jeremiah a birthday present seems frivolous, but to me it is important, even if he doesn't want one himself. Jeremiah may have proved to me that he's a real friend, but how have I proved it to him? I mean, I did save his life, but what if he thinks that's the only reason I'm sticking by him? So I won't have to have his life on my hands? I always thought that he might leave me, but I didn't worry about what he was thinking. To prove to him that I will stick around after this is all over, I have to get him a present. It is the only way. Unfortunately, I still do not know what Jeremiah would like as a present. I mean, as far as I know, he doesn't have that many interests. What if I get him a book? Walking downstairs, I see Jeremiah at our doorstep.

"Hello Paula," he says with a smile.

"Hey Jeremiah. Want to talk?"

"Sure."

We walk outside onto the grass covered with dew and I take a deep breath. Everything stays quiet before Jeremiah begins speaking.

"So… tomorrow I'm turning 15."

"Yes. That's cool. I'm still 14."

"Don't worry, you'll catch up to me soon enough. Hey Paula…"

"Yes?"

"Are you worried about the dream you had? That means something is going to happen, right? Do you think it will happen on my birthday?"

"I don't know Jeremiah. I just hope it doesn't ruin the day for you. There's going to be a lot of joy when… when we all… when we all eat dinner together," I laugh nervously,

"You know… today I was reading a book. It was a nonfiction one. I really liked it."

"What was its name?"

"I forgot. What kinds of books do you like Jeremiah?"

"I like ones that have to do about families and how they stick together through tough times. It kind of reminds me of what I never had, you know? Or what Mr. Switz had to give me. Even though I don't like being reminded of the event that happened with my parents, it doesn't mean I want to forget them completely. They gave birth to me, and without them, I would never be feeling these feelings. I can't explain whether I'm happy or sad I was born, because it comes with so many pros and cons."

"I'm happy you were. I mean, you are my best friend after all. Without you I don't know what I'd be going through right now."

"Without me everything would be fine."

"And there you go again! Please promise me that during these last few days where we don't know whether we will live or die, you will not blame yourself for what is happening right now. We've had to grow and mature faster, yes. We've lost some of our precious childhood, yes. But we both have made a friendship that will never end. Right now we have each other's lives in our hands, and even after, we will have each other's happiness. Isn't that really the same thing? Even if you hadn't been born with the curse, we'd still be here in this same situation, trying not to hurt each other and support each other at the same time. Can I say that for sure? No. But can I make a probable guess? Yes. Whether you like it or not we are stuck together, so become happy already. You're putting a damper on my mood," I pouted and Jeremiah laughed.

Thinking about how this is how it's supposed to be, I smile, because I know that as long as I hear that laugh... I'm doing my job right. I know that as long as I see him smile... Everything will be ok. Jeremiah and I come from two different worlds, when you think about it, but that didn't stop anything. Even if Jeremiah is supposed to be the curse, he's more of a blessing to me. Without him, I don't know where I'd be.

Another Time, another Fear

I wake up in the middle of the night and feel an urge to smell fresh air; an urge to feel free. Looking at the clock, it is 4:00 a.m. I don't feel very tired, so I take a stroll out of my room. Times such as this make me think of what it must've been like 200 years ago without light. If people wanted to stroll around the house, they would need a candle. Now, I do not have a candle and only have the moonlight to guide my way. I open the door to my room and exit, strolling down the hallway. It soon becomes darker, but I reach the stairs. Luckily, after living in this house for so many years, I seem to have an idea of how many stairs there are. I walk down each carefully, trying not to make a noise. Everything is dark downstairs, and my eyes are just beginning to adjust. I see curtains on the windows. No wonder I can't see. Walking over quietly, I tug on the curtains until a fragment of light enters the room. That's enough for me to find the doorknob. Walking near the wall, I slowly turn the creaking doorknob and walk outside onto the porch. From there, I make my way onto the grass, where I find myself staring at the moon and taking in the fresh air. The stars are out tonight, and it is very beautiful.

But I become curious as I notice the moon turning a darker shade of orange, soon into red. Is this what they would call a "Blood Moon"? I don't think our moon works like that, though. I can't seem to remember what happened in science class, either. The sky begins to form with a tint of red, the stars glowing bloody circles in the distance. I begin to see a shaking within the sky, almost as if it is to turn into something else. My fear begins to grow, and anxiety forms inside of me. Was this a bad idea? The moon begins turning a sharper shade of red, nearly blinding. The winds pick up, and I fear for my life. A circular cloud begins to form, seeming to laugh at my very face and a circular funnel crashes down near Jeremiah's house. Can they please leave him alone for once? I mean seriously. He's fifteen years old.

"Now is not the time, Paula," I yell out loud to myself.

Unfortunately, I know what I have to do. And unfortunately, it scares the wits out of me. I pull the front door open and walk toward the red tornado, and realize that the land around it is becoming entrapped in blood. Well, truthfully, I do not know whether it is blood. It could just be a red substance or tint, but either way it gives me a sense of disgust. I try to slow down time, but it doesn't work. Looks like it's time to fly. If you can't slow down a tornado, beat it with its own force. I jump up into the air, but the tornado nearly throws me. I'm going to have to use my strength to undo what is happening here. I fly into the tornado, noticing everything inside of it is not red. I fly in the opposite direction of the tornado, hoping to reverse its power, but it is too strong. I fly downwards, unsure of what I am doing, and stand in the center of the tornado. I have incredible strength, but even this is nearly impossible to fight. Despite the fact that I know it's being caused by a curse, it still is a tornado. It can be undone by reversing its effects. I put my hands out and nearly tip over. If this is going to work, I have to push the winds with all of my might. Already I am tired and the air is taking a toll on me. I cannot breathe, and it's becoming harder to stay awake. I am splitting the tornado in half, but I need to push. I just… I feel… Sleepy…

"Go Paula, you can do it! We're counting on you!" Jeremiah says.

Fear is apparent in his voice, but it begins to give me strength. I need to fight so Jeremiah can live. I push against the forces of the tornado, moving my arms in the opposite direction. I'm surprised my arms haven't flown off by now. Though I suppose my healing powers wouldn't let that happen anyway… I manage to push it a foot before I finally realize the true cause of the problem. I jump up and fly into the clouds above. Stinging sensations surround me, and lightning nearly shocks me. I fly forward and back, trying to separate the clouds the tornado is coming from. It begins to work, but I have to go a bit deeper into the clouds. I fly whichever way I can, careful not to get stuck in the tornado's whirlwind of power. The tornado does not disperse easily, but I manage. When I know that the tornado is over, my senses take over. I fall to the ground. My heart's beating is faint, and I know it's over. There's no way I could live through this. I'm sensible enough to know that I saved Jeremiah, but I'm also sensible enough to know that I might not wake up for a really long time. My energy is nearly completely depleted. Not to mention I fell at least 100 feet to the ground. Time seems to pass so slowly when you are in a coma… but for everyone else, time moves on.

6 Months Later

Every day, every second, every moment since that day, I've had nightmares of losing my family. I've had to deal with the fact that I might never wake up, and be stuck with this dream for an eternity. I was terrified... There were tears in my eyes... I screamed... I yelled... I cried... But ever since I woke up, my family was there right beside me. Exactly one month ago, five months after the incident, I woke up. But one month ago, I was in terrible shape. It took countless hours for me to come back, and even as I come back, I'm broken. The old Paula was brave, but I'm a coward and I'm fearful. The old Paula was sensible in dealing with time, but I'm over here wasting more time being mad about my life. I know the toll it's taking on Jeremiah, but I don't stop. Jeremiah thought this was his entire fault, I know it. And I wasn't there to help him. Looking back on who I was a month ago, I'm ashamed. I'm still ashamed of whom I am, but here I sit on the beach, feeling the sand. It is Wednesday, October 14. I am not here to swim, I am not here to enjoy the water or go fishing. I am here to find the old Paula. To take memories of what I used to be, and bring them into the person I am now. I get a sense of nostalgia, but I am not anywhere near being Paula. Even though Mr. Switz tries to hide it from me, I know that the tenth event is coming soon. And I know that I won't be ready. The thought gets me frustrated and I throw the sand away from me. It just happens to land on Jeremiah.

"Hey! What was that for?" he asks with a laugh.

"That's for trying to find crabs. I think if they wanted you to knock, they'd have a door."

"Instead they have holes in the ground, meaning that they want me to find them, but they don't want me to see them in the light. They are beach cave dwellers."

I roll my eyes and Jeremiah continues looking for seashells.

"Enjoying the view?" Jeremiah asks.

"The land out here isn't the same as it used to be when I was a little girl. The waters were cleaner, but I have to admit there is nostalgia. The seagulls squawk, but their calls are lonely. There are no children running after their parents trying to catch them, no flying kites. Times have changed."

"Paula?"

"Yes?"

"What if we just want to stay with the old times? Have everything like it used to be? What if you just moved on without us?"

"Are you forgetting that I was the one stuck in a coma? I didn't even know what life out here was like until I woke up. I missed my summer and I missed the chance to grow and mature a bit."

"Isn't that what we need, though? To keep our child-like minds? As we grow older, everyone worries about jobs and money and all of that, but what about being creative? What about having fun?"

"Adults just have different thoughts of fun, Jeremiah."

Jeremiah puts his bucket down.

"You know what I miss about you, Paula? You used to be so open-minded and had an answer even if there was no solution. You always thought out of the box. That was the Paula that I liked. Maybe the only reason you've changed is because you *think* that you're *supposed to* change. That everything is supposed to be different. But you don't Paula. You can be whoever you want to be."

"I have to figure that out for myself. And Jeremiah, maybe I don't want to be me. I'm missing everything. I just want to be a normal teenager."

"But you're not Paula! When we're fifteen is probably the only time that we get to be kids and make mistakes! When we get older, everything will disappear! We will have to work hard to get good jobs just like everyone else, and I don't want that to happen."

"It's just life Jeremiah."

"It's your version of life, not *mine*! *My* version of life just happens to be better."

I roll my eyes once again, but think about what Jeremiah said. If I keep wishing that none of this would've happened, then I'll be missing the things I have right in front of me. I stand up and follow Jeremiah.

"Let's go to the park," I say.

Jeremiah smiles and we ride our bikes to the park. After we got out of the hospital, I taught Jeremiah how to ride one. The sun is beginning to go down, and we can't stay out too long. Jeremiah and I walk around for awhile; climbing trees, jumping on park benches, skipping stones, and watching the sun go down. For that time period, I live in the present. I don't feel the same though. I'm doing everything the old Paula used to do, but I still feel lost.

"Who was I?" I ask quietly.

"As in what were you like?"

"Yeah. I mean, it'll come back to me eventually, right? I might as well start somewhere."

"The old Paula was determined even though she didn't think it. She always thought everything was her fault and tried to take the blame off of me. She didn't think she was special, but she was. She doubted herself often, but was very selfless even though she thought that she was selfish. And I bet that right now, you know that this is taking a toll on me. You think you're a different Paula, but you're the same person. Even if you don't feel like it yet, you are. You have your memories, you just got lost a little. You're a bit depressed. It'll go away Paula, just give it time and stop blaming yourself."

"Thanks, I guess."

"Oh, and one more thing. The old Paula used to tease me. Don't try to be like the old Paula, though. Your true personality will show itself, but trying to work for it will just cause you more anxiety."

"And what about the old Jeremiah? You started to mature, and I can tell by what you say."

"Everything I say is for your benefit, Paula. I don't want to hurt you. Of course I've matured. It happens. Just remember the cause you were fighting for. I don't know what gave you that much power to fight, but it surely was something. You were the bravest person I know. And you still are."

The cause I was fighting for was Jeremiah. It always was. Jeremiah is my best friend, and I can't lose him.

"Don't you ever get it?" I question.

"Get what?"

I sigh.

"Nothing. We should probably head back now."

"Yes."

The ride back to the neighborhood was quiet, but I felt happier. I may not be completely reverted back to the old Paula, but I have a reason to fight. I'm being a little bit more true to myself now, and I can count on the fact that my cause will not be taken away. The months I was locked away were filled with agony and sadness, but that doesn't have to change who I am. If anything, it should make me wiser. I suppose agony can make anyone change though. As for my powers, no sign of them has shown up since the event. It's almost as if they went missing. Maybe that's the part of me that's missing, though. I don't think powers would have such an effect on my personality. Perhaps... without them... I'd never be brave enough to save anyone. With my powers, I know that it's possible for me to save people, but without them, I could very easily die. I would be very fragile and that would be problematic. Even though I don't know what will happen after all of this is over, I can still hope for the best: that I keep my friends. That I can go to school. It seems everything has been sidetracked because of these powers. My whole life was put on hold. How am I supposed to continue after this? All of my friends that I used to have will fade away because I decided to stop hanging out with them for their safety. Life really isn't fair. Why does the thought of this curse have to be so ambiguous? We don't know when anything will happen, and when it does, we don't know whether we'll be prepared enough. This could very well turn out badly. And if it does turn out badly, we can't be there to help those that need us. This curse will live forever and ruin everyone's lives, which is why I have to stop it. I cannot let it take away lives that easily. Powers can't just be placed upon someone. We can't just expect them to save others. It's the same thing with the curse. You can't just put a curse on someone and expect them to die. We have no clue as to where this curse comes from, but we will soon find out, won't we? I need to win this battle for Margaret, who gave up her life to save Mr. Switz. Sure, I can easily die and save one person, but that would be the easy way out. This whole thing needs to stop. And I will be the one to stop it. There is no way I will continue to live like this. I can't live in fear, only protecting one person, because Jeremiah isn't the only one that needs saving, just the same that I can't rely on only myself to save them. This is a team effort, just as everything else. Jeremiah and I were put in this together, and we will end it together. I'm no longer just angry at the curse for taking *our* lives away. I'm angry at the curse for taking *everyone's* lives away. I fall asleep with peace for once, my thoughts set straight and my goals right in front of me. However, I cannot simply measure how far these goals are from just one angle. Time will pass, but I do not know how long it will take. My peace will soon be interrupted. I know that for certain. But I won't be filled with anger this time. I will be filled with an aspiration to achieve; to save; to fight my one and only true enemy: Death itself.

* * *

When I wake up in the morning, I am the old Paula, but stronger than ever before. Now it's my turn to help Jeremiah become just as strong as me. I need to let my happiness and determination fill the air. I do everything I need to do in an average fashion, but with each movement, each step, you can see the excitement that I have. I'm taking the initiative and staring at the curse in the eye. The curse may have roared at me once, but I am now roaring at it, stronger and louder than ever before. As I go for my classes, I can tell my physical abilities as well as my powers' abilities have advanced greatly. Jeremiah is also doing much better in his mental practice games. However, in the middle of our practice, Mr. Switz tells us to sit down so that we can have a chat.

"Based on my calculations, the curse should be coming within a week. It seems to have been held back for a little, but it will still be coming soon. We don't have much time and you are going to have to spend most of that time training together. As you may have noticed, fighting the curse requires teamwork, and without that, you're bound to fail. This curse, as far as I can tell, will be at least 10 times stronger than your fiercest event. The curse was just playing around then; getting you ready. Seeing what you could do. Paula, there's a certain power you must achieve in order to fully get rid of the curse. Obviously I do not know its form; otherwise I would be able to tell you more. I also do not know how you are supposed to achieve it. School will be lengthened by about 2 hours each day, until 5:00 p.m. After that you may relax, but traveling anywhere alone is not an option. It will be extremely dangerous, and we can't risk losing one of you; or both of you, for that matter. Our highest priority is keeping you two safe, and we will do that to the best of our ability."

"Excuse me, Mr. Switz. You say you want to keep us safe, but don't you realize that's not possible? Even if Jeremiah and I work together, this is a great task. If you guys try to pry into it, you will end up getting hurt. Our goal is to protect everyone. That's our job. I know that we have to work together, but putting people in danger will be taking the purpose of everything we have worked for away. It's our job to keep you two safe, and we will; which is why we need to leave. We can stay here for a few days, and believe me, I don't know where we will go, but that gives everyone a greater chance of living. If I have to run away from all of you, I will do it. Don't doubt me. At this point, I would do anything to protect you all, even if it meant putting me in greater danger," I finish.

"Paula, you need to depend on us, because we aren't the only people you need to worry about. If you decide to go alone and you get into trouble, you'll be ruining two kids' lives in the future. Do you really want that to happen? I'm sorry Paula. I would agree with you, but there are so many downsides to you going somewhere other than here. Promise me you won't leave Paula. Promise me."

"I promise."

He never said I couldn't leave the neighborhood. I have my reasons for promising on such an ambiguous idea. If I had pushed too much, then I couldn't do anything. He would've been more specific. Now the promise is only valid for one idea and one idea only. I will not die, but that doesn't mean I won't leave. Though, then again, I can't promise anything.

Same Old Classes

The toll that my powers have taken on my body has decreased quite a bit ever since I was in that coma. I hate to admit it, but I feel refreshed. I'm still not filled in on what happened during those five months, but I would like to find out. As for my studies, I didn't miss too much. School was obviously out during the summer, but Jeremiah told me Mr. Switz made him practice every day anyway. He said that time passed by normally, but I can't seem to believe him. He keeps bringing up the fact that in less than a month, I will be fifteen years old, as if that's supposed to cheer me up. If time keeps passing by like this, soon enough my whole life might end up being taken by the curse. Everything that I say seems to hold Jeremiah. The curse doesn't mean I'm referring to him, but in some ways... it does. This is why I have trouble speaking about it sometimes. If I were to say 'The Curse is the cause for everything.' Jeremiah would automatically blame himself. It's hard not having anyone else my age to talk to, but I can't bring Katelyn or Beatrice into this either. It's sad because I know that Katelyn and I won't be the same as we were before. I haven't let myself talk to her, so our best friendship may be slowly slipping away. This isn't what I wanted. But it seems like it's the only thing I'm going to get.

My body is stronger, but I am a bit stressed out. I obviously still come home tired. I usually just fall asleep for 30 minutes to an hour and then get up to go eat. Time is passing by under my finger tips, and I want it to stop, but I know that if certain wishes are granted, they will have a different effect than what you originally wanted. My powers won't fix everything. I can't go back. I can't treasure everyone more than I did. From today onward, I know what I'll have to do, and it won't be easy. It feels as if an invisible sheet of armor is around me, silently protecting me from anything that comes my way. But a sheet of armor can't protect you from what you feel on the inside. Perhaps I'm trying to convince myself that everything will be alright, when I know that it won't. Perhaps I'm trying to make myself brave. Throughout everything, I just wanted to be Paula; the real me. Not a superhero, not just a normal girl. I don't know who I am yet. I know I don't like the fact that if I didn't have these powers, I wouldn't be special. And I know that these powers will fade. One day they will all be gone and I'll be left with the question 'What do I do now?' I have no answer for my own questions because I'm at a loss of time. I'm at a loss of breath, and a loss of words. I want to go back and breathe in the refreshing air, filling my lungs, giving hope to my heart, that one day I'll be more than just Paula Berney; that one day I'll be more than a person with superpowers. Maybe the person in the comic that has the powers is the coolest. I've always thought that all of my life. But sometimes the person that seems the bravest is actually the weakest. Perhaps they want to see other people live the life that they don't have themselves. Maybe they're living through those other people. I don't know. What I do know, though, is that I cannot judge myself based on my powers. No one can call me brave! I'm only brave because of my powers, and this bravery that people say is real, is actually fake! I'm afraid of everything. I'm still a child. I tremble in the cold. I have tantrums in the heat. And I can't take feelings that are overwhelming me right now. My mind has been filled to the brink; my heart has been so pushed to the limit that I'm surprised it hasn't gone out yet. Perhaps instead of a heart, instead of a brain, I have a candle. And that candle might light into a fire one day, burning everything in its wake. Is that what I want? Do I want to destroy everything? That's why I need to leave soon; maybe not today, maybe not tomorrow, but soon. After today, I have about 6 days until the curse comes. Am I really ready? My powers have grown stronger and I believe my mental capabilities have grown, but don't we need more than that? Sure, we've had to train for a long time, but it just seems too simple. Mr. Switz said we need teamwork, but I'm going to have to do this alone. No one else can find out I'm going to be leaving, especially not Jeremiah. He will try to convince me to stay, and I'm afraid that it might work. Leaving will not be an easy thing to accomplish, but I'm going to have to try. I'll bring snacks, a blanket, some clothes, and maybe I'll camp out in the park or in Jeremiah's parents' house. I hope they don't mind. Even if they're not living, it still once was their home. I shouldn't be intruding in such a place. I suppose now I will have to spend my time planning. I will be leaving the night before we are supposed to be fighting the curse. If I leave too early, they will notice I am gone, so this would be the perfect chance. I need to leave late in the night, too, because I can't risk anyone seeing me leaving. Walking back to my house and up to my bedroom, I lie on my bed and begin to plan everything out. Not one thing can be out of place. For a plan like this, everything must be perfect. The only thing is perfect doesn't exist.

* * *

It is now October 17, 5 days before the curse is going to come. The thought hits me as I wake up, and I groan. As far as patience goes, I don't have much right now. Waiting 5 days so that I can fight a curse when I'm ready to face it now? What's the point of that? Is the curse not ready now? My thoughts put me into a grumpy mood, but then I remember it is Saturday. At least we get a break from school. Then again, I don't know what Mr. Switz has up his sleeve. He might make us go to school anyway. I get up and walk downstairs, planning on eating something. I didn't eat dinner last night because I fell asleep early, so I'm really hungry today. As I eat my cereal, I think about what I will be leaving behind and whether this decision will really benefit all of us, though I can't seem to get my thoughts straight. It is, of course, the morning, and I just woke up. My brain was hardly ready to pour milk into my cereal, so thinking straight becomes a bit difficult. After I finish my cereal, I walk over to the faucet and rinse my face off, making sure I put cold water on my eyes to wake me up. Though I may be able to help my eyes wake up, my brain is still fast asleep. My shirt is a bit wrinkled from sleeping, but I walk out onto the porch anyway. I don't plan to stay outside for long, but I need to get the fresh air on my face. Out of the corner of my eye, I can see Jeremiah throwing a basketball. I walk back inside of my house and go get ready for today. There's not much to do except go outside, though… Maybe I could text Katelyn--just this once. I mean she's still far away from me, right? It would be safe to text her now. And she has school on Monday, so there's no way she could travel over here. It would be a complete waste of money. My conscience is telling me not to, but I miss my other best friend. She meant so much to me, and it seems as if I am just throwing her away. I want to protect her, I really do, but sometimes you need someone to talk to other than Jeremiah. Do I really want to risk it though? I suppose not. I trudge back into my room and take a shower. When I get out, I brush my teeth and get dressed. Looking out of the window, I don't see Jeremiah playing with his basketball anymore. He must've gone inside. I would go knock on his door, but for some reason, I feel like this is for the best. Talking to him now will just make it harder to leave later. It'll be a boring day, and I know it, but what else is there to do? If I go on my phone, I'll get countless messages from my friends. Did my mom tell Katelyn that I was in a coma? I guess not… I mean, if she told her that, Katelyn would come to visit… That wouldn't leave me in a good situation. I need to find out, though. Just because I have had no contact with Katelyn, doesn't mean my mom hasn't. Walking back down the stairs, I prepare myself, because I have no clue what I'm about to hear.

My mom was in the living room watching TV and invited me to sit next to her. I sat down and looked at the screen for what seemed like a few minutes and began to speak slowly. If Katelyn knew about everything that is going on, why wouldn't my mom have told me? It doesn't make sense to ask her, really. She would definitely tell me if she was talking to Katelyn, right? I almost chicken out of asking her, but then I think about how much I've really got to lose. There's so much going on my life right now that I think I'll be able to take some small news such as this.

"Hey mom?"

"Yes, honey?"

"Did you ever tell Katelyn about what is happening here in Maryland?"

"I couldn't Paula. She'd ask why you haven't texted her, and what was I supposed to say? That your phone broke? And if I had told her you were in a coma, she'd definitely come to visit. I'm sorry sweetie, but it seems as if your friendship is breaking apart. I'm just telling you the truth, because I'd rather have you face it now than right before the battle."

My mother's face goes sour at the word 'battle' and I know she doesn't want to talk about it anymore. That's ok though, because I got the answers that I need. Katelyn is safe, and I have to stop myself from telling her anything. I have to stop myself from talking to her completely, just as I have this past year. So much time is passing, and I don't know how to deal with the fact that I'm growing up already. But… Even more… I can't accept the fact that my life might be over. It could all end here, and what would Katelyn be left with? No last words… from a year ago… I feel extremely guilty for not talking to her, even though I know it's better this way. I wonder how she is dealing with all of this…

Katelyn's Point of View *
Saturday, School Fundraiser

My whole life, I had dreamed of Paula and me growing up together and becoming famous movie stars, or working together in the fashion industry. Maybe that was more of my dream, but even so. It has been one year since Paula last spoke to me. We promised our friendship wouldn't end, but look at what is happening… I'm not mad… I just should've expected it. Paula will always remain my best friend, even if we haven't talked in awhile. She was there for me when I needed her, but I couldn't be there for her. I tried texting her, but maybe it was too late. And as for Jeremiah, he left without even muttering a goodbye… it just seemed so weird… I mean, I know he liked Paula and everything, but he went *this far*? I don't even know why his parents would allow such a thing. Though, Jeremiah and I were never good friends. We just managed to pretend around Paula. When she was in a coma… it was easy for us all to seem like friends then, but it wasn't the truth. Now I seem to have an extreme dislike for Jeremiah. I mean, obviously he took Paula away from me. He took my best friend. Though, I don't hold grudges. I'm just happy that Paula is happy... But none of this would've happened if we never had to leave! So much time has passed, and I'm fifteen now. I'm in high school. My friends that I originally made here have gone to different schools, and now I don't really talk to people. You would think I would be the person who becomes captain of the cheerleading squad, right? Well... Instead ... I'm sitting in the corner of the lunchroom wishing I had my old life back. There's nothing that can change how everything is now, though. Maybe Paula will talk to me again one day. I hope so. I hope that whatever I did to make her mad is soon forgiven. I don't know how long I can go without my best friend... I'm alone...

Sunday Calls

As I am asleep in my bed, I see a dream… far away… almost as if it were from a place other than mine. But within the dream, I see a blur of lightning and hear the faraway sound of thunder roaring in the air. I should feel afraid. I should be scared. But I'm not. For some reason, there is a starry kind of comfort that moves on with the lightning. Every clap of light, every boom of thunder, makes me feel a comfort that I haven't felt in so long. My heart is racing, but this is not a nightmare. However, the light I desire to brighten up my way seems to be disappearing. But it always manages to come back. I hear heavy rainfall, and open my eyes. Large drops of water are on my windows. My dream simply reflected the weather, though; perhaps it made me feel a bit more like a normal girl. Every child has to face the thunder sometime, and every child may become scared during that point. Maybe we cry, maybe we hide, or maybe we wish it would stay like that. Despite the frightening aspects of a storm, it seems to be a part of my childhood, and therefore it is something that reminds me of home: all of the times I had to be comforted because of the loud thunder roaring in my ears; all of the times I was able to be with my family, simply putting it, and hear the sound of their voices; hear the sound of the people that I have cared so much for during these last 14, almost 15 years, of my life. I wish I could have that back, even though I know wishes like that don't come true. I roll under the blankets, and prepare for a long day of staying inside. But a noise interrupts me. Under my bed, I hear the ring of a phone. I do not recognize the ringtone, but I answer the call anyway.

"Who is this?"

"Hello Paula. It's me."

And the clap of thunder races to beat down on the ground like no other, threatening to burn everything you have, everything you love, into flames.

* * *

My heart was racing. Why would she call me now after all this time? Doesn't she hate me? She's not supposed to be calling me. I mean, I didn't block her number or anything, but that's just because I was so sure she wouldn't call. Should I just pretend that I'm someone else? She might call the number again though… What else can I do? I can't just hang up. And Katelyn knows my voice… or at least knew… But even now my silence is just proving that something is wrong. I need to speak before she assumes that I'm trying to avoid her or something, but that's what I'm doing. It's for her safety, so I shouldn't feel bad… But I do. She was my best friend and I just threw her away. The thoughts keep coming back. I need to speak up now.

"Paula, I know you probably don't want to talk to me,

but I just need to know what I did wrong. Please tell me. Maybe I can apologize or try to make up for it."

She thinks *she* did something wrong, when I was the one basically ignoring her for a full year? This makes me just the least bit annoyed, but how can I be annoyed with someone who I have hurt so much? Then again, maybe she doesn't care that I stopped talking to her. Or at least, she did.

"It's…" I try to speak, but my voice comes out like a croak.

"What?"

"It's not your fault Katelyn. There's just a lot going on right now, and I didn't want to bring you into it. I figured it be easier if you weren't enveloped into the… things… that I am now."

"What do you mean? Paula, are you ok? Are you hurt?"

"Not exactly… Just trust me, I'm ok now. I just thought that after not talking for a few months, you wouldn't want to talk to me. It might be better for you that way, anyway."

"How could you possibly think that Paula? I don't know whether this will make you feel better or worse, but without you, my whole world has been a complete mess. I had a feeling you were going through something, but I didn't have the bravery to contact you until now. I just want to make sure that our friendship is still ok. Maybe we have drifted apart a bit, and maybe I'm a different person than I was since you last saw me, but trust me, I still remember you."

"The question should be whether you're ok, Katelyn. Tell me how school is going. Tell me what I've missed. I mean, falling into a coma really confuses your mind a bit."

"Wait… what?"

"Um… yeah… about that…"

"Paula, you let things slip way too easily. That's one flaw about you, but good for me in my case. How long were you in the coma?"

"5 months. It's nothing big, really."

"What caused you to get into the coma?"

"Just stuff," I say nonchalantly.

"What kind of stuff?"

"Stuff that's really complicated and will make me out of breath if I try to explain," I say taking a deep breath.

"I'll be here for awhile. You can tell me."

"The thing is… I can't. I'm sorry Katelyn; I'll explain it to you one day, but right now isn't the best time."

"When can I come to visit?"

"In a bit. Just give my mom some time. She's going through a bit too. How about during winter break? That's the last time I saw you."

"Ok. I will. And how is school going?"

"It's going."

"And Jeremiah?"

"He's doing fine. We've become pretty close over the past few months."

"So… Has he told you he likes you yet?"

"NO! WHY DOES EVERYONE ASSUME THAT HE LIKES ME?" I shout.

"You obviously like him so…"

"Katelyn, we're just really good friends. That's it."

Well, other than the fact that our lives depend on each other and we've been training for months to fight a nearly indestructible force that may kill us.

"Uh huh… Sure you are. I haven't talked to him in

awhile either, but that's a story for another time," she replies, laughing.

Katelyn and I talk for a few hours. I can't explain how good it feels to have my best friend back, even if it's not permanent. I'm out of breath from talking about everything. Tears start flowing down my face, and I can't hold them back anymore. There's no way to stop myself. I cry because I want my life with my best friend back. I cry because I miss her so much. I cry because I know that I haven't been there for her. I feel the pain in her voice. My heart drops little by little, and it's hard to repress. I want to cry out loud, I want to sob, but I don't, and instead I wash my face off. My nose is running and I'm trying to ignore what I feel. The feeling of having my best friend back is a relief. I never thought that I could miss someone this much. But I know that our conversation will have consequences. I'll form stronger bonds with Katelyn, and that'll make me become weak, because I don't want to fight. I'll want to just talk to my best friend like a normal person. It's hard to be strong in times you feel so weak. My heart dropped one hundred feet, and it's taking 1,000 tow trucks to pull it back up. The tears are no longer there, but I still feel the burning, the heat, which was left on my face. The cool water did nothing other than show to me that I'm burning. Sometimes the things that you think might help you will actually make your situation more apparent. I want to run again. I want to get away. I want to nod my head, and scream no. But I don't. Save my energy, right? Well… I think it's taking more to keep my feelings bottled up inside. The days are passing and I'm trying to keep going. I don't even know how I have any energy left. But I do. And I'll try to be the strongest I can be. Everything is changing, and I may be at a loss looking for myself, but things will eventually come to light. They have to. They must. Just because something "has to", it doesn't mean it will, though. I open my windows and feel a blast of fresh air on my face. A new beginning, I suppose? New beginnings don't come that often, however. Perhaps I'm simply dreaming of what I want... Perhaps I need to wake up to reality.

Back to Work, Back to Solitude

As school begins, I complete my training. I do what I'm supposed to, just like every day. When I think about it, October 20th will be the only day I've ever done something that's really reckless. Sure, I ran away from home once before, but this time I might not actually be coming back. It's scary to think that I might have so little time left. Today is October 19th, two days before the tenth event. I don't feel prepared. I thought I knew who Paula was, but I feel more lost than ever. Maybe it's just because I'm getting closer to the 10th event, but either way, I don't feel like myself. It's almost like being sick when you have to give a presentation or going up on stage in front of thousands of people. You feel like you're going to mess up because your health isn't 100%. Well, for me, it's my confidence that's being stripped away. Jeremiah told me who I was. Back then, I thought I was beginning to find myself, but my life is being pulled in so many different directions. I don't know which Paula I should be. The normal Paula? The confident Paula? The depressed Paula? What should I feel at times like this? Should I feel afraid? Could it be possible I'm trying to block out my own feelings? I shake my head and begin to focus on my work more. If I'm going to be able to defeat the curse, I need to be as strong as I can possibly be. I think. Without assurance, I become nervous, and soon enough, my palms are sweating. I ask Mr. Switz for a break because I'm starting to become dizzy. As I sit down, Jeremiah follows me.

"Are you ok?" he asks.

"Yeah… I'm just a little dizzy."

"Maybe you shouldn't train anymore."

"I have to. Plus, I think I'll feel better in a few minutes. It's just that thoughts are clouding my mind."

Jeremiah narrows his eyes at me, as if he doesn't believe me. He leaves without saying a word, but I'm almost sure he knows that I'm not telling the full truth. I don't want to tell anyone I've talked to Katelyn, either. That will just get me into more trouble than I am already in, and I don't want to have guilt on my back when I leave tomorrow. Though I already know there's going to be heaps of it. I feel a cool breeze and I shiver, but my dizziness begins to fade. Jeremiah enters the room again with some water.

"I thought you might need something to cool you off. You looked a bit pale."

"Thanks, Jeremiah."

"No problem."

I'm lucky to have Jeremiah as my friend. He understands me and what I need. Unfortunately, time is passing, and that's what he can't help me with. Sometimes I just want to stop time and enjoy life as it is, but if you have regrets, mistakes, or burdens on your back, you can never enjoy life to the fullest. For now, though, I'm starting to feel a bit more like myself. I just hope things keep going well.

* * *

I walk outside, and Jeremiah follows me. I stop and sit on the grass, waiting for him to sit next to me. It's funny how we can already expect certain things to go a certain way. It's almost as if, after a while, we learn the person's habits, and become accustomed to them. It takes time, but eventually everything comes into place. When Jeremiah makes it over to me, however, he does not sit down.

"Want to go to the park?"

"So no talking on the grass or is that later?"

"I just want to see my parents' house before... Wednesday..."

"That's all you had to say. Walk or bike?"

"Walk. If we bike, we'll miss seeing the neighborhood."

I get up and tell my mom that I'll be going to the park with Jeremiah. We begin to stroll down the street, taking a careful look at each of the houses.

"It's funny," I say while sighing.

"What?"

"I remember when you first came here; you asked if we could go to the park. I was really suspicious because I didn't know you that well at the time. And when I saw you in school, you kept on making up lies about why you had to stay here. It seems like such a long time ago."

"That's because it was. And you know why I made the lies. I couldn't tell you what was really going on. Plus, you ended up learning why I liked going to the park so much. My parents are there... even if they're not alive; they're still there in spirit, watching over me. I just know it."

"Did anyone ever know your parents?"

"What do you mean?"

"Did your parents have people they talked to?"

"I was a baby when I last saw them, so I don't know, but I would assume yes. My parents obviously had jobs and co-workers, so they must've been friends with somebody."

"Why didn't you ever try asking about them?"

"I was afraid, mostly. I didn't know what I would find out about them."

"You know, if they had friends, they must've been good people."

"That's not exactly what I was afraid of. People would know my parents died, and they would take pity on me. They would tell me that my parents were great people, without sharing the bad side of things. I didn't want that to happen. Everyone has a good and bad side, and the only way I could really get to know them was if I saw every part of their personality, even if that's pretty much impossible now."

"Nothing is impossible. It may be difficult, but definitely not impossible."

"You know, some people say it's harder when you lose your parents at a young age, and I understand that, because you never got to learn or get to know them, but because I never got to know them, I can't feel as deeply for them as I would for someone like Mr. Switz. He's been taking care of me so long that he's like a father to me."

"I think your parents would understand if you cared about him."

"I hope so."

"Trust me, they would. I have a feeling they're a lot like you."

"Then they'd be very jealous."

"You really don't know yourself, do you? Looks like I'm not the only one that's lost."

"I just know I'm a kid, originally born in Maryland, with a hard life. But there are people with harder lives than me."

"Yeah, that's true. We're very fortunate to have people caring about us. Though, I think everyone has someone that cares about them. Someone loves you, even if you haven't met them yet. The same thing happened for me and you. What's important is that we don't give up and that we keep on trying. The curse has brought our lives up and down, and we can't control all of the sinkholes that we might fall into, but eventually, we will learn how to climb out. Even if we have to spend years making stairs, we will climb out."

"Do you think this will keep on going on?"

"I think that after we defeat the curse, obviously the extra bad luck and danger we have in our lives will be gone, but that doesn't mean we need to stop watching out. I'm not saying we can't make mistakes, but we should be careful with the mistakes we choose to make. Sometimes mistakes can ruin our lives forever. And yes, we will still have bad luck at times. I would say we actually have supreme good luck for being able to stay alive this long."

"That's your side of the deal. You got the blessings, and I got the curse."

"Even though mine are considered blessings, there are still downsides to them, just as there are good sides to your curse."

"What's the good side?"

"We became friends. Wasn't that obvious?"

I smile at Jeremiah and he laughs.

"Ok, maybe that's a good side."

"Maybe? I think it's the best side you've got."

"Hm... I don't know... I mean, I did get to meet Mr. Steve the tree over there. Hello Mr. Steve!" he says while waving to a random tree.

"It's too bad Mr. Steve doesn't talk."

"He waves back."

"But he needs the wind for that. I think even nature counts on friends."

"Are you saying you count on me? Hm?"

"Well, yeah. I'd probably be dead right now if it weren't for you."

"No need to make the conversation serious."

"Too late, egghead," I mock while laughing.

"What kind of insult is that?"

"It's not an insult, it's the truth. You have an egg-shaped head," I say while smirking at him.

He gets up and I quickly make a beeline for the park. I hide behind a tree and hear him calling my name. However, I manage to elude him. While he's near the playground, I silently crawl up to him and yell "Boo!"

And Jeremiah screams like a little girl. I immediately start laughing hysterically because that was the highest-pitched scream I had ever heard in my life.

"Geez, Paula. Do you have to scare me like that?"

"Yes. Yes I do. By the way, you might want to work on your scream a little. Your pitch just sounds a bit high."

"Thanks for the advice," he says with a laugh.

"Jeremiah, since we're going to fight the curse soon, maybe you *should* see your parents' house."

"Good idea. Are you going to come with me?"

"I'll meet you later."

I watch as Jeremiah walks off, and I walk off in the opposite direction. I've been to that side of the park so many times that there is no possible way I could forget it, but the idea of how the other side looks has become a bit of a mystery to me; a faded memory. I want to try to remember my life as much as I can, and this park has countless memories that I don't want to fade away. Looking, for a specific tree, I walk towards the one with roots that are circular, rounding into the floor. The roots have grown since I last saw them, which was much too long ago. This was the first tree I climbed, and the first tree I fell off of. I remember Katelyn screaming "You can do it!", and I was so happy when I reached a branch about 8 feet off of the ground. The tree branch, was not strong, however, and broke while I was sitting on it. I hurt myself pretty badly, with a deep scrape on my arm. Luckily, Katelyn and I were only 6 at the time, and my mother was sitting on a park bench nearby. The worst part about that was getting the scrape cleaned out, but after that, my mom applied a big band aid. Katelyn was crying when I hurt my arm, worrying about what to do. She thought it was her fault because she was the one who encouraged me to climb up the tree in the first place. I never blamed her, though. It just happened that the tree branch wasn't strong. No one could've known. I laugh at the thought, and continue on my walk. I pass a park bench, where I remember having countless picnics; however, I cannot form an actual image in my head of these picnics. I remember the park being covered in a winter coat, and making snow angels with Katelyn. So many of my past memories have been of my best friend and me, and now that's gone. Sure, I miss those times, but I understand why Katelyn had to leave. I'm not mad at her.

Sometimes I wonder whether I would care more if Jeremiah left, and maybe it would be a yes, maybe it would be a no. Katelyn knows more about me, but Jeremiah understands me more. The two are so different, however, that I can't compare them. It *is* crazy, however, how close Jeremiah and I have become. Sometimes I want my old life back, but I never really thought about the things I would be losing. As time passes by, I'm starting to think that maybe I don't want things to go back to the way they were. Maybe I want things to stay like this. And lose Katelyn? Would it all be worth it? There's a voice inside of me saying that I need to learn that what has happened, happened, and that I cannot change it. I mean obviously I want Jeremiah and Katelyn to be my best friends, but eventually one of them will leave me. I understand that Katelyn is feeling depressed without a best friend to talk to, but she can learn to find new friends. There's a difference between someone who wants you around, and someone who needs you around, right? There will come a time Katelyn will be tired of talking over the phone, and it'll fade. I know that. But as for Jeremiah, I can't leave him behind, and he can't leave me behind. I'm debating whether I would prefer to have Jeremiah or Katelyn as a friend, but I think I already know. Am I holding back the answer because I feel bad for Katelyn? I don't really know. Or maybe I just don't want to admit it. My past created who I am today, but every second passing by is another moment of my history. Someday, my life will end. Even if it isn't now, I'll die sometime, and there's no one that can stop that from happening. Losing someone is very painful, like a part of you has been taken away. The hole in my heart will stay there for the rest of my life, and there's nothing that can change that, but my heart has also grown in size from the love I've received. I'm truly thankful for everyone in my life, even if some have hurt me; even if some had to leave. I don't deserve these people. They've been there for me when I can't be there for them, but I'll make it up to them. One day. I'll try my best, and I'll live. For everyone that loves me, for everyone that I love. I know I make mistakes and I know that things will never be the same, but that doesn't mean I have to be sad because of it. The wind begins to pick up and a shiver goes down my back, though, I can't help from smiling. The wind, the air, the ground, and the water in this world are all cheering me on, telling me to live. I am a part of this world, and I want to keep it that way. I was born here, and I'd like to die here on my own terms, not because something or someone else is forcing me to. I let my arms fly into the sky and let the wind blow my hair around, and I laugh. I have a chance to be free, to be the best friend I can be, and I'll take those chances for me. Not just for others.

Coming Back Home

How did I find people that would mean so much to me? When they came into my life, I couldn't control how I felt. They mean so much to me. They let me feel happy in my saddest times. Every second, every minute of every hour is filled with happiness thanks to them. There are bad times, but as I'm walking home next to Jeremiah, I find myself laughing for no apparent reason, skipping down the pavement. Maybe I look like I'm five, but I don't care. I need to be happy if these last few hours are going to be the last time I see them. I'll hold onto these memories. The idea of me leaving them makes me sad, but I need to accept my fate if I ever want to get through this with them. I don't want to die depressed, I want to die happy. Jeremiah chases me down the block because I'm racing ahead of him. The wind is still blowing in my face, and my hair is being blown back. Walking down my last pavement will lead me to a choice. Living or dying. When we get home, I sit down on the grass, right next to Jeremiah. The grass is becoming cold, and dying little by little, but it always grows back. Maybe when the time comes, my life will be like that. The clouds began forming in the sky, and I notice that it's about to rain. Jeremiah suggests that we go inside, but I tell him that I'm staying here. I love sitting in the rain, watching the raindrops flow down my arm, covering the grass in dew for tomorrow morning. The rain is cold, but every drop counts, creating a pool of water in the grass. Jeremiah looks at me like I'm crazy, but I won't budge.

"If you're going to stay out here, you might as well do something fun rather than sitting down and getting soaked in water," Jeremiah says.

"Hey, we've got to have fun. Tomorrow is dangerous, and I don't want to think about that."

Jeremiah looks at me as if I'm a little baby and says "I'll be right back."

I give him a curious look, and he returns with two jackets from his house.

"Put this on."

"This jacket is way too big on me. Is this Mr. Switz's jacket?"

"No, it's mine."

"Are you sure?"

When I put on the jacket, the arms are way too long on me and I look tiny.

"You either keep that on, or I'm bringing you inside."

I pout at Jeremiah but keep the coat on. What else can I do? Plus, I don't have any really warm jackets.

"Put the hoodie on, Paula. Please."

"No. If my hair doesn't get wet, what's the fun of staying outside?"

"Are you trying to get sick for the fight?" he asks with a suspicious glance.

"Oh please. I have healing powers. You're the one that needs a jacket."

"Do you seriously want to be cold?"

"The icy, frigid air of the outdoors doesn't affect me. I mean obviously I feel cold, but I'll be fine."

"I suppose I can't control you then, but I still think you should put the hoodie on."

I roll my eyes and begin twirling.

"What are you doing?"

"I am feeling the rain."

"How, exactly, are you supposed to do that?"

"I can slow down time. Here, come hold my hand. You'll be able to feel the rain as it's coming down instead of being stuck in slow motion."

Jeremiah's face goes red for a bit, but he gets up and holds my hand. I don't know whether that was a blush or just from the cold, but either way, it disappeared quickly. His hand is warm, and I would let go of it if I could, but unfortunately, in order for him to see things the way I do without me getting exhausted, we need to have physical contact. I look at him as he marvels at the raindrops coming down slowly.

"If I touch the raindrops, will they move fast?"

"They wouldn't move fast and you'd be able to see the raindrop break up into pieces, forming into different raindrops. It's really quite amazing, if I do say so myself."

Jeremiah reaches his hand out, and catches a raindrop before it falls. Each raindrop looks solid in its form, but each moment they are changing. They are like the clearest ice crystals I have seen, except they aren't frozen. When time is slowed down, they look like jewels. I tell Jeremiah to look at the mildew on the grass, and we can see small crystals covering each one.

"It's like a wonderland. You're lucky to be able to see life like this, Paula."

"I know, and these are my favorite times to use my powers. You get to examine life in slow motion. It allows you to pay attention to the little details you never saw before, like the way everything looks upside down as you look into the raindrop, or how when it hits the grass, the grass moves with the raindrops. Everything has a rhythm, and that's crazy to see. I think after I lose my powers, this will be the power I will miss most. I drag Jeremiah to the trees, and we watch as the raindrops fall down on the leaves.

"Hold on, Jeremiah."

I begin to climb up the tree, and Jeremiah follows me. It's a small tree, but strong enough to hold the both of us. I pull a branch toward us, careful not to break any leaves off.

"Look at the raindrops on this leaf. If we pull the branch away, the rain will not hit it, causing the grass to be drowned in water. We need this branch so as to not disrupt the rest of the surrounding life."

I carefully return the tree to its former place and look at Jeremiah.

"Just like the grass, I need branches in order to survive so I don't get drowned in depression. You are the branches, Jeremiah. I need you in order to survive, so don't leave me, ok? Promise me. Something is going to happen to me tomorrow, and I need you to promise me that you won't be mad at me. Promise me. Please."

"What do you mean something is going to happen to you tomorrow?" he says as I look away from him, "Paula…?"

I begin to tear away from Jeremiah.

"I care about you… A lot… So don't leave me, ok?" he asks.

"Unfortunately, that's a promise I cannot keep."

Jeremiah chases after me, and I don't realize that I stopped using my powers. I run to my door and pause when he yells my name. I continue to go inside, but before I'm able to close the door, he stops me.

"You leave me wondering whether I'm going to ever see my best friend again, and you expect me to not be the least bit angry. Actually I'm not mad. I'm sad. I'm depressed. I don't want to lose someone that means so much to me."

"Don't you see what this has turned us into, Jeremiah? We're kids acting like adults. We don't know how to deal with any of this."

"We're partners; we're a team. That's all you need to know. If you go, I go with you."

"I don't think you know what that means."

I close the door and lock it, then walk upstairs. Why did I make this any harder than it needed to be? Look at the predicament I'm in now. I need to leave, but I don't want to. I want to stay. But I know that I can't. I stay up the rest of the night, staring at the stars, wondering how much life will change after this. Before I fall asleep, I look at the time. 10:04 p.m. That means I have about 24 hours until I need to leave. What do I say to everyone that I care about? One of the hardest parts about this is that I can never get in a proper goodbye. It's just going to be 'Goodnight.' Maybe I'll see you, maybe I won't. But everyone knows that. The truth of the matter is, people that I love will be lost if I stay, which is why I must go. If I leave, I'll be hurt, but no one else. I want to yell, I want to scream, but it's better if I use that scream to power my attacks, and win this battle. Time is passing, and all I can say is goodnight; never goodbye, because nothing will ever end. I'll always be there for the people I love, even if it's in spirit. I guess it's time to accept my fate. But I don't want to...

Sometimes I want to run away into the starry night,
Never thinking about a single fight,
But with life passing by, and times that are hurting,
I can never find the words that will stop
everything from immersing,

I find people I care about,
Losing them all at once,
Because I could never accept,
That maybe I was the true dunce.

I've always thought about losing everything,
But never thought how to prepare,
Never thought how to move on,
And now I'm left to pay the fare.
~ Paula Berney, an Infinite Entity

Goodbye

I wake up late in the morning, at 10 o'clock. We don't have school today because Mr. Switz wanted to let us rest before the big day. Tomorrow I will be fighting the curse, whether it is in the morning, or at night, I don't know. Perhaps it will be in the afternoon. I throw the cover off of me, but remain in bed for a few seconds. I don't want to get up yet. I want to remain a normal girl for a few more seconds. I know that after I get up, everything, including the mirror, will remind me of what has happened so far. I do look different than I did 1 year ago, that's for sure. More mature, I suppose, but you couldn't tell as much from the deep frown imbedded in it. I'm still tired, and I would go to bed if I could, but I have a feeling that I won't be able to. After taking a shower, I get dressed with my eyes still drooping. I only lost two hours of sleep from going to bed at 10. Why does this have such an effect on me? Before I walk down the stairs, I close my eyes for a few moments, hoping that everything goes well today. I open my eyes and walk downstairs to get breakfast.

"Hello Paula. I made you eggs," my mother says with a smile.

"Thanks mom."

I quickly eat the eggs, and still feel hungry afterwards. Thinking about it, I realize that eating is taking time away from me spending time with the people I'm probably going to lose. A tear falls down my face and hits the plate. I keep my head down and throw the plate out, then return to my room and close the door quietly. I push my back off of the door, and sit on the ground. I curl up into a ball while sitting down, and cry a little bit. The thought is complete torture, and it won't leave me alone. It feels as if someone is kicking my head around and playing a game of soccer with it. It doesn't hurt, but I feel unable to lose the depression being put upon me. It seems so strong, and it begins to take over my emotions. Not again. I won't let this happen. I slowly get up and drag myself to the door. If the curse wants me to stay in bed for two days, then I'll be strong enough not to. I'll show my tears to my mother. This way, the curse can't take over. My body becomes weak, but I continue walking. I travel down the stairs, and make my way to the living room. I see my mother sitting down and watching TV, so I run to her and hug her. She doesn't look at my face because she already knows how I feel. She knows that I need her now. I cry into her shoulder until there's nothing left to cry about, and when I look up, my mom has a tissue in her hand. She wipes my face and tells me to go to bed. I lay down on the couch, and she covers me with a blanket and plays with my hair until I fall asleep. I know I shouldn't fall asleep because I'm supposed to be leaving, but I can't help it. And when I wake up, it's more than 12 hours later.

6:00 P.M.

The TV is still on, and I slowly get off the couch, and silently climb up the stairs. I need to be as quiet as possible. When I make it to my room, I check my bag under my bed, and make sure it has my clothes and everything I need. I wait 3 hours, grab a piece of paper, and quietly drag my bag behind me downstairs. My mom is still sleeping on the other couch into the living room, so I write on the piece of paper that I'm going to see Jeremiah and that I'll be back by 11:00. I quickly run to the door and open it, trying to stop it from creaking, and place the bag behind a chair. When I see that the cost is clear, I pick up the bag and leave it near the side of the house, behind a bush. I then run to Jeremiah's house and knock on the door. Jeremiah answers.

"Paula? What are you doing here? I tried to talk to you, but your mom said you were sleeping."

"Yeah, I was, but that's beside the point. Want to talk?"

"Yeah, just let me get my jacket."

Jeremiah runs to his closet and grabs a black jacket. He puts the jacket on and closes the door behind him. When we make it outside, I interrupt him before he can say anything.

"Sorry about yesterday. Tomorrow we'll be fighting, and it seems as if everything is going to be lost. I still don't know what the curse is or how to fight it, and I'm still figuring out who I am."

"I told you who you are already. You're Paula."

"You say that, but do you even know who you are? The way we see ourselves is so different from the way everybody sees us."

"Paula, sometimes I wonder whether we really are ourselves around other people."

"What do you mean?"

"We are only ourselves when we are around people who truly know us. We've been fighting for so long, that I don't know if we ever really got to know each other."

"Jeremiah, we've gotten to know each other through actions and words. I know how you feel before *you* know it. I can expect certain emotions during certain times."

"But people are unpredictable, Paula. We never really know who anyone is, I guess, because we are always changing."

"And I guess that's how you know that you know a person."

"What?"

"When you get to see them grow up and turn into something else. Good or bad, you know which path they're taking. I can't say you really know someone if you influence them, because some people can be influenced easily. If you know how to help that person is when you really know them."

"That's true, I guess. Whenever I blamed myself for everything, you always made me feel better. We're best friends, and I don't think that can change."

"But after all of this is over, you'll meet more people and I'll meet more people. Even if we still are best friends, it won't be the same."

"Are you saying you'll meet someone you like better than me?"

"No, but I'm saying that we might stop hanging out with each other. We will grow up and things will change."

"I told you I like you, Paula. What else is there to say?"

"I like you too, Jeremiah," I say while blushing, "But like I said, I'm going to be leaving. This might be our last time seeing each other, so I wanted to say goodbye."

Jeremiah stands there, his face looking extremely saddened and depressed.

"Listen Jeremiah, there's nothing I can-"

"Paula, we're supposed to fight together. And we will. You won't die, because I won't let you. So stop acting like this is the last time we'll see each other, because it won't be." Jeremiah says with a tear falling down his face, "You can't leave, so stop saying that. You're not going to… Please…"

This is what happens every time I make friends. I always lose them, and they end up living a hard life because of me. I can't let this continue. I can't let what happened to Katelyn, happen to Jeremiah, which is why I need to leave.

"I'm sorry Jeremiah. I can't. Go back inside."

"Why should I? If you're going to leave me, then what's the point? I'm going to end up dying anyway."

I slap my hand against my forehead and grab Jeremiah's arm. He's heavy, but I drag him to the porch. I literally drag him because he would not stand up. I knock on the door and tell Mr. Switz what happened, except I left out the part about me leaving. He asked me why I was still up, and I told him I figured getting a jog before the fight would help me. Mr. Switz brings Jeremiah inside, but I don't look at him. I can't, because if I did, I couldn't leave. I know I couldn't. I did my job, but there's one more thing to do. I grab my phone and call Katelyn. However, she doesn't pick up. I leave her a voicemail.

"Katelyn, I know you're probably busy right now, but I

need to say something. You were a really good friend to me; my best friend, and I don't want to lose you. I'll be leaving, and I don't know if I'm going to return. If I don't return in 2 days, I need you to do me a favor. Call Jeremiah and talk to him. I can't leave him like that. I'll feel better knowing he has someone to talk to. I know that this is a big thing to ask, but please. If something does happen, you'll know. I promise. I know this doesn't make sense now, but my mom will tell you everything. I promise, Katelyn. So please. Help him." I hang up the phone and leave it under a chair on the porch. I can't have anyone tracking my whereabouts. I grab my bag and run to the park without looking back. Luckily, there are some lanterns hanging up in the park so I can see. I put my sleeping bag down and climb inside. I look at the tree branches, some blocking the stars, some not. It reminds me of the conversation Jeremiah and I had yesterday. As I replay the conversation in my mind, everything begins to fade to black…

The Final Battle

When I wake up, I feel a wind pulling me, and I sit up. There's a circular whirlpool in front of me, looking like a million stars mixed in with a large cloud, spinning around and around, beckoning me forth. My hair is being pulled into the portal, and I begin to stand up. It's becoming hard not to be pulled in, and every few seconds I lose my balance. I take a step forward when I hear a voice. "Paula, no!" I hear a familiar voice scream. When I look, I see Jeremiah.

"You don't have to do this!"

The portal is growing larger and larger.

"I have to! You don't understand, Jeremiah!"

"Please don't leave! I don't want you to die!"

"I have to… before it swallows us whole."

I quickly jump into the portal, but someone grabs my hand. As the portal pulls me in, this hand comes with me. I look back and Jeremiah is with me in a grey room. When I walk, my feet dive into the ground. I don't sink, but ripples form, and they spread across the walls. They almost look like metal bending its form very quickly, but without quite the shine. Almost like a rubber. I trace the ripples across the walls, and notice that the farther they travel the softer they become. I try taking a full step, but big waves form that nearly push me over. Still holding Jeremiah's hand, I slow down time. I try to fly, but there's something blocking me from doing so. I take a few steps, and when I make it to the next wall with the ripples slowly bouncing, everything shifts. Suddenly one of the walls has become my ground, and I'm able to walk on it. When I look back, the waves are hitting each other in slow motion. We have to hurry. I run to the door, dragging Jeremiah along with me, and dive inside. The place that we enter is circular, and the only place that is actually stable is the floor. When I try to walk, the bricks collapse and fall into a dark abyss. My heart beats loudly in my chest. These are puzzles, aren't they?

"Paula, I-"

"Shhhh!"

The ground began to rumble when he spoke. Everything settles down, and I think about when I was younger. There used to be tiles on the floor in stores that we used to shop at. Some would be blue, some would be red, but no matter what, they would invert. When I bend down, I can see that these tiles are squares, but they are all the same color. The one I stepped on was the middle one, so the correct one must be either on the left or on the right. I try the left first, and it stays still. That means that the next tile that's safe to step on must be the middle one.

"Jeremiah, follow me exactly and do not step on any other tile," I say in a whisper.

"Ok," he whispers back.

I step to the left, but it wasn't the right one. I quickly make a leap to the right one, and barely stick the landing;

265

however I manage to catch my balance. Jeremiah, on the other hand, is about to topple. I try to slow down time, but it doesn't work. He nearly topples forward when I grab the back of his shirt collar and pull him up. It seems my strength is working.

"Thanks."

"No problem."

"How many of these do you think we'll have to do?"

"I'm not sure, but let's keep on going."

I'm 8 tiles away from the end of this tunnel. I quickly jump in the middle. Jeremiah jumps on the one I last stood on, and I jump to the left. This time, the tile stays. I jump to the middle again, with Jeremiah right behind me. It's a bit difficult to do this, considering that I can barely focus because my heart is racing, but I give myself a bit of confidence. Now I only have 6 left, and I think I understand the pattern. Jumping to the right, I notice that the tile wobbles a little. It begins to crumble while I'm standing on it. I quickly jump to the middle, and this one does the same.

"Quickly, Jeremiah!" I whisper.

I then jump to the left, then the middle, then the right, but this one falls and I'm left hanging on the end of the tunnel. Jeremiah quickly makes a gigantic leap towards the end of the tunnel. He sticks the landing and makes it into the next room. I didn't notice I was holding my breath until now.

"Jeremiah, let go of my hand. You'll fall. I can climb up."

"But-"

"Let go."

He does as I tell him, and I pull myself up. Jeremiah nearly topples and almost sends us falling into the abyss.

"That was close."

"Yeah."

I sit down on the safe ground and pull Jeremiah down will me. I feel as if I want to cry, but I know I can't; even so, a tear falls down my face. Jeremiah looks at me with a hint of pity.

"Paula, relax. I'm you're shield, so please, let me protect you." He says with a smirk.

"We're-not-i-in-a," I quickly take a breath, "soap opera, Jeremiah. It'll be fine."

"You know, the way you're breathing doesn't tell me that."

I shake my head and get up. When I turn around, I notice we are in a room with lights and a garden. The lights turn around and around, in every which way, and the plants are killed as soon as the light touches it. My heart starts beating more quickly, and I try sneaking over the dead plants. I make small noises while walking on the grass, but I don't think the lights have the ability to hear. I giggle at this thought, and Jeremiah looks at me.

"You know, Paula, I know that we're not in the best situation right now, but I don't think laughing will make it better," He whispers.

"Says the person who smirked before. Nice smile you've got there. It totally calms me down," I say while rolling my eyes.

I grab Jeremiah's hand again and we slowly walk forward. The light hits my jeans, but all they do is smoke. They don't burn.

"Looks like your shield is doing his job," He says, pretending to act like a superhero. I start running again and luckily, nothing happens to me. I keep running and nearly get hit by the light once more. Making my way to the end, I see a door knob, but I can't open it. I find a mirror on the floor and use it to redirect the light on the door. It's dangerous, however, because if the light even touches me one bit, I could die. The last time I got lucky. I don't know if I'll be so lucky this time. Jeremiah stands behind me while I carve a circle in the door. After I am done, the light begins to fade and I climb through the hole, making Jeremiah go first. We are in a hallway where there is a red carpet and bricks surrounding us. The sides of the carpet are golden, and are very shiny. Suddenly the lights go out. When they turn back on, I notice a pool of blood, and Jeremiah is missing! My heart beats really fast, and I stop breathing. *Think Paula, think!* So far, the path has been straight, left, straight, right. I had to go through the door, and then I had to get through the tunnel. I might as well try it. However, there is no straight path. When I walk to the wall, I notice one brick not shaped like the others. When I take it out, a hole crumbles in a wall, and I'm able to get through. The walls in the past room go dark, and I realize I made it out just in time. The walls disappear behind me, leaving me with four paths. This time, there is no wall stopping me from going somewhere. I choose left, just like the pattern before. A wall appears behind me, and I hear the lights go black behind the wall. I keep walking, and this time there are no paths. I keep walking straight, however, and find a small jigsaw puzzle waiting for me. There are only 4 pieces, but I have a feeling that if I mess up even once, that will be the end of me. I take the four jigsaw puzzle pieces and arrange them in a way that only makes sense. I hesitate for a bit because

I see the apartment that burned down, causing my dad to die, but I place the puzzle in quickly. I can't stand looking at it anymore. I just need to get out of here. I make it out of the room with not a second to spare, because the lights turned off immediately. When I enter this room, there are keys covering the floor, and one door. I know what I have to do. The keys are, however, imbedded into the carpet. Which one do I choose? What will happen if I choose wrong? I think about what Jeremiah said before about being my shield. I really hope he's with me right now. I take a deep breath. I begin to think about how I hid my clothes under my bed. I walk forward into the middle of the room, and tear a piece in the carpet. It begins to melt away, and I find a key under it. I walk to the door, but instead of placing the key in it, I walk to the edge of the room. The real door is hiding behind a curtain. I place the key in the real door, and find myself in a trophy room. There's something at the head of the room. There's a statue that looks eerily like Jeremiah. The statue is behind the 3 trophies, which are all stuck to the ground. There's a sword, a cape, and a wand. The statue is golden, and it seems to be thick, but as I take a more careful look at it, it can actually be cut very easily. I break open the statue with my bare hands, and find a tiny key inside. I look at the cabinets under the trophy cases. There are 3 keyholes, but only one is the correct one. Looking carefully at each of the cabinets, I see different figure in each one of them. On the sword, there is a dragon. On the cape, there is a man riding a horse, and on the wand, there is a cage and a wizard. When I look at the cape, I see that the man on the horse is moving. Instead of putting the key in the keyhole, I see that a new one appears on the man's chest. I quickly put the key inside before it disappears. When I unlock it, Jeremiah appears behind the trophy case, with a big cut in his arm. I grab Jeremiah by his other arm, and the trophy cases move out of the way. A doorway appears, and I walk through it with Jeremiah. This time, I have to balance on a line, one foot wide. When I look down, I see whirlpools that confuse me, and I begin walking off of the line. Jeremiah pulls me back, however, and tells me not to look down. He nearly screams out in pain as he does this, however, because the cut in his arm is extremely thick. I place my hand on the cut and focus all of my energy on it. When I look at it again, I notice that there is a scar in its place. I smile and nod at him, thankful that he's on this trip with me. I am nearly at the end, when I become extremely curious. At this point, the line has become thinner. Jeremiah holds me back when I look down, and pushes me to the end. I shake my head and continue walking until the surroundings change. This is the 6th room, and this time, we are back in a garden with a path on it. There are many flowers, and when you inhale, you almost become in a trance. I want to walk to them, but I know that I can't because something will happen to me if I do. I mean, this one is pretty obvious. As far as I know, most flowers don't give off gases that can kill you.

"Try to slow down time now. This way you can run across without needing to breathe as much."

"I don't know if that'll work, Jeremiah."

"Either way the fumes will move around slower."

When I try to slow down time, it works, and we run across the stone path. However, I become dizzy from holding in my breath. I take a deep breath and nearly fall to the ground. Jeremiah picks me up and throws me through the hole into the next room. I hurt my head and I'm still dizzy, but at least I'm not dead. The air is very thin here, once again, and after a few moments, I nearly faint from loss of oxygen.

"Run into the sand dune, Paula."

"Why?" I say weakly.

"Sometimes, in order to fight, you need to do the things people least expect."

Jeremiah runs, this time dragging me along, and we make it into another tunnel, but this one is different. It seems... closed off, in a way. There is a rectangular hole in the wall, about 8 feet wide and 2 feet high. There are two of these, both in opposite directions. It looks as if light is shining through the left one. There isn't a way to exit. Unless...

"Jeremiah, follow me," I say, breathlessly.

I climb up into the hole, and suddenly my ground is what would normally be part of the wall. I walk downwards, where there is an opening, and Jeremiah does the same. Inside the opening it is dark, but you can see certain pathways. I take the pathway with the light, since I cannot see the rest. There is a wooden door at the end. When I open the door, I am in a large theatre with a stage in front of us. This is the 9th one we have to go through. I walk around until I find stairs to the stage. There is a trap door in the middle of it. There is also a curtain hiding the back of the stage. Which one do I pick? I repeat the words Jeremiah said to me earlier. Sometimes, in order to fight, you need to do the things people least expect. I pull the trapdoor open, and jump down. I land on solid ground and tell Jeremiah to come down. I don't know whether this is the right choice or not, but I guess I'll have to stick with it, because I don't see a way up. We keep on walking, and the tunnel forms into a big room. It is white with a tree in the middle. The land behind us curves into a whirlpool and disappears. Jeremiah is with me, but I feel alone. Maybe that's because when I look back, he isn't there. Instead, I see a root. Afraid to touch it, I instead follow it into the tree. I see a new form into the tree. It is still charcoal and as depressing as it can be.

"Come, child. Take the power. Take the curse, and let it take control. You'll be fine, I promise," the tree says in a scratchy voice. I feel compelled to what it says. The tree moves with each word, and you can hear the tree bending and cracking at each movement. The tree smiles at me, and I turn away. I know what I have to do, but I don't want to be covered by the darkness. The face on the tree forms into something else… Jeremiah's face.

"Come on, Paula. You can do it. Make everything easier for me. I am a part of the curse, right? You can help me live. If you get rid of the curse, you get rid of me. You've known that from the beginning. So why try to stop it now? Come help me, and we can be friends again."

I say nothing.

"Paula, come on. Time is running out. If you join then we both can become stronger. Paula…"

"No."

"What did you say?"

"I said no."

"You will do as I say!" the tree screeches in a miserable voice.

The tree's branches come to grab me, and I jump back. I know what I must do. I run at the tree, jumping over every obstacle. However, I wasn't prepared for the roots. I struggle to get out, but I can't. The roots are squeezing the life out of me. I'm losing breath… I'm dying… Wait. I was going to fight the middle of the tree, but the tree can't survive without its roots. No tree can. Not even a cursed one. I smile and regain my confidence. The tree gave me what I wanted, so I'm going to use it. I let every happy moment I've ever had with any of my friends, Beatrice, Katelyn, Bryan, Michelle, and Jeremiah, fill my mind. I keep thinking about that, and I notice the tree is losing its grip. But I can't lose my grip on it. I keep holding the roots, but the tree begins screaming. I all at once remember the fact that Katelyn left me, and that Jeremiah might die… The tree makes me think that he *will* die. My power begins to weaken. It makes me think about all the arguments we've had… how much I hate myself because of it. But here's the thing: I don't hate myself. I fight back with tremendous power. I've blamed myself for everything, but none of this is my fault. The curse was the one at fault. Jeremiah wasn't at fault either. The curse was placed upon *him*. He didn't ask for it. Jeremiah is an amazing person, and *no man or woman or curse* can take that away from him! I become extremely powerful, but the Curse reminds me of me hating my normality once again, and I weaken. However, I still fight. Yes, I'm normal, but I don't care! I'm still different from everyone else. My personalities, my speech, even my thoughts. And I don't need someone to tell me otherwise.

"I'm perfect the way I am, and NO ONE can take that away from me. Not even some stupid curse! You never controlled me. You just thought you would! You use hate to take control over people, and that isn't right! I'm a person, not a rag doll. You can't throw me around! I was hurt before because of you, but now I suppose I must thank you. Because of you, I'm stronger! Because of you, I'm a better person! And that's why, because of YOU, I'll never stop fighting! You did exactly the opposite of what you wanted! I'm Paula Berney, and I love who I am!"

A burst of power makes me hit the wall, and my back begins to hurt. The tree is transforming into something else... It looks living... it looks happy... it looks cheerful. And sitting right beside it, is the one and only Jeremiah. I'm happy with myself and with everyone else. I accept who I am, and that's why we're going to get out of here together. I laugh and grab Jeremiah's hand. A doorway appears, and we fall out of the portal onto the park grass. It's sunset. I suppose we spent a few hours in there.

"Paula... Thanks for helping me."

"No problem. How do you feel?"

"Different... But somehow, I feel the same. I don't think the curse is still on me, but I don't feel any happier or sadder than usual. I'm just grateful."

"That's because you have to make your own happiness. Even good luck can't offer you eternal joy."

"Well, I know that I feel happy right now, even though my head hit the grass pretty hard. Ow..."

"You're happy because everything is over, right?"

"It's not just that. It's because I'm here with you."

I smile at Jeremiah and stand up.

"Well, I guess we better return."

"Yes, I guess so."

There's a bond between us now that can't be broken. We are best friends; maybe more than that. We've gone through a big part of our lives together. As I think about everything that has happened, I realize how much he really means to me.

"Jeremiah?"

"Yes?"

"Thanks for being my best friend."

"Paula?"

"Yes."

"I think we can say we're more than best friends now."

"Super Ultra Best Friends?"

"Nice try, Paula." he says with a laugh.

"Come on. Let's go before people really think we're dead," I say with a groan.

Back Home, But Not Quite Done

When we get home, we hug our parents. My mom started crying and Mr. Switz was so happy he lifted Jeremiah into the air. We all spent time watching TV, debating, and playing a few games. Every so often Jeremiah and I would share a glance or two and laugh because our parents were really competitive, even more competitive than us. I suppose some parts of them didn't grow up, but then again, I guess that's a good thing. I was relieved to see my parents so happy. I don't think any of us would forget this day. When Mr. Switz gets tired, he heads home, telling Jeremiah to be back by 10:00 p.m. We walk outside once again, the sun nearly out of the sky. You can hear the wind rustling throughout the trees.

"It's kind of relaxing, isn't it? Hearing the trees, I mean."

"Um… I think I've had enough of trees for one day."

Jeremiah laughs.

"But wait… Paula, you never told me what happened in there. All I remember is running away from a tree. Is that what you had to fight? You had to fight a *tree?*"

"Yeah, but it was harder than you think."

"I never said it was easy, I just said you had to fight a tree."

"I can hear the sarcasm in your voice."

We both pause for a minute, reminding ourselves that the wind rustling in the trees isn't the only thing that nature has waiting for us.

"Hey Paula… About what I said earlier…"

"What's up?"

"Are we more than best friends?"

I stay quiet for a few minutes.

"That depends because I think that now we have a deep psychological bond that cannot be interrupted but-"

"You know that's not what I meant."

"Are we? Jeremiah, I've never dated anyone. Plus, you're my best friend. How is that going to work out?"

"I don't know, Paula. If I have to ask it the proper way, then I will. Paula, will you be my girlfriend?"

The wind blows in my face, making my skin cold. Do I want to risk our friendship? I'm only 14, turning 15 in less than a month. I know I like Jeremiah, but I'm afraid of being hurt, too. Are risks meant to be taken?

"My answer is…"

Jeremiah looks at me with hope. I can tell that if I say no, he'll be hurt. It'll cause a gap in our friendship. But I can't worry about now. Do I want to date him?

…

…

…

"Yes."

And like that, another path has been chosen. I'm afraid, I'm nervous, but I'm also extremely happy. This is one of the few times in my life where I feel like I haven't made a mistake. As the wind blows, I can see my future forming ahead of me. But will that future come to be? I suppose it depends on the choices I make. So let's hope I make good ones. As for my mistakes... they're meant to be made. So here I am, 14 year old Paula Berney, telling you this message:

Don't be afraid to be yourself. You're going to
make mistakes. Learn how to fix them.
There are many paths that you can take.
Try to pick the best one, but if you make
a mistake once in awhile, that's ok.
And lastly, there's always someone that loves you. Even
in my darkest times, I had someone who cared.
It's up to *you* to find those people, because
they won't come to you all of the time.
Oh, and one more thing:
You have a story; don't be afraid to share it.